DARK DANGER

April found the light switch; dust motes skittered in the glare of illumination. Then the pungency of earth and dust and wine-soaked wood rushed at her from every corner of the vast cellar chamber. In spite of her determined bravery, she braced the cellar door open with a cardboard box. Her heart pounded.

Wine racks crowded the room in a haphazard pattern. Each was six-tiered, and they towered over her like heavy bookshelves, filled with dusty bottles reposing in downward slants. On a rack near the back wall, she found what she was looking for—the French Bordeaux. She lifted the bottle. The ancient framework creaked.

Shivering, she hastened to the wine cellar door, gave the bottle a swipe with the cloth she carried, and set it on the floor. April caught a movement out of the corner of her eye. Her imagination? Rats? Or . . .

"Is someone there?"

No answer.

Calm down, April. Don't do this to yourself.

Forcing herself to continue, she moved between the racks hunting for another bottle . . . a Zinfandel. Gingerly, she hoisted it. The rack vibrated and screeched.

To her right she heard a different sound. Somebody breathing? Her head snapped around. She caught a movement of shadow on the wall. Her pulse zinged. And then the full-packed wine rack came crashing toward her. . . .

ENDLESS FEAR

ADRIANNE LEE

*For Marge:
Happy Reading.
Adrianne
Lee*

ZEBRA BOOKS
KENSINGTON PUBLISHING CORP.

To Larry, for always believing I could,
and
To Carol Hurn, Mary Alice Mierz, Nadine Miller,
& Judy Strege, for making the dream come true.

ZEBRA BOOKS

are published by

Kensington Publishing Corp.
475 Park Avenue South
New York, NY 10016

First printing: August, 1992

Printed in the United States of America

Prologue

Angry voices!
Echoing from the landing above the basement stairs.

Fourteen-year-old April clamped her palms over her ears, effectively blocking the words. But not the anger.

Who was arguing with her mother? For it was her mother's voice she heard; there was no mistaking that singsong lilt it always took on when she'd been drinking.

An awful dread filled April. She hated her mother, and this was the way she hated her most. Drunk. Sometimes she even wished Lily was dead.

Lily! She wasn't allowed to call her Momma, or Mom, or Mother. Just Lily. While she was to answer to *Baby!*

As if of their own volition, her hands slid from her ears and caught hold of the braids at the sides of her head. She gave them a disgusted yank. Pigtails! And this horrid dress that hung like a pillowcase from her shoulders. She wasn't a baby. Why did her mother make her dress like one? Couldn't Lily see she'd started to change from a child into a young woman?

Or was that the problem?

A loud slap resounded through the open room.

April flinched as though she'd been struck. Had she been? She could swear she felt her cheek sting, and her ears rang as if from a blow.

The normal dusty dank scent of the basement dissolved in the tinny odor of fear burning April's nostrils, coating her tongue. She tried to edge away from her mother's wrath, but Lily stood between her and the door.

"April?" Her mother's voice was shrill with disbelief.

This time April listened, straining to identify another voice. Instead she heard the tinkle of breaking glass.

"You'll be sorry . . ." Lily hissed.

April slammed her eyes shut. Suddenly she didn't want to see, to feel. She threw her hands in front of her and shoved hard as though she could push aside the bad voices.

Lily's scream startled her.

April's eyes flew open. Lily was falling. Tumbling down the stairs. Frantically, April reached for her. *Too late.*

Thud!

A shriek.

And then silence.

Running recklessly down the steep staircase, April stopped halfway, clung to the railing, and gazed in horror at her mother's sprawled form below. Her chest squeezed with pain.

Until that moment, Lily Cordell-Farraday had always seemed more alive than everyone else. No longer. She was still. Too still. Her long blond hair was in wild disarray, spread about her ivory face like discarded gold silk. Her aqua eyes were huge with glassy terror, and her graceful neck was twisted at an unnatural angle.

April stumbled down the remaining stairs, fell to her knees and caught her mother's lifeless hand to her chest.

"I'm sorry," she sobbed. "I'm sorry."

One

The ominous note arrived two days after the invitation.

April's stepbrother was getting married May first. The invitation from her father was not for the wedding. That was still four months away. Rather, he was asking her to attend the formal engagement party her family was throwing three weeks hence at Calendar House.

The note warned her to stay away.

Shakily, April scanned the unsigned paper for the umpteenth time. The message was simple: "If ever again you set foot inside Calendar House you will regret it!"

"What do you make of this?" she asked, dropping the note on her doctor's file-cluttered desk. Obviously, Nancy Merritt, the psychiatrist at the Phoenix sanitarium where April was an outpatient, had been in the middle of evaluations when she'd agreed to this appointment. "I haven't been home in twelve years. In fact, this has been my home for most of that time. And now, when I'm well enough to face them, someone sends this!"

Dr. Merritt was a plain woman whose cropped

brown hair hugged her head like an overturned bird's nest. Her features lacked beauty, but not strength. The preteen shapelessness of her figure had long ago convinced April the woman fed more on nervous energy than food. The doctor read the mysterious note, then turned her warm brown eyes to April. "How does this make you feel?"

How did she feel? Angry. Offended. A little scared. Although morning shafts of winter sun spilled in through two windows, April hugged herself against a sudden chill.

In the background the soft upbeat sounds of Kenny G filtered from concealed speakers. Usually the music lifted her spirits and soothed her. Today it annoyed her. She stormed to the shelf of books which also housed the stereo equipment and punched the off button.

Dropping her head back on her shoulders, she stared at the ceiling, and drew a deep breath. There was, she noted absently, the usual overlaying scent of pine cleaner in the utilitarian office, a distinctive sign of normalcy. It should have helped her pull things into perspective. It didn't. Slowly, she faced Nancy.

If the psychiatrist was surprised or offended by April's actions she showed no sign of it. Irrationally this annoyed April all the more. She paced, waving her hands in the air. "How do you suppose I feel? I'm upset."

"And . . . ?"

Avoiding the real issue, April said, "And . . . I want to know who sent that vile note. Other than Daddy, I haven't seen any of those people in twelve years. Oh sure, they've written, sent birthday and Christmas presents, but none of them cared enough to show up on my doorstep."

"Was that their idea . . . or yours?" asked Nancy in her gentle persistent way.

Some of April's bluster deflated. "You know it was mine."

Nancy nodded. "I've never understood why."

April opened her mouth, but didn't speak. She still couldn't bring herself to tell Nancy the whole truth. Nor anyone else either. Until she remembered all the details, she couldn't even admit out loud that she might have killed Lily. With her blood the temperature of ice water, she eyed the foreboding note. Perhaps the person who'd sent it already knew and was afraid she'd murder them all in their sleep. Her mouth felt as dry as the desert outside, her palms as damp as the dew on the cacti.

"It's all right, April. You can tell me your reasons when you're ready. Look, I realize this is unsettling. But I strongly caution you about giving this" — she tapped the note again — "such importance. I'd hate to see it undo all the good we've accomplished, or to keep you from achieving a complete recovery."

April was used to Nancy's unobtrusive way of letting *her* figure out what she wanted. And more than anything else, she wanted to be well. She steeled herself against giving the note and its unknown author even a modicum of power over her. "You know what? Nothing is going to deter my plans to return to Calendar House."

Twelve years in Arizona had disaccustomed April to the cutting chill of the San Juan Islands in winter, but the pungent bite of seawater invading her nostrils brought a smile to her lips. Without realizing it, she had missed the aroma of home. But not the rain, she admitted, watching it gather on the windshield.

Resigned to getting wet, she stepped from her rented car onto the bobbing deck of the Farraday family's working ferry. Moored in Friday Harbor, the bargelike affair was all flat deck and wooden railings, and large enough to accommodate two medium sized cars. It smelled of creosote and brine-soaked timbers.

"Go on into the wheelhouse," Karl Winston, the ferry's captain directed. "I gotta secure the car."

She didn't need to be told twice. April dashed for the forward deck and the snug five-by-eight structure from which the captain steered the motorized craft. The words *Farraday Island* were emblazoned in huge red letters on three of its four walls. The paint looked fresh.

Somehow the whole ferry seemed smaller, April thought, entering the compact cabin. She shut the door against the drizzle, slid onto the bench seat, and watched Karl ready her car for the journey ahead.

Seeing him again had been a shock. She was still having trouble accepting that the scrawny, spoiled mama's boy she had once played with had grown into this handsome man. Now in his late twenties, Karl looked as striking as some Viking god.

A blast of icy air rattled the rain slicked window at her back, and April shrugged deeper into her red parka.

Karl cast off and hastened into the wheelhouse. "Here we go," he announced, grinding the engine to life. "The heater will warm this place in no time."

A moment later they were cruising across the choppy waters out of the harbor. April's heartbeat fluttered as Karl veered recklessly past oncoming boats with no apparent regard to who had the right of way. The hard wooden bench beneath her was smooth from wear, and she struggled to hold her position.

Intentionally arriving one day early, April had planned to spend the night in Friday Harbor, reacquaint herself with the town where she had attended school, and go to Farraday Island in the morning. No such luck!

"I 'bout had a stroke when I saw you in the Electric Company." Karl laughed, and much to her chagrin, glanced over his broad shoulder. She wished he would pay more attention to his navigating and less to her, but that seemed to be a futile hope. "Man, I thought for sure it was Lily Cordell come back to life."

April cringed, hating the unavoidable comparison. Unwittingly, she caught her reflection in the glass. From her shoulder length gold blond hair, to her round aqua eyes, right down to her fine boned features, she looked hauntingly like her famous mother.

The noisy engine chugged and whined inside the tight confines of the wheelhouse which suddenly seemed to contain too little air. Why couldn't Karl quit staring at her?

As though he had read this thought and was determined to defy it, the corners of his generous mouth curled. Heat spiraled into her face. Was he flirting with her? She knew men found her attractive; she was, after all, her mother's daughter. In appearance anyway. However, the few experiences she had had with men had taught her that sending mixed signals could be disastrous, especially when you weren't aware you were sending them.

Flustered, she raised her voice to be heard above the raucous engine. "Well, if you hadn't introduced yourself, I wouldn't have recognized you, Karl."

The smile reached into his ice blue eyes. "Yeah! I came into my own."

That was putting it mildly, April thought, realizing for the first time that this whole visit would likely be one confrontation after another with change. She had best be prepared.

At last Karl devoted his attention to maneuvering

the unsettling swells. Her stomach felt queasy. Taking advantage of his silence, April leaned her head against the vibrating wall, and gazed at the gloom-shrouded afternoon. Prepared or not, was she ready to see Spencer? His image came to her in a flash, and her heart quickened. Twelve years would have changed him, too. Why had he never married? Why did these feelings for him persist? Why had she avoided finding out all she could about him?

Karl interrupted this scenario she had hashed through too many times over the past four years. "Got a real storm brewing."

April nodded, but said nothing. Karl, she decided, had a penchant for stating the obvious.

"How come you ain't got much of a tan? I thought Phoenix was sunny year round."

"It's usually sunny, but not always warm. Besides, I'm too busy for sunbathing."

"Doin' what?"

The question sounded like simple curiosity, but was it? "Working and going to school." She didn't want to talk about herself. "What about you?"

"Your pa just promoted me. I got my daddy's old job lookin' after the grounds, the cars, the ferry—you know, a little of this, a little of that."

April's memory of Karl's father, Jesse Winston, remained clear. Jesse had had dark hair and pale eyes, and he was a man whose job kept him fit, kept his skin perpetually tan. As a young girl she'd thought him quite a hunk. Of course that was before she'd lost her heart to someone else.

Tragically, Jesse had died soon after the car he'd been working under slipped off its jack and crushed his chest. The accident had occurred two months before her mother's. With a start, April realized Karl and she had both lost a parent at about the same time.

Before she could comment on this, Karl said, "Say, my old lady's eyes are gonna bug out when she sees you. She loved your ma."

April forced a smile. Karl's mother had been the cook and housekeeper at Calendar House for as long as she could recall. A wayward thought struck her. Had his mother loved Lily enough to send the mysterious note? Involuntarily, April shivered. *Don't jump to conclusions,* she reminded herself. "How is Helga?"

"Same as always. A little thicker around the middle since you last saw her. 'Course she's got her hands full readying for the party. Gonna be some shindig. Lotta important people coming . . . even some reporters."

April's neck muscles ached with tension. Could the fact that the press would be attending her stepbrother's engagement party explain the motive behind the anonymous note? She knew her resemblance to Lily was bound to cause a stir, but surely her absence would also have created unwanted speculation. Which was worse? Hugging herself, she gazed toward the heaving waters of Haro Strait. "How much longer before we reach the island?"

"A few more minutes." He moved aside and gestured toward the ship's wheel. The grin was back. "You wanna steer awhile?"

"No, thanks." What she wanted at the moment was to be alone. "If you don't have any objection, I think I'll wait in my car for the remainder of the trip."

"Suit yourself. It won't be as warm out there."

The colder confines of her rented car sounded preferable to the sudden oppressive warmth inside the wheelhouse. April picked her way gingerly across the slick deck of the swaying craft. Rain pelted down, saturating her in seconds. The going was rough. With every rise and fall of the waves, the aged planks creaked and groaned as if they were struggling to hold

15

together. The eerie sound stirred goosebumps on her neck.

Inches from the car a gust of wind stole her balance. She slipped, caught hold of the car's door handle and righted herself. Maybe this wasn't such a good idea. In these rough seas the car might decide to jump ship.

Scoffing at her fears, she stubbornly climbed into the driver's seat, determined not to be intimidated by the weather, or her own active imagination, or Karl's overly friendly manner. Oh, he seemed nice enough. And God knew, he was easy to look at, but she had no right to encourage — however unintentionally — any man. *Even Spencer.* A pain centered in her chest. Until she broke through her memory block and learned to deal with whatever she discovered, her future was one big question mark.

Unshed tears obscured her vision as much as the rain on the windshield. She daubed her eyes dry with a tissue and checked the rearview mirror for mascara smudges. Finding none, she started the engine and flicked on the wipers.

A full five seconds passed before she realized what she was seeing.

Farraday Island.

It rose out of Haro Strait, a crudely shaped horseshoe consisting of nearly two thousand acres of forests and beaches, rocky shores and dangerous cliffs. The house and its outbuildings occupied the southernmost arm.

The ferry smoothed as Karl left the open waters and navigated into a sheltered cove. Directly ahead was the landing dock. April tensed. In the pit of her stomach a swirl of panic rose. Forcing herself to breathe deeply and evenly, she strained for a glimpse of the house that dominated the promontory.

On a clear day it was impossible to miss from this

vantage point. Now, however, the misty downpour obscured all but the massive roof line. It was enough to start her heart careening.

Within minutes, Karl had moored the ferry, lowered the ramp, and removed the blocks securing her tires. Maneuvering the car ahead, she rolled down the window, actually welcoming the cooling rain on her flushed face. "Would you like a ride to the house?"

"Naw, I got a few things to finish here first."

"Okay. See you later."

April disembarked. The car's tires spun and caught as she drove onto wet asphalt and began a steep ascent. Although the narrow lane seemed to wind aimlessly away from her destination, she knew it eventually circled back and led to the spacious parking apron in front of the house.

Leafless madronas lined the road like a naked garrison guarding the way. They'd grown so tall.

The boathouse had disappeared from view, and seconds later she was passing the six car garage. Wind railed against the rented compact. Trees bobbed and bent and moaned. Branches snapped and leaped into her path. The wipers were useless against the onslaught on rain and debris.

April squinted into the failing light, recalling the beauty of this place in high summer. She shivered. This was January at its ugliest: soggy, matted grass, flowerless bushes, and puddled water. The bleakness struck a chord within her. Arizona and Dr. Merritt suddenly seemed far away, too far away.

Her headlights pierced the darkness as she peered uneasily into the shadowed gloom.

In the distance to her left she spotted what appeared to be a cluster of sporadic lights. The housekeeper's cottage. Even that cozy abode looked forlorn today.

17

Trying to ignore a chilling sense of foreboding, she managed the final curve.

Lightning speared the sky, illuminating the area for a split second.

Her foot hit the brake. April blinked.

Calendar House!

It hid in the rainy mist, angling this way and that, like some huge stone and mortar monster waiting to destroy her.

TWO

Bone-chilling wind drove sheeting rain against April's back as she rushed to the porch and knocked on the heavy pine door.

Once.

Twice.

Three times.

Where was everyone? Granted she wasn't expected until tomorrow, but there were lights on inside; surely someone was home. Finding the door unlocked, April stepped into the immense foyer. Her stomach seemed to be in her throat. Swallowing hard, she wrestled the door shut, then set her single suitcase on the planked floor.

For a long moment, she stood motionless, listening for approaching footsteps or the sound of voices. All she heard was the pelting rain and the thundering of her heart. She drew a quavery breath. The faint aromas of roasting beef and lemon oil tangled in her nostrils. Inexplicably these homey touches lifted the fine hairs on the nape of her neck.

Her gaze flicked uneasily from the sweeping staircase at her left to the rough-hewn, open-beamed ceilings, to the hammered pewter chandelier overhead, and lastly, beneath her feet, to the gleaming pine floors which sported a hodgepodge of subtly-shaded Oriental rugs. *Nothing to be frightened of,* she chided herself.

It did look different though. Redecorated. Except for its grander size, Calendar House brought to mind an old English hunting lodge, best suited to antiques, natural woods, and overstuffed furniture in natural fabrics. Twelve years ago it had looked that way.

April frowned in disbelief. Black lacquered tables and low slung couches with frilly flowered throw pillows and matching drapes adorned the sunken living room and valuable-looking Oriental vases the foyer. It was so inappropriate she wondered if someone had deliberately tried to remove every trace of Lily and her era here.

Trying to shake the unsettling notion, April removed her wet parka and dropped it atop her suitcase. A blast of wind slammed against the leaded windows on either side of the door. She jumped. It felt nearly as cold inside as it had outside. Had it always been so?

A sudden lull in the downpour exposed heretofore unheard voices coming from the vicinity of her father's den.

With her nerves taut, April headed into the wide hallway at her right. As she neared the den, she realized her Aunt March was speaking; the elderly woman's grating tones were unmistakable.

"Not thinking, as usual." The clack of knitting needles punctuated her words. "If ever you'd consider the ramifications of your actions, brother dear, instead of leading with your heart . . ."

"For the love of God! Must I remind you, April is my daughter. Your niece! She belongs here as much as either of us."

April froze. Her pulse skipped, her mouth dried. She knew she should walk in and let them know she had arrived. Unaccountably she stood rigid, inches from the doorway, listening.

"Humph! How do we know she's strong enough?" Her aunt had neither dropped a stitch nor a beat. "What if the shock of returning to Calendar House sets her off again?"

"Really March!" Her father's voice resounded in anger. "Hysterical amnesia is hardly schizophrenia!"

Another furious clack of needles followed. "Bad genes! That's what. Never been insanity in the Farraday family . . . till you married that actress, August. Show people! Hah! Unstable, the lot of 'em."

No insanity in the Farraday family? April pressed her palm to her mouth, stifling an angry "Hah!" Generations of Farradays named for the month in which they were born. Perhaps not insanity, but definitely a strain of eccentricity.

"Shame on the both of you." The reproach pulled April back to the conversation. The soft Southern drawl, she realized, was that of her stepmother.

"I want no more of this, this ancient history," declared Cynthia Farraday. "We have the future to consider. Promise me you'll refrain from this distasteful subject while Vanessa and the twins are here. I won't have my son's fiancée—the governor's niece, for heaven's sake—gettin' the wrong impression of our family. Not to mention the press. Why, if some snoopy reporter heard the two of you and dragged up all that old business, it could ruin the engagement celebration, the weddin'—or possibly Thane and Spencer's careers."

April had heard enough. She stepped into the room and, for the first time since her return, into the past. Her father's den was exactly as she'd remembered: the rock fireplace dominating one wall, the red leather sofa and high-backed chairs on either side of it, the cluttered bookshelves, the even messier desk, the old braided rug and knotty-pine paneling. Taking heart from it, she moved closer to the three people seated before the roaring fire.

A nervous quaver stirred in her stomach. "None of you need worry. I'm not insane."

Three heads jerked toward April.

Above the crackle of blazing logs she heard a tight gasp escape March Farraday. The old woman's hand flew to her ample bosom and color drained from her florid face as she sank back into the worn leather of the highbacked chair. "Dear God! It's Lily."

"Don't be absurd, March." Sitting on the sofa next to his wife, August Farraday smiled up at his daughter, but made no move to rise. At sixty-nine, he was three years younger than his sister, and, whereas March was plain with a mannish jaw, a prominent nose and hair the color of corroded steel, August was still head-turning handsome. The only signs of aging were the silver strands in his thick russet hair and a slight stoop, a by-product of years bent over a workbench bringing his inventions to life.

His navy blue eyes suddenly clouded with confusion. "I thought you weren't due until tomorrow, April. Did I get the dates wrong?"

"No dear, you didn't. April honey, we weren't expectin' you today. How did you get across the strait from Friday Harbor in this foul weather? Surely, Karl didn't come get you?"

"I had intended to spend the night in Friday Harbor, but the working ferry was at the dock."

There was the slightest twitch in Cynthia's cheek as she clasped hold of the gold cross hanging from a lengthy chain around her neck. April wondered if her stepmother's discomfort sprang from her presence, or from worry as to how much of the conversation she might have heard.

Cynthia sighed, then smiled sweetly at her. "Y'all

must have made it back just as the storm hit. You look chilled to the bone." She lifted a silver carafe from the coffee table and poured steaming brown liquid into a mug. "Here's some hot spiced tea. Come warm yourself by the fire."

Wind wailed against the double French doors and lifted the sheer curtains in a ghostly dance as April strode to the fireplace, accepted the cup, and curled her icy fingers around it. The hot glass burned her skin, but she didn't mind.

It smelled of apples and cinnamon and tasted delicious. Taking a second sip of the steamy brew, she sank to the raised hearth. The sudden heat at her back felt as unnatural as being in this room with these three people. Too many years had passed.

"Now doesn't that feel better?" Cynthia piped.

April nodded and hid her discomfort in another swallow. For the life of her, she couldn't figure out why her father had married Cynthia less than one year after Lily's accident. As much as she had hated her mother, April would not have chosen her social secretary as a replacement.

Oh, there was no denying Cynthia had a certain exotic appeal, with her long dark brown hair pulled severely off her face, accentuating her almond-shaped, dove-gray eyes, but at fifty, she was young enough to be one of August's daughters. Was that the attraction? Her age?

The knitting needles clicked anew, startling April. She eyed her aunt through lowered lashes. The elderly woman stared back, boldly, assessingly. *Probably waiting to see me fall apart,* April thought angrily.

The leather sofa swicked as Cynthia shifted position and leaned closer to April. "Welcome home, sugah. We intended to have the red carpet, so to speak, rolled out for you, but you caught us unawares. I do hope you won't be sneakin' up on everyone the whole time you're here visitin'?"

Cynthia's tittering laugh grated against April's nerve endings. It was a struggle to keep her voice level. "I knocked. No one answered."

"Never mind about all that. You're here now, safe and sound, and that's all that's important," August said.

"Of course it is." Cynthia smiled at her husband. "Now give your daughter a hug, dear, or she'll think we aren't glad to see her."

"What? Oh!" August's confusion lasted but a second. Always a bit preoccupied, her father often forgot amenities. Usually April found it an endearing trait. Today it hurt. He was the one ally she felt certain of, and he hadn't thought to welcome her on his own. However, now that the defect had been pointed out, she couldn't fault the speed with which he strove to correct it.

Setting aside the tea cup, she rose to meet him, allowing herself to be wrapped in his comforting embrace. He pulled her to his chest, flattening her nose against his breast pocket. The smell of pipe tobacco clung to his shirt, evoking bittersweet memories from her childhood.

"Of course, we're glad to see her," he said. "Why wouldn't we be?"

Several reasons occurred to April, starting with the anonymous note and ending with the conversation she had just interrupted.

August grasped her by each shoulder. "Why, April, your sweater is damp. You must be freezing. Let's show you which room you'll be using and you can change out of those wet clothes."

"Which room I'll . . . ?" April frowned. "Won't I be staying in my old room?"

"Humph!" The knitting needles silenced, drawing more attention than when they clacked. "Imagine . . . expecting to move back in here as though the past twelve years hadn't even happened."

The breath in April's throat seemed as hot as the fire. Obviously, Aunt March was unhappy about her presence here. Unhappy enough to have penned an anonymous note? April wouldn't put it past her, but it would take more than a sharp-tongued old lady and a scrap of paper to intimidate her.

No longer the meek fourteen-year-old her aunt remembered, she returned the elderly woman's stare. "You're right, Aunt March. It was silly of me to assume I would have a room I haven't seen for twelve years."

Making a silent vow to curtail all future impulsive presumptions about anything, or anyone, as long as she remained in Calendar House, April swung her gaze up at her father. "Life changes so many things. I'm glad to see though that this room is exactly as I remembered it."

Chuckling, August caught her around the shoulders and steered her out into the hallway. "Can't change me. Don't even try. Your little sister has your old room, by the way."

"It really is the best room for a child, what with the eastern exposure and all." Following on their heels, Cynthia continued, "July is so excited about meetin' you. It's all she's talked about for days."

In the foyer, April retrieved her suitcase and coat. "I'm anxious to meet her, too, but Daddy's right. I'd better get out of these wet clothes."

"Certainly." Cynthia's eyes widened, telecasting a frantic message to her husband.

He stepped forward and caught April's wrist, loosely. "When you do meet your little sister please don't mention the sanitarium."

"Why not?" A frown weighed heavy on her brows.

A blush stole across her father's face and he looked relieved when Cynthia saved him from answering. "Small children ask such embarrassin' questions and have the most vivid imaginations. We wouldn't want her to have nightmares, hon, now would we?"

More likely Cynthia was afraid July would ask some of those "embarrassin' " questions in front of the reporters who had been invited to Thane and Vanessa's engagement party. Oh yes, April understood. Better than they thought. Anger swirled in the pit of her stomach.

She gazed from one to the other. "Where exactly does July think I've been—traveling the world—too busy to ever come and meet her?"

This time Cynthia was the one with the red face. "Well—I must admit, sugah, we were less than honest. However, I do believe we came up with an ingenious story. She thinks you're a, ah, missionary, workin' in some obscure little town in South America. We even showed her on the map."

Wide-eyed, April stared at them both, opening and shutting her mouth, unable to do more than sputter.

"It was my idea." Her father's look pleaded for her understanding. "It seemed right at the time. Please, darling, say you'll go along with it."

The bellowing wind matched April's screaming inner protest. For the last few years everything in her life depended on the truth, no matter how painful. Now they were asking her to lie about the very thing she'd had to confront to overcome. Her illness.

The prospect of meeting her seven-year-old half-sister was becoming less and less appealing. On the other hand, she'd decided before setting out on this journey, she'd do whatever it took to unlock the truth about

Lily's "accident," and if that meant lying, so be it.

Nodding, she said, "All right. But what about Thane and Spence and Karl and Vanessa?"

"The twins and Karl know and will maintain our little deception, but Vanessa will be told the same story as July, for now. We'll tell them both the truth after the weddin'."

"I know this will be hard on you and we appreciate your cooperation." Her father's relief was evident.

If only she shared his confidence. Fielding questions from a child didn't worry her, but Vanessa was an adult and might inadvertently ask some "embarrassin' " questions April would not be able to answer.

Aunt March tramped into the foyer like an army drill sergeant. "I'm going to take a nap. Vicious headache. Lordy, girl, haven't you got out of those wet clothes yet? All we need around here is some fool catching pneumonia. Come along. I'll show you which room is yours."

A clap of thunder drowned April's muttered retort as she grabbed her suitcase, slipped her damp parka over her arm and hurried up the stairs after the formidable figure of her aunt.

When she reached the landing, April paused, letting her eyes adjust to the reduced light. Peering down the darkened hall at the line of closed doors, she felt an ancient familiarity creep around her as cold as the air sneaking through the drafty walls. She shivered and let her gaze flick to the master bedroom door, then on to her old room beyond. Her sense of loss seemed to echo through the long corridor.

A brilliant flash exploded next to the window at her back, and, for a few seconds, light danced through the hallway. Momentarily blinded, April blinked. Dear God, it was unbelievable. The Oriental decadence extended to the upstairs as well. Her mind reeled in confusion. Had Cynthia also hated Lily—so much so that she had needed to erase every reminder of her existence?

Thunder boomed overhead as though a cannon had fired from the rooftop.

Suddenly, the thought of being alone held no charm and April hastened after her aunt, who had just disappeared around a corner. As she reached the turn, she stopped, engrossed by two huge doors on her left. "Aunt March, why is the west wing closed off?"

Slowing, the old woman glanced over her shoulder. "No sense heating a ballroom and servant quarters no one uses. You want to see your room or stand here jabbering all day?"

April said nothing, but hurried to catch up. "When will the others be arriving?"

"The others? Do you mean Vanessa and the twins?"

"Of course."

"They're due sometime tomorrow. But then so were you."

Sometime tomorrow. The thought sent an anxious twinge to her stomach and a bittersweet lump to her throat. She'd been as close to Cynthia's sons as if they were her older brothers, yet neither had made any attempt to see or talk to her during her recovery or since she'd left the sanitarium.

Attorneys now, Thane and Spencer Garrick shared a practice in Bellingham, Washington, and according to her father, aspired to the hierarchy of politics. Thane was campaigning for state representative while Spence actively sought the mayorship. But busy careers didn't explain their silent rejection of her.

Following her aunt around another bend, she shoved the old hurt aside. Dwelling on the twins' thoughtlessness was counterproductive. There was mystery enough to solve without taking on more. In truth, she could've contacted Spence and Thane anytime during the past four years, but something always held her back, something related to her confusion over Lily's accident.

The elderly woman pushed open the door at the end of the hall. "Here you are. Hope the smell of fresh paint doesn't make you ill."

She stepped through the doorway past her aunt and let out a sigh of relief. The room was small, almost an afterthought, but the decor was strictly Laura Ashley, all peaches and creams with lots of bleached pine. "This is a lovely room." Setting down her suitcase and coat, she turned back toward her aunt, but March had gone, closing the door behind her, leaving an abrupt void.

Hoping to ebb the encroaching gloom, April switched on her overhead light, but wind-whipped madrona trees outside her windows shrieked and moaned and beat angrily against the house like demons demanding entrance, deepening her unease with each passing minute.

Hurriedly, she unpacked, wishing she could empty her mind as readily. The more she thought about the ridiculous sham her father and Cynthia had perpetrated the less sense it made.

Exactly *how* had Daddy managed to keep her illness from reaching the press? And why? Did he know something about the accident he didn't want revealed? A chill knifed through April. The sooner she recovered her missing pieces of memory, the better. She pulled on beige slacks and an angora sweater, brushed her wavy, shoulder length hair and left her room.

Outside her door, she stopped and glanced left, then right, down the hallway, momentarily disoriented. She hadn't paid much attention to the direction her aunt had led her and the strange decor yielded few familiar landmarks. It was like trying to read a favorite nursery rhyme in a foreign language.

With her eyes closed, she mentally rummaged through her treasure house of long unvisited memories. Of course! She was in the east wing, and, unless she missed her guess, her bedroom had once been Aunt March's sewing room. Then there should be a back staircase leading to the kitchen around to the left. There was.

Perhaps she could pass through the kitchen and slip into the basement unnoticed. Confronting the past immediately held real appeal for her.

With her insides trembling, April headed down the steep, enclosed staircase. The slap of her beige flats on the bare, timeworn steps duplicated the slam of her heart against her rib cage, but halfway down she stopped and pressed her palm against the faded wallpaper. A shiver tripped down her spine. On the other side of this wall was the landing above the basement stairs.

She drew in a shaky breath. The passageway smelled musty and aged and summoned an image of herself curled on the fifth stair from the bottom with her ear tight to the wall, listening to the twins. As children, they often excluded her from their games, using the landing as a private hideout, but one day, quite by accident, April had overheard voices coming through the wafer-thin wall and discovered a way of having her own secrets. A nervous laugh discharged in her throat. It was silly, a childish prank.

Why did it feel like something more?

She peeled her hand from the wall and continued down the few remaining steps. The door into the kitchen was ajar and the aroma of pot roast brought her to an abrupt halt. Was someone in the kitchen? It was a chance she'd have to take.

With a determined shove, April pushed the door open and stepped into the room, but her resolve turned to rubber at the sight that met her eyes. The warm and wonderful, old-fashioned farm kitchen of her childhood had been replaced by a cold and awful, stainless steel, black and white update.

Outside, the wind and rain lost power while inside April's pulse thudded in her ears too loudly for her to notice the abating storm. Judging the wear and tear on the cabinets and appliances, she estimated the modernization had been done several years ago.

Shaking her head in disgust, she turned toward the basement door and froze.

It was gone.

Three

Staring at the solid wall where the basement door had been, April felt her hopes of unlocking her memory begin to shrivel as surely as the dying storm.

"April?"

The vaguely familiar, masculine voice drowned out the quieting patter of rain against the windows. She turned to find a tall, handsome thirty-year-old man, looking at her with his head cocked to the side. One of the twins. Cynthia's sons had inherited their mother's coloring, but not her exotic features; his were bold, masculine. But twelve years had passed without contact, twelve years in which nature had molded teenagers into adults, and April couldn't discern if this was Thane or Spence.

Spencer Garrick's breath caught in his throat. God, she looked like Lily. A floodgate opened inside his brain, washing old memories and feelings to the surface. And the guilt, always the guilt. Dammit, he should have been better prepared for this. Rubbing his palms on his gray Levis, he realized her face was as pale as his felt. An insane urge to touch her had him cramming his hands into his pockets. "Are you all right?"

April read dismay in his dove-gray eyes. It struck

her there was something unapproachable, even dangerous about this man. And yet . . . she felt an inexplicable attraction to him. "What happened to the basement door?"

He took a step closer.

She tensed, then noted the concern on his face and willed herself to relax.

"The way to the basement and wine cellar was rerouted through the laundry room. The new stairway's closed in and not so steep."

The image induced by his reference to the steep staircase had April swallowing hard. Strangely, his words also revived her hopes. She could still reach the basement. Then another thought cut short her relief. Had Daddy torn down the landing and the old staircase? She wanted to ask, needed to ask, but the question lodged in her throat. It might sound odd. *Or insane.* Aunt March's words rang in her head, reminding April to choose her allies with care. There was no cause to trust the twins; in fact, for some unknown reason, the notion sent up red flares.

"Mrs. Winston?" A little girl with russet-colored French braids and navy blue eyes bounded into the kitchen. Spotting April, she stopped dead in her tracks and hugged the blond Barbie doll she carried to her tummy. "Are you April?"

Overwhelmed by a rush of emotion, April fought the unexpected urge to embrace the darling seven-year-old whose eager expression warmed her chilled insides. The proper procedure in greeting a half-sister for the first time hadn't been included among the new things she learned in the past four years. Would the child bolt if she moved too fast? Deciding to take the little girl's lead, she said, "Yes, and I'll bet you're July."

"Yes, I am." The child closed the distance between

them. "Gee, you're pretty."

"Why, thank you." Bending at the waist, April added, "And so are you."

July reached out and took her older sister's hand. "Do you think I look like Daddy? Everyone says so."

Biting back a smile, she pretended to think about it for a moment, then said, "I have to admit, you do look a lot like him."

July flung her arms around April's neck and squeezed tight. "I'm so glad you're home."

Tears stung her eyes as April hugged this fragile, precious person to her, marveling at how loved a child could make one feel.

Too soon, the child squirmed free of her sister's grasp and glanced up at her brother. "And Spence looks just like Thane, doesn't he?"

"Yes, he does." The adults' eyes met and held, and April felt her heart jump. Inexplicably she had sensed this was Spencer. Not that it made any difference, she chided herself. Sure, she'd had a slight crush on him, but that was twelve years ago. For a long moment, she studied his face intently, amending her outdated memories with this older version of the handsome young boy who had once owned her heart.

Spence caught July against his side and ruffled the top of her head. "Thane and I are supposed to look alike, kiddo. We're twins."

The little girl stretched her neck to see his face. "Who does April look like?"

"Myself," April answered, sounding harsher than she'd meant. Why must she be reminded of her resemblance to Lily at every turn? She caught the slight lift of Spencer's brow, but he didn't contradict her claim. Surely, he could appreciate how it felt to constantly be compared to someone else.

"Why doesn't she look like you or me?" July

persisted. "She's our sister."

Spence pulled out a dinette chair and sat down, dragging the child onto his lap. "No, sweetheart. She's not my sister."

July tilted her head in the same way Spencer had earlier. Her navy blue eyes clouded in confusion. "How can she be my sister and you be my brother and April not be your sister, too?"

"Well, it's pretty complicated, and I'm not sure I'm the one who should explain it to you."

"I know." July sighed dramatically. "Go ask Mom."

"Hey, you're pretty smart for a twerp."

"I'm not a twerp." She smacked him on the belly. "Oh, I'm supposed to find out when dinner will be ready. Where's Mrs. Winston?"

"I'm right here, child." A blond, rosy-cheeked woman in her early forties, who brought to mind the Swedish countryside, came bustling through the laundry room door. She was slightly breathless, shorter by several inches than April's five foot six and rounder by at least four dress sizes. "Been getting extra potatoes from the basement larder. Tell your ma dinner will be ready in about half an hour and then come back and help me peel these."

"Okay." July scooted off Spencer's lap and hurried out of the room, clutching the Barbie doll around the middle.

The housekeeper dumped the armful of potatoes into one of the stainless steel sinks, then wiped her hands on her apron. Facing April, she grinned and extended a hand. "Don't know if you remember me or not? Helga, Helga Winston? I've been the cook and housekeeper here since you two were wearing rompers."

The twenty or more pounds Helga had gained altered her facial features, but not enough to make her unrecognizable. April felt her cheeks warm as she accepted the housekeeper's hand. "Certainly, I remember you. It was Karl I didn't recognize. We ran into each other in Friday Harbor, but until he introduced himself I had no idea who he was."

Helga's chest puffed with obvious pride. "Every bit as handsome as his father, don't you think?"

April nodded, but to her way of thinking the two men were total contrasts. Karl's father Jesse had dark hair and a crude, undefinable handsomeness. Karl's features were male-model perfection. However, something about the man put her off, and she couldn't really say why. Perhaps it was nothing more than his eagerness to know everything she'd been up to and her unwillingness to satisfy his curiosity. She managed a smile. "You must be very proud of him."

"It's not easy to raise a boy without his pa. Not that I was left a choice in the matter." Surprisingly there was a bitterness in Helga's voice that struck April as odd. Surely it should have lessened by this time.

"Well, you've obviously done a fine job."

"Thanks." Helga's smile flashed a little too brightly as she abruptly changed the subject. "You sure do look like your ma."

"I don't think April is comfortable with the comparison." Spencer hadn't meant to blurt that out, but the truth was he wished everyone would stop comparing the two women. For God's sake—Lily was dead! Lurching to his feet, he shoved the chair back against the table.

The housekeeper's rosy cheeks turned to a dark crimson. "Sorry. I didn't mean any offense. It was a compliment. Why, I was Lily Cordell's biggest fan."

Helga's blue eyes were as guileless and friendly as the woman herself. April cringed inwardly. Her hang-up about resembling Lily wasn't the housekeeper's problem. Nor should she have made such a big deal out of it that Spence felt he had to leap to her defense. Striving to make amends, she offered the housekeeper a grin. "No offense taken, Mrs. Winston."

"You call me Helga. Your folks sure have been excited about your visit, but none of you were expected today." Digging into a drawer, she extracted a peeler. "Good thing I got the bedrooms ready this morning and fixed a big pot roast."

"It smells wonderful, Helga." Spence leaned against the counter.

As he pushed the sleeves of his pink and gray cable knit sweater up to his elbows, revealing muscular forearms, furred with sleek sable hair, April felt her pulse bounce. Quickly, she forced her gaze elsewhere. "Do you need any help, Helga?"

"As a matter of fact, Spencer could do me a big favor. Fetch a bottle of wine from the cellar. A full-bodied red."

"Sure." Spencer shoved away from the counter.

April wasn't about to let the opportunity to see the basement pass. "I'll help."

Spencer stiffened. The last thing he wanted was to be in the basement with April. "That's not necessary. Why don't you stay here and visit with Helga?"

She moved toward him. "Actually, I'd like to see the wine cellar. My education is lacking in numerous fundamentals and I could use a lesson in wines . . . if you wouldn't mind playing teacher."

One look at her eclipsed the protest Spencer had started to voice. The stubborn determination in the set of her slender shoulders and delicate jaw said she intended to go to the basement with or without him. Any argument he might put forth would only seem

37

suspicious. Resignedly, he motioned her to follow, and headed toward the laundry room.

April felt an anxious twinge in her stomach as she fell in step behind him, but soon her attention veered to his lilting stride. With rapt fascination, she watched the shift of his jean-snugged hips and the flux of his broad shoulders beneath his loose sweater. His walk emitted a raw sensuality April found unsettling. There was no room in her life for men—not until her lost memory returned. And maybe not even then.

He switched on the light. To April's chagrin, the laundry room had also been enlarged and windows added. The glass threw back their reflections and their gazes met and held. The dismay she felt was written on her face for all the world and Spencer to see.

Despite his resolve to remain indifferent to her during the next two weeks, Spencer couldn't help but respond to this lovely, tormented woman. He spoke without thinking. "It can't be easy coming back to find so much changed."

The tenderness in his voice was too much. Sympathy was the one thing April hadn't hardened herself against. Tears burned the back of her eyelids and a lump clogged her throat, forcing her to swallow hard. "No, it's not. Even the rooms that haven't been . . . redone . . . show more wear than I expected to see." The smile hovering on her lips felt weak.

Realizing the danger of encouraging this conversation, Spencer pulled his gaze from her entrancing aqua eyes and changed the subject. "Sounds like the storm is over."

He skirted the dryer and waited by a wide archway to give her, as well as himself, a moment to regain composure. The fierce silence was punctuated by the patter of dripping water from the eaves and down-spouts. Ducking through the arch, he proceeded down the steps. "Come on."

April caught hold of her courage and mixed it with a deep breath for good measure, reminding herself her stay here was only temporary. Once she recovered her lost memory, she could go back to the life she'd established in Arizona. And the first step toward that goal started with these stairs. "I'm right behind you."

With her heart pounding wildly, she followed Spencer down and down, colliding into his solid backside when he stopped abruptly at the bottom stair.

"Sorry," she stammered, too conscious of the intimate touch of her fingertips against his muscled back, too conscious of his heartbeat beneath his soft sweater, too conscious of Spencer Garrick the man. Levering for balance, she leaned away from him.

The door swung inward, releasing a dank smell and a breath of cool air. The cellar was medium-sized with an unswept cement floor and an overbright ceiling bulb. The light glared yellow across the cold, dusky room, conjuring creepy shadows in corners and along ledges.

Proceeding into the room, April glanced from the metal shelves lining the walls — crammed with home-canned foods in every size and shape glass container imaginable — to the heaped gunnysacks of potatoes and onions on the concrete floor.

Spencer moved ahead to a door stuck between the metal shelves. As he reached for the knob, uncertainty tangled with expectancy inside her. Her voice held a telltale quaver. "Everything is backward. We used to get to this room through this door."

Spencer heard her misgiving and suspended his hand on the doorknob. Perhaps she'd changed her mind. He glanced over his shoulder. "Are you sure

39

you want to go on?"

"Absolutely!"

The nod of her head set her golden hair dancing wildly about her arresting face. Spencer stared, mesmerized. She looked so like Lily just now, younger of course, but the similarities, the place, aroused unwanted memories—memories better left forgotten, he reminded himself. He twisted the doorknob and pushed. "The door is stuck. It swells in this damp weather. Move back."

April retreated to the center of the larder and watched him apply his shoulder to the stubborn door. A second later it scraped across the cement floor, setting off an eerie echo in the large open area beyond.

Spencer stepped over the threshold and flicked on the light switch. The dim bulb did little to dispel the darkness or ease the shadows in the vast room. It felt as cold and damp as a mausoleum. Indeed, over the past few years it had been designated as a graveyard for August's failed inventions. Discarded metal skeletons peered around stacked cardboard boxes that looked more like bulky tombstones draped in cobweb shrouds. He heard a rat skittering into a corner and felt a shiver slice up his back.

This was the moment of truth, but he wasn't ready. His pulse was beating too fast for his liking. Deliberately, he positioned his body to block April's range of vision.

April gazed through the doorway at Spencer's back. Why didn't he move aside? Impatience skipped along her nerve endings and crept into her words. "You'd never make it as a tour guide."

He wheeled around to face her with his dark brows crooked in a frown. "Huh?"

Barely containing the urge to shove past him and into the room, she fought to keep her tone light, teasing. "The object of any tour is to let the customer *see* the scenery."

The frown turned into a scowl. Shifting position, he further barricaded himself between April and the doorway. "Tour? What tour?"

Heat rushed into her cheeks at the inadvertent admission, but the chill emanating from him quickly sobered her. "I want to see what changes Dad has made to the basement."

Spencer narrowed his eyes as anger licked through him. He knew he was probably going to be too blunt, he always was when he cared about something. It was a flaw in his nature he had never been able to overcome, the one thing that would always keep him from receiving the political success that came so easily to Thane. "April, I assume you have your reasons for wanting to see this room and I suppose you have a right, but we can't afford to have you fall to pieces again. Lily is dead. Accept that fact and get on with your life. And let us get on with ours."

April blanched, then felt her face flame anew, this time in anger. In her elation at being reunited with him, she'd actually forgotten how single-minded Spencer could be. Always thrusting his opinions on people as though he, and only he, had the solution to the world's problems. "I—"

Cutting her off before she got started, Spencer raged on, "You can't know the torment the family has suffered at the hands of the press. Politicians are under intense scrutiny these days and there are any number of unscrupulous opponents who will win an election however they can. Every election year, including the one four years ago, some byline-hungry reporter digs up the whole mess again. The engagement festivities should be Thane and Vanessa's celebration. But I'm afraid this year your presence here is going to stir that hornet's nest worse than ever."

Alarms went off inside her. Had Spencer sent the note? "Are you telling me to leave?"

He sighed loud, frustrated. "It would have been better if you hadn't come—but you're here now."

She could no more contain the fury building inside her than she could contain her need to see the room beyond him. Arching one brow higher than the other, April glared at him. "Don't worry. I won't do anything or say anything that will ruin the family festivities."

The tartness in her voice made him wince. "You won't have to." He grabbed her by the shoulders, but when he pulled her near and gazed into her eyes, his breath and his anger snarled in his throat. His words came out whispered, sounding husky, sensuous, even to him. "Your beautiful face will do the damage."

As his heated breath embraced her face, April's ire gave way to a much stronger emotion, a deep yearning to be kissed, to at least once in her sterile life know the secrets of intimacy most women her age took for granted.

The unmistakable invitation in her bewitching aqua eyes was his undoing. Lowering his lips to hers, Spencer kissed her gently, then possessively and felt her innocent response as her body arched instinctively toward his. His arms snaked around her, pulling her closer. God, she felt good, tasted good. She was everything he'd always dreamed she'd be, and more.

The stirring deep in his belly brought him to his senses with a jolt. He released her as though he'd been bitten instead of kissed. Anger twisted his gut, anger at himself. He hadn't meant to take advantage of the situation, nor let the situation take advantage of him.

Bracing his frame against the open doorway, he spoke to April with all the reproach he felt toward himself. "Go back upstairs. I'll get the wine."

Her spirits felt as bruised and abandoned as her lips. How dare he dismiss her like a naughty child! Damn, he was arrogant! Was that what politics did to a person? With every ounce of willpower she possessed, April managed to rein in her shortened temper, realizing it would do more harm to defy him than to let him believe he was getting his way. She couldn't quite eliminate the ice from her gaze, but she did manage to tip her head in acquiescence. "All right. I'll go."

Scrambling through the larder, she ascended the stairs, pausing halfway up. Her fingers strayed to her swollen lips, gingerly caressing them. The kiss had been wonderful, but now she felt humiliated. She'd allowed him to think he could deter her from seeing the basement by using the oldest trick in the book. Seduction.

Now, he was probably laughing at her naivete, judging her a pushover, a fool. Heat burned into her cheeks and she knew they were undoubtedly as red as the wine Spence was selecting. The only consolation was that he had sorely underestimated her determination.

As soon as she heard him cross the basement to the wine cellar and close the heavy door, April hurried back down the stairs. In seconds, she'd moved through the larder to the door. Her heart raced with anticipation, then skipped two full beats as she stepped into the large open room. The temperature was definitely several degrees lower in here, yet April felt flushed with heat.

The low watt bulb offered inadequate illumination and several precious seconds passed before April's eyes adjusted enough to survey the room that spiders and neglect had veiled in webby, ghostly mantles. Her nose wrinkled at the musty smell. As children, the twins, Karl, and she had been allowed to play in the spacious room, roller skating almost daily in the winter.

Now there was only a narrow pathway between boxes and metal hulks leading to the wine cellar.

At length, her seeking eyes located the coveted spot.

The muffled sound of a scuttling rat brought April to her tiptoes, but her hopes fell flat. As far as she could tell the landing was intact and being used as a storage shelf, but the staircase had been removed.

Yet, as she stared at the desecrated site, April found she could see the staircase distinctly in her mind's eye. And something else, too. Something indefinable, intangible, something April sensed in the hidden recesses of her memory banks. New hope sprouted inside her. Perhaps even without the staircase she would be able to retrieve those lost minutes so vital to her full recovery.

The creak of unoiled hinges announced the opening of the wine cellar door and shattered April's musing. She scurried through the larder and back up the stairs, arriving in the kitchen, slightly breathless, only seconds before Spencer. A telltale blush warmed her cheeks, but April was counting on the arrogant man to think that she was blushing because of their kiss, and not because she had disobeyed his edict to leave the basement.

July and Helga were bent over one of the huge sinks peeling potatoes. As Spencer strode toward them, the cook dried her hands on her apron, then reached for the dusty bottle. After daubing at the filthy glass with a damp paper towel, she read the la-

44

bel, then looked up at Spencer. Her smile included April. "This is exactly what I had in mind. Now you two had better get on into the living room."

"Yeah," the little girl chimed in, "Thane and Vanessa are here, too."

The moment Thane Garrick's eyes met April's, his face paled, but his recovery was so quick, so complete, she doubted anyone else saw it. The master of diplomacy. The exemplary politician. However, he looked nothing like a rising young political star in his white chinos and a white hand-knit cotton sweater which would have better suited Phoenix than the San Juan Islands in wintertime.

His appraising gaze swept her. "Good Lord!" There was a note of surprise in his voice. "This can't be little April."

Wincing inwardly, she reminded herself this was the last of these innocuous greetings she would have to suffer. "Hello Thane. It's nice to see you again."

April watched Spencer greet his twin with a handshake. Lord, the likeness was uncanny. Except that Thane was slightly shorter she would be hard-pressed to tell them apart. As Thane moved toward her, she noticed a tiny crescent-shaped scar near the corner of his left eye that she couldn't recall having ever seen. For some inexplicable reason, it made her uneasy.

Thane planted a kiss on her cheek. "You're looking well."

His faux pas landed in the room like an unexploded bomb. Her father choked on his cocktail, Cynthia went ashen, Aunt March coughed into her lace hankie, and Spencer scowled at his twin. The only person unaffected by the gaffe was a pretty blond-haired young woman standing with the night-darkened picture windows at her back.

April gave Thane a dazzling smile. "Thank you, Thane. I *am* well."

The tips of Thane's ears glowed red. April was assailed by myriad memories, little things she suddenly recalled about the twins like Thane's ears turning red when he was embarrassed and Spencer's turning red when he lied. Did Spence still have an impassioned nature with the hair-trigger temper, quickly fired, then spent? Was Thane still able to control his temper to the point where it seldom emerged? His greater success on the political battlefield would seem proof of it.

Thane's arm on her shoulder made her too aware that everyone was looking at her. He led her toward the blond who appeared to be near her own age. "I want you to meet my fiancée, Vanessa O'Brien. Darling, this is April."

Vanessa's golden hair was cut to align with the curve of her jaw. Straight bangs covered every inch of forehead above the greenest eyes April had ever seen. Contacts? She was tall and her delicate-boned frame gave her an underfed look, bringing to mind the phrase "You can never be too rich or too thin."

She grinned at April. "I've been dying to meet you — especially after Thane told me you were Lily Cordell's daughter."

Uncertain what to expect from this obvious fan of her mother, April tensed.

"I love old movies," Vanessa enthused, "and your mother's are my absolute favorites. Has anyone ever told you how much you look like her? God, it's like having her ghost right in our very midst."

A nervous laugh escaped Thane as he and Spencer locked gazes.

Damn! April shouldn't have come home. The ache

between Spencer's temples exploded to a crescendo, pounding the inside of his skull like the relentless surf pounding against the cliffs outside.

Vanessa was right. Watching April move and talk, it was as if Lily had come to life, was here with them in this house, in this very room she had loved. A chill settled in his stomach. Why wouldn't Lily stay dead? Wasn't it enough that guilt stalked his every waking hour?

His gaze stole to April. White cold fear seared across his heart, and he knew with a certainty what he must do. April had to leave. Willingly or otherwise. And soon. Before the other guests arrived. Before the reporters. Before her mother's old friends.

Before she discovered the truth.

Four

The truth was, April felt as out of place at dinner as the black-lacquered dining table and chairs looked in the pine-paneled room. With the sole exception of July, no one made an effort to engage her in conversation. The main topic revolved around politics, a subject she knew and cared little about.

In all honesty, April was relieved that she was no longer the center of attention. It gave her the chance to study her family unobserved. Which one had sent the nasty little note?

Aunt March? She had always treated April with a touch of disdain, always daring her to stand up for herself, always managing to make April feel a failure. Yes, the old woman was certainly capable of threats and had expressed her opinion of her niece in no uncertain terms. *Insane!* Somehow, the hurtful label and her aunt's cold indifference bothered her more than she would have thought possible.

April sipped at her wine as her gaze shifted down the table. Spencer? She watched a stray lock of dark hair fall across his handsome forehead, obscuring one of his compelling gray eyes as he expounded the virtues of a bill he was endorsing. Absently, he shoved the wayward strand back into place and April heard her heart-beat hammer in her ears.

With a sudden rush, she felt again the touch of his lips on hers, the surge of desire in her bloodstream, the sting of rejection, the ache of humiliation. Unwelcome heat grazed her cheeks. He *could* have sent the note. Hadn't he told her she should have stayed away from Calendar House?

Roughly, she wiped her napkin across her mouth, subconsciously trying to wipe away the memory of his kiss, and forced her attention to Thane. She found him faintly disturbing, but couldn't say why. They hadn't had a minute alone. All she really knew about Thane consisted of her twelve-year-old memories and the momentary paling of his face when he had first seen her today. But did that prove he hadn't expected her to show up, or merely that he was startled by her resemblance to her mother?

April took a bite of the pot roast, finding it as tough to chew as her thoughts. Her gaze veered to the head of the table.

Her father? The small piece of meat hit her stomach like a chunk of stone. She refused to cast him in the role of malefactor. That would be the cruelest cut of all. It took a mouthful of wine to wash down the rancid notion. August Farraday would never be able to keep his mind on something that devious long enough to carry it off. Even now she could see the vague gleam in his navy eyes that always signaled his mind was a thousand light-years away on one of his inventions.

April freshened her pallet with a bite of mashed potatoes and gravy and glanced at Vanessa. She couldn't imagine one reason for the outgoing young woman to harbor any hatred for her. In fact, she seemed the only person in the group willing to admit Lily Cordell had even existed.

49

But what about Cynthia? April found the idea the easiest to digest. She watched the woman fuss over her future daughter-in-law, waving her bejeweled hands in the air for emphasis, then curling her fingers fondly, possessively, around the beloved girl's. There could be little doubt as to where her stepmother's loyalties lay, or that she had tried to obliterate Lily's memory. But was that so unnatural for a second wife?

Still, letting prejudice color her logic this early in the game was ill-advised. Give the woman the benefit of the doubt, she was urging herself, when the huge emerald ring on the middle finger of Cynthia's right hand caught her eye. Disbelief chased her good intentions aside. The filigree setting was as gaudy as the ornate chandelier above the table, but April knew the glorious stone was as real as the orange blossom centerpiece. It was her mother's emerald, reset. She would swear to it.

Her sharply indrawn breath snared unwanted attention.

July tugged at the sleeve of April's angora sweater. "Why are you looking so funny at Mommy?"

April blanched. With expressions ranging from confusion to curiosity, everyone at the table turned their collective attention to her, waiting for her answer. What did she have to lose by being candid? Nothing, she decided, swallowing the lump in her throat and squaring her mental shoulders.

She set an unwavering gaze on Cynthia. "I was just admiring your mother's pretty green ring. It reminds me of another ring, one I remember from my childhood."

Cynthia's right hand went immediately to the gold cross resting between the ruffles of her vee necked, purple silk dress. Her fingers worked the smooth surface of the small crucifix as though the gesture would cleanse her of unconfessed sin, but her almond shaped eyes showed no distress. She looked at April with all the innocence of a puppy. "It sounds like a fascinatin' story, sugah. Do go on."

April's confidence faltered, but she was saved the necessity of further explanations by Helga's arrival with hot apple dumplings à la mode.

As the housekeeper replaced the dinner plates with dessert bowls, Vanessa broke the stilted silence. "Mr. Farraday, Calendar House is charming. When was it built?"

April smiled to herself at Vanessa's tactful maneuvering of the conversation to safer waters. Thane's fiancée had obviously cut her teeth on diplomacy.

With a forkful of dumpling and ice cream halfway to his mouth, August blinked, looking slightly taken aback at having been addressed by his stepson's fiancée. His older daughter's heart warmed with love for him. He seldom had to deal with everyday matters, like polite conversation, and was undoubtedly not aware of the group around him in any real context. But he thrived on family history and welcomed every opportunity to talk about it. Vanessa couldn't have asked him a better question.

He chewed and swallowed, regarding the slender girl with sudden interest as though reassessing her, favorably. "The house was built and named in 1894 by April's great, great grandfather, Octavius Farraday, and is basically unchanged, with the exception of a few necessary structural repairs over the years."

"How did Octavius come to select such a remote spot?" Vanessa's green eyes shone with encouragement.

August was warming to his subject. He dipped the fork into the dessert bowl again as one of his rare smiles made an appearance. "Quite naturally I should think. Octavius was a sea captain, but a rogue and a pirate would better fit the legends of him."

"Why?" Vanessa's pale brows lifted in amused arcs.

"Well, you see, the San Juans total one hundred and seventy four islands in all. There are hundreds of coves and winding passageways. That, plus their location — their close proximity to the mainland of the United States as well as Canada — made them ideal bases for smuggling."

Her voice rose in surprise. "What was worth smuggling in this part of the world in those days?"

August's face grew grave. "In 1792 John Meares introduced Chinese to the Puget Sound area as a source of cheap labor. In later years this commodity was big business to the unscrupulous."

The clank of a spoon against a bowl sent April's attention to her Aunt March. The elderly woman was scowling at August. "How dare you let this impressionable young woman believe any Farraday, past or present, would deal in slavery! The very idea — duping naive Chinese into using their life savings for safe passage to America only to sell them for cheap laborers. . . ."

"I believe the girl is intelligent enough to figure out this was before our great grandfather's time, March, but the history is too colorful not to be told."

Spencer cocked his head to one side in the distracting gesture that was beginning to annoy April. "Weren't the islands also noted as the headquarters for hoodlums, adventurers, disappointed gold seekers, and all sorts of other lawless characters in those early days?"

August nodded, obviously finding his subject as delicious as his dessert. "Absolutely! The locale offered excellent hiding places. Opium and diamonds were also prime smuggling items, then later wool and, of course during Prohibition, liquor. Great-granddad had his fingers in at least one of those messy pies, because this old house is full of secret passages and underground tunnels."

"Really? What fun! I'd love to see them. Thane you must take me on a tour." Vanessa twinkled at her fiancé.

"Don't get too excited, darling," Thane interjected. "Most of the passageways have been walled off—for the obvious reason of safety."

"Ohhh . . . that's too bad." Vanessa's disappointment lasted mere seconds before she returned her attention to August. "Is there some history behind the family being named for different months?"

Before he could answer, Helga brought in fresh coffee and began refilling cups. August took the opportunity to finish the last of his dessert.

April shoved her bowl aside and reached for the sugar. She added a lump to her coffee and stirred slowly. Her gaze wandered to her father. While the others either doctored their coffee with sugar or cream or merely accepted it straight, he reached into the pocket of his beige corduroy jacket for his pipe and tobacco pouch. By the time he took his first puff, spoons had been set on saucers, expectant glances on August.

He laid the pipe in the ashtray. "Octavius's fascination with chronology is the source of the house's name. As to the family, he married six times and buried all six wives. He lived to the age of one hundred, and he was a prolific old devil—had lots of children with each wife. He named the first seven after the days of the week, then started with the months of the year, then the signs of astrology. 'Course not all the children lived, but fourteen did, and they passed the tradition on through the generations."

"How wonderful! Not every family can claim a genuine black sheep." Vanessa spoke with enthusiasm.

"Isn't she a darlin'? As if a family's black sheep are somethin' to be proud of." Cynthia grabbed for Vanessa's hand, causing the emerald to glare at April and bounce her thoughts back to the question of Lily's jewelry.

What had become of the other expensive pieces? she wondered. It took little imagination to conjure a picture of the dazzling gems ensconced in Cynthia's bedroom wall safe. An odd sense of jealousy warred inside April. It wasn't that she wanted any of the jewelry herself. She had no use for such high-priced baubles, and in any case she didn't deserve to inherit Lily's jewelry, especially not if what she feared were true. In fact the very idea of owning any of it, of touching it, of wearing it, stole all breathable air from the room.

Lurching to her feet, April excused herself. She retrieved her parka from her bedroom closet and wrestled into it on her way down the back stairs. In the kitchen she came across Karl. He was alone, seated at the black and white table, drinking from a mug. Eyeing the dirty dishes scattered about him, she assumed he'd just finished eating his own dinner.

He gave his shockingly blond hair a shake and cast an assessing gaze at her. Then, half rising out of his chair, he asked. "You need me to fire up the ferry?"

"No. I'm just going for a walk."

"In the dark?"

"It's not that dark."

Karl shrugged. "You look like you could use a friend. I'm a good listener, if you want company."

"Thanks. Maybe some other time."

Helga chose that moment to arrive with an armload of dishes. April turned toward the laundry room, but she could feel Karl's eyes on her. As she opened the back door, she heard Helga say, "Karl, do you think you might help me with these?"

Outside the brisk post-rain air stung her cheeks and filled her nostrils with its clear sharp scent. Her lungs reached for the sweet breath, and April felt her distress begin to disperse. Through the scudding clouds overhead, she could make out an occasional star, but the roiling black masses darted across the moon, blinking its illumination off, then on, in erratic sequence, bringing to mind a lighthouse beam searching the ground for survivors after a storm.

Over the years she had survived many a storm. This time would be no different. Trying to ignore her niggling doubts, she pushed the deep collar of the red jacket against her ears, shoved her hands into her pockets, and set a course for the stand of firs at the left side of the house. She strode along the timeworn path leading to the cliff above the bay, letting go of her tension with each step.

As she neared the source of the noisy surf, pungent salty air rushed at her from all sides, nearly drowning April in a gigantic wave of familiarity. How often had she walked this path, struggling to understand some new cruelty foisted on her by Lily? April ground to a halt, shook her head and expelled an exasperated sigh. God, how Lily had managed to hurt her. The old pain crowded into her mind as dark and agitated as one of the clouds overhead, carrying with it the sting of tears. Why had Lily been so afraid of growing old that she'd rejected the love of her only child, making her dress like a ten-year-old at the age of fourteen?

The memory provoked her to scoop a twig from the ground and smack the nearest tree trunk. April cursed out loud, then tossed the leafy whip away, and picked up her pace as though she could outrun her thoughts. So, she wasn't as immune to her mother's behavior as she liked to think. At least now she understood the problem was Lily's—an obsession—not something lacking in herself. But being unable to confront her mother left a lingering frustration she hadn't quite learned to let go of.

She was breathing hard by the time she left the woods behind, but the anxiety stayed with her. Buried somewhere in the recesses of her mind was a possibility April still couldn't face. Had she already confronted her mother—twelve years ago—at the edge of the basement stairs?

If only she could talk to Dr. Merritt. Yes, Nancy had said she was only a phone call away, however, April doubted the good doctor would qualify her present state as an emergency. They had already discussed her apprehensions, and until she regained some significant memory, there was nothing Nancy could do but reassure her. Maybe that was all she really wanted. Reassurance—that she couldn't have done what she feared the most.

Lost in thought, April had no idea how long she'd been walking along the edge of the cliff. Foggy patches had sneaked unnoticed across her path. She shivered. Having grown used to the arid climate of Arizona, she'd forgotten how quickly fog could occur here at this time of year.

Ahead, she spied an old friend: a massive rock, shaped significantly like a huge turtle. A wistful smile tugged at her mouth and stilled her steps. She'd spent many hours perched on that humpy "shell" watching the bay for pods of killer whales, but the rock was a mile from the house. She hadn't meant to walk this far. Promising herself to come back one day soon, she reversed direction.

The return trip seemed somehow longer, the path more precarious. It was the swirling fog and the increasing breezes, she told herself. As she picked her way along, the wind whined across the precipice, touched her with ghostly breaths, and escaped into the trees beyond, whispering through the gnarled timbers like a moaning phantom.

Then she heard it. "A-a-pril-l-l-l . . ."

The fine hairs on the nape of her neck prickled. Was the sound some trick of the wind?

Nearby, a twig snapped. April spun toward the woods at her side, feeling her heartbeat triple. "Is someone there?"

No answer. Was it an animal? The island teemed with nocturnal critters. A deer perhaps? Or a mother raccoon scavenging food for her babies? Yes, that was it. She willed herself to relax, fighting the urge to walk faster. Her imagination was too good, too open to suggestion.

Then she heard it again. Low. Eerie. Riding on the breeze. "Aapril-l-l-l . . ."

And something else. A heavy footfall. Crashing through the trees at her side. Coming closer.

Alarm put wings to her feet. Running parallel to the woods, she fled along the precipice as fast as the limited light and the slick ground allowed. Her pulse thudded in her ears, simulating the resounding tide. She heard only the wind and surf. Was it following her? April glanced over her shoulder. It was too dark to tell. She swung back around and lurched ahead.

Her feet struck loose pebbles.

She pitched forward.

Off balance.

The wind knocked from her lungs as she landed half on and half off the edge of the cliff. A thunderous splash exploded from the dark void below her, and briny spatters of water reached to graze her face. She felt herself slipping. Dear God, she was going to die.

April flailed the air. Her fingers caught something leafy. A bush. She grasped for dear life, kicking and pulling, relinquishing her beige flats to the watery abyss.

At length she managed to wrench herself to solid ground. Fear and pain dissolved in the joy of being safe, alive. For precious seconds, April savored the dank smell of the earth, thinking it the sweetest odor she'd ever encountered.

Then the sound came again.

"A-a-pril-l-l-l . . ."

Although her breath burned in her lungs, April staggered to her feet and stumbled on. A few minutes later, she was forced to stop again. The ground ahead was a mixture of gravel, broken seashells, and sand. It would flay the skin off her bare feet. She'd have to take her chances in the woods. Her frantic gaze searched the section of cliff she had just traversed, seeking any sign of her pursuer. Good. So far she was alone. At least through the cover of the trees she could travel slower and incur less injury.

Before she could stir, the clouds parted, illuminating a figure on the path about a hundred feet behind her. The wind carried off her startled scream. It was a man. A man she knew.

Why was he chasing her, deliberately trying to scare her? For a split second pale gray eyes met aqua eyes, then the churning clouds squelched all light. April stood stock-still with her heart threatening to explode inside her chest.

Was the man Thane or Spence?

She ducked into the trees. Right now it didn't matter who was chasing her, it only mattered that she get safely back to the house. She could figure out the identity of her hunter and why he was hunting her then.

Staying clear of the path, she moved gingerly, picking a makeshift trail through the tangled undergrowth. The damp earth sucked at her numbed feet like the hurt sucking at her spirits.

Camouflaged stickers and taloned limbs clawed at her hair and stabbed her feet, but the shock coursing her bloodstream, and the certain knowledge that her pursuer was near, that he was one of her stepbrothers, deadened her awareness to physical pain.

After what seemed an eternity, April spotted the lights of Calendar House glowing through the trees and patchy fog like bright yellow beacons. The sight gave her heart.

Panting, she rounded the last stand of trees and veered toward the house. A dark form reared up in her path.

The message telegraphed from her brain to her feet too late for retreat.

They collided.

Her screams fled on the wind.

Two strong arms snapped around her like a sprung trap, pinning her upper arms to her sides, her hands against the man's chest. She tried ineffectually to struggle free, to pound her fists, but his grip was as restrictive as a straitjacket.

Five

Even through her heavy clothes, he could feel the erratic thud of her heart. "Hey, it's all right. I'm not going to hurt you."

Recognizing Spence's voice, April felt her knees go weak. Without questioning why, she quit struggling, and buried her fear and her cheek in the rough suede of his sheepskin coat. It smelled of spicy aftershave and cold and rain-freshened salt air. Her breath slowed. Within minutes she realized she felt warm, secure, and wondered how she could have been so frightened of this man one moment, then feel so safe in his arms the next?

Spencer felt the trembling in April's body dissipate while deep inside himself a subtle quaking commenced. The swift tenseness in his gut startled him. What was he doing? This was a mistake! Hell, under the circumstances, it was dead wrong. He had no right to harbor such feelings toward this woman. Even less right to act on them.

The nervous clouds overhead abandoned their jealous vigil of the moon at the same time Spencer relinquished his grip on April. She stumbled backward, blinking from the sudden effusion of moonlight as much as from Spencer's abrupt release.

All the worry he'd felt when he'd spotted her running along the cliff rushed into him with a renewed vengeance. "What were you thinking, wandering about with a fog bank rolling in? Do you have any idea how dangerous that is?"

Confusion and hurt tangled inside April. She stepped farther away from Spencer. Where did he get off berating her? "The only danger I faced was you!" What a fool she was, falling into his arms and clinging to him like some shrinking violet. Everytime she got near Spencer, her reasoning took a leave of absence. "Why were you following me?"

His dark brown eyebrows rose, but his voice was menacingly low. "Do you have any idea what time it is?"

Unexpected, this question brought April up short. "No. What does that have to do with anything?"

"It's after ten. Your father has the whole household looking for you!"

Heat furled into her cheeks. Good Lord, she'd nearly plunged off a cliff trying to get away from Spencer, all because she'd let her imagination run wild. Embarrassed at her own foolishness, she couldn't meet his reproving gaze. "Oh. . . . Well, I . . . I hadn't realized how late it was, or that anyone would fret."

For the first time, Spencer noticed the twigs and leaves in her hair, the scrapes on her face and hands, the mud on her clothes. And lastly, her bare feet. "What the hell happened to you? Where are your shoes?"

His harsh tone uprooted April's chagrin faster than a gardener pulling weeds. Her hands landed on her hips and this time, prodded by the defiance heating her blood, she met his icy gaze with one of her own. "I lost them when I stumbled at the edge of the cliff."

"My God, woman! You could've been killed!"

61

"Well, I wasn't. Granted, I'm muddy and my pride is hurt, but otherwise, I'm fine." Her body ached in places she suspected she'd be too aware of in the morning, but she'd be damned if she'd let him know that.

She shoved past him, but he caught her by the arm. "Fine my hide! You're quivering like a jellyfish. You'll catch pneumonia standing barefooted on this damp ground."

Before April could protest, Spencer scooped her into his arms and hauled her against his chest so hard she could have sworn a rib cracked. If the gleam in his alluring gray eyes hadn't stopped any struggle or objection she'd started to raise about being carried back to the house, his words would have. "Save your breath. This issue is not open to discussion."

Accepting the inevitable along with the welcome respite from the pain biting at her feet, April lifted her arms and locked her fingers behind Spencer's neck, capturing the thick coffee brown hair at his nape beneath her palms. The intimate contact sparked a wild memory of his lips on hers, and for a few uncomfortable seconds he, too, seemed to be remembering.

Thane and Vanessa emerged from the woods. Like children caught playing doctor, April and Spencer flinched.

"Well, thank God you found her. Is she all right?" The tension in Thane's voice was as subtle as the perpetual murmur of waves in the background.

However, Spencer knew exactly what his twin was thinking. He'd promised Thane he'd steer clear of April and here he was, caught like a groom ready to carry his bride across the threshold. The analogy struck his heart and drew blood. "She lost her shoes running along the cliff. She's a little cold and muddy, nothing a warm bath and some hot brandy won't cure."

"Lost her shoes . . ." Vanessa hugged her arms around her middle, rustling the slick Irish green fabric of her ankle-length, quilted coat. "How in the world . . . ?"

"She can explain in the house." Spencer boosted her higher in his arms. "It's freezing out here.

As Thane and Vanessa hurried ahead to inform the others that she'd been found, April tried to ignore the gentle jostling of her body against Spencer's strong arms and his firm chest. Her inner turmoil ground her emotions until they felt as grimy and achy as her feet. Why had she been so quick to believe he had been chasing her on the cliff with intent to do her harm? Was it this place, this time of year? Whatever the cause, she knew instinctively it had its origins in her lost memory and Lily's fatal accident. But how was she going to explain that to her family?

The family gathered in the den, warming themselves before the fire and fussing over her. April didn't know what to think. All this unexpected concern was somewhat overwhelming. In Arizona, she lived alone. No one monitored her comings and goings. It felt strange and rather nice.

Cynthia, who had surprisingly assumed the role of nurse, knelt over a pan of water, tending her injured feet. April knew the woman was being as gentle as possible, but nevertheless, soap in an open wound stung.

Pressing a warm snifter into April's hand, her father said, "Drink up, honey. This is guaranteed to cure what ails you."

If only it were that easy, she thought, catching a whiff of the sharp-scented liquor. The first sip burned a fiery path across her tongue and drew tears into her eyes, but the warm sensation it created inside was

63

amazingly pleasant. With her eyes closed and her head thrust against the high-backed leather chair, she could almost block out the pain.

She took another swallow of brandy, then, leaving out the theatrics, she explained as simply as possible how she had come to be in this condition.

"Where and what is Turtle Rock?" asked Vanessa. "Is it a famous landmark?"

Thane draped an arm around his fiancée's shoulders. "Nothing famous or historical about it. It's just a big rock about a mile or so along the cliff that looks like a giant turtle. April named it. She used to sit on it for hours when she was a kid, just staring out to sea, lost in her own little world."

Vanessa seemed disappointed by the explanation.

"Fool place to go in the dark. And right after a storm!" Aunt March sat next to April in the matching chair. Her arms were folded under her ample chest and her ruddy face was heightened by her irritation. "You could've got yourself killed. A fine how-do-you-do that would have been for the wedding festivities."

Raising her head from her task, Cynthia glanced over her shoulder at her elderly sister-in-law, then back at April. "I'm sure she didn't mean to worry any of us, did you, sugah?"

There was a slight reprimand in Cynthia's soft drawl, but April wasn't sure if it was meant for March or herself. Nor did she care. The brandy tasted better with every sip. "No."

"Of course not. There, all done." Cynthia wrung out the washcloth, set it aside and rose. "None of the cuts are deep. Rub in a little salve just before you climb into bed."

She wasn't sure if it was the mention of bed or the effects of the brandy, but the need to clean up and go to sleep hit her in a rush. "I'm going to take a bath and hit the hay."

Setting her empty snifter on the end table, she stood. But the soles of her feet weren't ready to bear weight.

Without thought to the consequences, Spencer leaped to her aid and swung her once again into his arms. He could feel his twin glaring at him, but surely Thane realized he was the most likely person in the group to help April upstairs.

"This is getting to be a habit," she whispered, then giggled unexpectedly. The outburst both surprised and embarrassed her.

Spencer only chuckled. "Say good night, Gracie."

"Who's Gracie?" April was totally puzzled.

Silence fell over the room. The expressions turned her way ranged from disbelief to pity.

Vanessa's eyes rounded incredulously. "You *must* have been in South America a long time."

The silence grew heavier. To save April any more embarrassment, Spencer whisked her from the den, and a short while later deposited her atop the fluffy toilet seat cover in the upstairs bathroom. "There. Now you're within easy reach of the tub faucets."

"Who's Gracie?" she asked again.

"No one for you to worry your pretty head about." He stood bent-kneed with his face on a par to hers. The willpower to pull away from her had deserted him. She seemed as unaware of the leaf caught in her hair and the dirty smudges on her face as she was of the effect her innocence had on him. He plucked the leaf free and flicked it into the wastebasket, wishing he could absolve his guilt with as little effort. The lack in her education was a direct result of his actions. If only being sorry could change that.

"Was she a friend of Lily? Was that why everyone got so quiet?"

If she'd stomped on his foot he couldn't have straightened faster. "No. It's a joke. An old television show. Start running your bath water. I'll get you something to put on."

By the time the tub was filled, Spencer had returned with a beach towel and a man's teal terry cloth robe with the initials S.L.G. on the breast pocket.

The room was as steamy as a sauna and felt just as restrictive to Spencer.

Feeling altogether lightheaded and unaccountably naughty, April smirked at him. "I do have my own robe, you know."

A hint of color tarnished his neck. "I didn't want to prowl around in your room. You can return it tomorrow. Now climb out of those filthy clothes and into that hot tub."

Another giggle spilled out of her. "Are you planning to stick around and scrub my back?"

Imagining that scenario unhinged Spencer's poise. The misty air clogged in his lungs like wadded cotton. He backed up and bumped into the wall. A second later he was in the hall, pulling the door shut after him.

Grinning, she limped across the room and locked the door. Standing there, she heard Spencer retreat, heard the opening and closing of a door farther down the hall and then something akin to muffled voices raised in anger. *Probably just the brandy buzzing in her ears,* she decided, turning toward the tub.

A while later, clean and dry and dressed only in Spencer's robe, April padded on tender feet across the thick carpet and down the darkened hall to her room. Apparently, everyone had retired for the night. She couldn't reach her own bed soon enough. The effects of the brandy were wearing off, and her fatigued body felt like the loser in a twelve-round boxing match, with the bruises to prove it.

The old house seemed in as much pain as she, creaking and groaning, settling deeper into the cliff above Haro Strait. Or was she hearing the moans of Farradays past, ghosts, who could find no peace at Calendar House until their slayers were brought to justice? The thought and the noises set her nerves on edge.

April entered the sanctum of her tiny room. Rather than the relief she'd expected to feel, she was surrounded by a prickling sense of something amiss. Warily, she moved about the room, trying to calm her accelerating heartbeat. The weird sensation that someone had been here, invading her private haven with their unwelcome presence, refused to go away.

Outside the wind keened through the madronas like banshees wailing at the moon. April made a perfunctory search of the room, but nothing seemed to be missing. Finally she came to the conclusion her mood was playing tricks on her. Again. Or maybe it was the relentless wind.

Worry nettled her as she donned a nightgown, laid Spencer's folded robe on a chair, and headed to bed. Was she losing her ability to differentiate between fact and fancy? Maybe she'd better put a call in to Dr. Merritt after all.

April pulled back the bedspread. A startled squeak leapt from her throat. She wasn't imagining *this*.

Someone *had* been here.

On her pillow lay July's Barbie doll. But April doubted her seven-year-old sister had pulled off the doll's head or spread its long blond hair across the pillowcase or arranged its headless body in a sprawl reminiscent of her final images of Lily.

The dreaded vision flooded into her mind, bringing with it both the inexplicable guilt and her desperation to know the whole truth. April pressed her balled fists against her closed eyelids in an effort to coax the buried memory out of the darkness and into the light. But it did no good. The futile attempt only gave her a headache.

Opening her eyes, she immediately confronted the dismembered toy. Someone's idea of a cruel joke, or another warning to make her leave Calendar House? Well, too bad, she thought, plucking up the doll and jamming its head back in place. Her anguish gave way to a revitalizing determination. Someone had wasted their time. The harder they tried to make her leave, the deeper she'd dig in her heels.

She unbent the Barbie's limbs and tucked the doll beneath her sweaters in the dresser drawer.

The next two days April stayed off her feet as much as possible. July promptly appointed herself entertainment chairman, seemingly determined to keep her older sister from boredom. It was a new experience for April, being revered for her existence, freely given and accepting hugs and kisses. She discovered forty-eight hours could pass swiftly when spent with someone you loved. They played everything from Nintendo to Checkers. However, the little girl made no mention of her missing Barbie doll.

By the third day the rain had returned, railing against the windows in icy sheets, and April found she could walk without a wince. She dressed in faded blue jeans, hightop Nikes, and a gold Arizona State sweatshirt. Drawn by the aroma of frying bacon, she headed down the back stairwell into the big country kitchen. The Barbie doll was tucked into the waistband of her jeans and concealed by her sweatshirt.

Helga was at the stove, A grease-spattered, beige

apron trussed her ample middle, protecting her tan-and-white checked dress. August, Thane, and Spencer, the epitome of casual in Levis and soft hued sweat-shirts, huddled around one end of the black formica table drinking coffee and dissecting some sports item in yesterday's newspaper while at the other end Vanessa and Cynthia had their heads together as they discussed wedding details.

Spencer heard her come in, felt his pulse joggle, but didn't look around. He'd never have the right to claim April and for both their sakes, he had to stop wishing it were otherwise.

Aunt March shuffled into the room with July at her heels. "Well, whadda ya know . . . She can walk again."

The remark made April feel as self-conscious as she suspected it was meant to. Trying to ignore the heat stealing up her neck, she smiled at the old woman and then at the other upraised faces. "Yes, the feet are good as new."

As the family exchanged "good mornings" April strode to the coffee maker and filled a white mug to the rim. Why she let that crusty old lady get to her, she couldn't say. She sensed eyes boring into her back. Aunt March, again? Had she been the one who'd left the gruesome doll on her bed? She balanced the hot cup with both hands and turned to face her family, but caught no one looking at her.

"Better all take your places before the food gets cold," Helga declared, hefting a platter of scrambled eggs, bacon, and toast toward the table. The rustle of folded newspaper and the scrape of chairs followed straightaway.

April walked to the vacant seat next to her young sister. Setting the coffee mug on the plastic placemat, she extracted the doll from her waistband, set it in the center of the table and said with practiced calm, "Look what turned up in my room, July."

The child let out a squeal as April's gaze sped from one adult face to another in pursuit of any betraying flinch. The effort proved a waste of time. Disappointment followed her into her chair. Whatever enlightenment she'd hoped to gain by this ploy hadn't materialized. She'd never seen a more innocent looking bunch. Not one guilty twitch, not one clenched jaw, nor one telltale red eartip in the lot.

What the hell was that all about? Spencer wondered, covertly studying April's fallen expression. The pointed way she'd plopped the doll on the table and drawn everyone's attention to it reeked of something rehearsed. And the failure to elicit a reaction from anybody but July seemed to have taken the wind out of her sails. The urge to touch her hand consolingly stole over him. *Don't!* he warned himself. Whatever her problem, his involvement was guaranteed to make it worse.

Several days later, April congratulated herself on the boldness of her actions with the Barbie doll. She may not have smoked out the culprit, but apparently she'd shown her tormentor anonymous notes and childish pranks couldn't frighten her away from Calendar House.

Intent on taking advantage of the unusually mild afternoon, she left her room and headed down the hallway toward the main staircase. Nothing and no one, she determined, must stop her from regaining her memory. But when would that be? What few recollections she'd experienced this past week had had nothing to do with Lily's fall, just her cruelties. April chewed the inside of her lip. The hatred she felt at each of these times only increased her fear that she had been the one

70

arguing with her mother on the landing above the stairs.

She descended to the foyer, thinking the house seemed unduly quiet. Sun refracted through the leaded glass windows on either side of the massive pine door, emphasizing the purples, greens, and blacks of the Oriental carpets. Adding yet another slash of color, her red parka hung from a hall tree hook. Catching hold of it, April padded across the rugs and stepped over the threshold onto the porch outside.

She slipped into her jacket and hastened down the steps to the deserted apron in front of the house. The air was crisp, and few clouds littered the sky. It was much like a spring day; only the occasional lick of a winter gust said otherwise. The sun felt good on her face, but the glare was blinding.

Squinting, April reached for her sunglasses in her pocket, then remembered she'd left them on the dashboard of her rented car which, along with the other family vehicles, had been relegated to the garages earlier in the week. Well, she had to get them or the glare would give her a headache before she even began her walk.

Leaving the asphalt, she started down the grassy slope toward the garages. The sudden roar of a motorboat engine belched from the belly of the boathouse, startling not only April, but a pair of sea gulls who had been perched on its rooftop. Squawking like a couple of disgruntled old maids, they lifted into the cloud-patched sky, wheeled over the protected bay and out across the glistening water.

April moved down the path toward a stone and mortar building—a miniature copy of the house, laughingly called a shed. Strange how much smaller it appeared than her memories of it, she thought circling the elaborate structure.

As children, the twins and she had been fascinated by it and its cache of ladders, rakes, nails, hammers, shovels and various garden sundries. They were allowed inside only when accompanied by an adult. Of course, when they had reached their teens and understood its function their curiosity had died altogether.

Now her curiosity was piqued by the powerful boat motor. Momentarily forgetting her sunglasses, she crossed the road. The tide was in. The ramp, bridging shore and dock, stretched as flat as the water today. April advanced onto the dock, enjoying the bob of motion.

As she neared the metal boathouse, the engine silenced. The flat notes of Karl's off-key whistling, accompanied by a metallic clank, echoed from within. Was he alone? Why did the thought of that make her hesitant?

Stifling the inexplicable feeling, she strode through the open door. The light inside was fluorescent, dull after the sun's radiance. She blinked, peering at the exposed framework walls and the score of orange life jackets, fishing nets and poles, gaff hooks, and buoys hung about on nails. The dock cuffed the inside of the building on the front and two side walls like a giant U. Aged creosote and brine tangled with the odor of fresh motor oil.

Her gaze fell on the sleek royal blue and white speedboat taking up the body of the boathouse. It skimmed the water, slung on large straps supported by a ceiling hoist as though it were in traction, April mused, realizing the purpose was more likely to protect the boat from the tide's whims. Seeing two heads dipped close together over its motor eased her tension.

"Okay," her father instructed Karl. "That should do it." August shifted to the boat's wheel and stopped. His eyes widened as they always did when something unexpected intruded on his train of thought. "April, this is a pleasant surprise. What brings you down here?"

"The noise." April acknowledged Karl's friendly grin with one of her own. "What're you two doing?"

Her father leaned toward her and dragged a grease-stained rag from his rear overall pocket. He wiped his hands, then poked the cloth back. "Karl and I are installing one of my gadgets. A keyless ignition."

"Something new?"

"Nope. Never found a buyer for it though. Still, it's a convenience *I* appreciate. No good inventing things if you can't use them." The subject seemed to draw his attention back to the project. He fiddled with something beyond her line of vision on the dashboard. "Okay, Karl, here goes."

The motor sputtered. Sparks flew at Karl. He swore and stumbled backward. August rushed to him. "Must have crossed the wires. Are you all right?"

"Sure. Surprised me, is all."

All but forgotten, April left them to their work.

The garages were a couple hundred yards from the dock, up the asphalt lane. Made of stone and mortar like the house and tool shed, the building had originally been a stable. With the advent of electricity and motorized vehicles the barn gates had been replaced with garage doors, the packed earth floor with concrete, and the oil lamps with electric.

Six truck-wide doors graced the front, while two human-sized ones allowed access at either end of the building. The one nearest the dock stood open. April hastened inside.

Murky light slithered through the grimy window set eight feet up the back wall, but it was enough for her to see the cobwebs massed on the high open beams supporting the roof, and that the car parked here was not the one she sought.

From somewhere deep inside the garage a car motor started.

Imagining how the building must have looked in her great-great-grandfather's era, April proceeded through the swinging doors separating each stall from the next. The individual chambers were huge, better suited to the luxury cars of the sixties than the compact, gas-efficient models now occupying them. And yet, for all the modernization April felt the old building had retained a sense of its original form. She could almost smell the hay and horse manure lingering in the shadowy corners.

The idling motor grew insistently louder with her progress. Evidently, whoever had entered the building before her and left the door ajar was going somewhere, most likely Friday Harbor.

In the fifth stall, she found her rented compact. The rumbly engine emanated from the sixth. Although the cells were partitioned the ventilation left a lot to be desired, April thought, getting a whiff of exhaust.

Best to get her sunglasses and leave. She spotted them on the dashboard, and seconds later was stuffing them into her pocket.

The running motor revved. Exhaust crept beneath the wall like smoke from a blazing room. April coughed, frowning disgustedly at the wall as though the person in the unit beyond could see her and would stop the car. Or exit the garage. Surely the engine was warm by now.

April felt an uneasy prickling. Maybe she'd better see if the driver in the next stall was all right.

She pulled the separating door open and leaned into the garage. Her father's Cadillac Seville hogged the chamber like the old white elephant it was, wheezing foul air from its bent tail pipe. No one was behind the wheel, and as she'd suspected the huge door was shut. "Hello? Is someone here?"

Holding her nose, April stepped across the threshold. The swinging door bumped shut against her backside. Intent on turning off the engine, she sank to the driver's seat. The aromas of pipe tobacco and childhood memories surrounded her as she reached for the key. Her hand froze. "What the . . . ?"

There was a hole where the ignition should have been. Obviously her father's handiwork. Lord, why hadn't she taken the time to look at the device so she'd know what she was supposed to do to turn it off?

Well, she certainly wasn't going to sit here and wonder about it. Rushing into the smog-laced cell, she sped to the single outside door on the side wall. Locked. Exhaust fumes burned her eyes and stole her breath. With her hand cupping her mouth and nose, she fled to the swinging door leading to the unit containing her car. She gripped the knob and pushed. The door wouldn't budge. Alarm burst through April.

Dear God! She was trapped. Cold curled in her belly. This was no accident.

She threw her shoulder against the door. It resisted. April hit it again. Nothing. She gulped a lungful of fumes, then coughed. Her head started to pound.

Frantic, she raced to the big door and clutched the chrome handle. The lock refused to release.

"Help!" she screamed.

The powerful boat motor roared to life.

"Help!" But even as the word left her mouth April knew it was a waste.

Coughing, she flung her gaze around the door frame, then the room. She spied an electric door apparatus attached to the ceiling. Was there a remote opener in the car? A second later she was again in the car. No opener.

The smoke was robbing the life from her. As April stared death in the face, she realized no matter how bleak her future might seem, it was better than this alternative.

She closed the car door. It took two tries before her trembling fingers managed to hook the seat belt. The pounding at her temples worsened. Shaking her head, she eased the shifter into reverse, and slammed the gas pedal to the floor.

Six

The garage door burst apart with a boom as loud as a detonated dynamite stick. Wood flew high and wide and clunked on the car's roof and hood. Yelping, April ducked reflexively.

The car roared backward, over the parking apron, across the road. It rammed into a madrona tree and stopped. April pitched forward. The seatbelt cut into her chest and stomach and yanked her back against the seat. Leaves rained onto the car.

Jerkily, she shifted the gears into park, then dropped her head on her forearms on the steering wheel. Her heart raced in sync with the motor. Drawing trembly breaths, April tried to calm herself. The thought wouldn't leave. Someone had tried to kill her. Why?

Panic regrouped and gathered force. Wanting out of the car and away from this place, she shoved the door open with adrenaline-powered strength and stepped from the vehicle onto broken hunks of garage door. The boards beneath her feet cracked. Exhaust continued to spill from the engine, but now the stench was softened by sea air and the scent of fresh-split pine.

Weak-kneed, she staggered into the sunlight. The

brilliant rays spilling through the madrona branches no longer held any warmth. April shivered, gazing impassively at the damage she'd rent. The urge to run had deserted her.

Shouts of dismay and concern eclipsed the rumbles of the car engine. Startled, she spun in a circle. The whole household seemed headed her way issuing from various directions.

Spencer reached her first. His face was as white as the old Cadillac. "Are you all right?"

She simply stared at him. Was she all right? Would she ever be again? Did he realize there was a spot of grease on his cheek? Answers eluded her. But questions came rapid-fire.

"April . . . ? Are you okay?" Her father arrived, breathless, looking as much in shock as she felt. The freckles on his face stood dark against his pale skin.

"Lordy," March railed. "What kind of craziness is this?"

August glared at his sister.

The fury storming her father's navy eyes penetrated April's stupor and stirred her own anger at what she'd been put through. "I'm . . . fine, Daddy." The words came out in a croak.

"How . . . ?" he sputtered, sweeping a hand and arm at the debris. "What . . . ?"

"The car . . . motor running . . . exhaust —" April's voice broke on a cough. Her lungs ached. She must have swallowed more fumes than she'd imagined. Another shiver stole over her. She glanced from one face to the other. Which of these people had nearly succeeded in killing her? "All the doors locked . . . Couldn't get out." She coughed again.

"August, obviously she's in shock." Spencer caught April's arm.

"I'm not in shock!" April yanked from his grip, glaring at him, ignoring his sudden hurt expression. "I know . . . what happened."

Spencer scowled. "All the same, these questions can wait until later."

"Spence is right, August. The girl is as pale as a whitecap. And you are, too. I think we'd best get you both to the house." Cynthia snaked her arm around April's waist. Her hold brooked no argument. "Come on, sugah, let's go inside. I want to make certain you don't have any hidden injuries."

The bluster left April as quickly as it had arisen. With the will of a zombie, she let herself be led to the house.

Behind her, she heard the car motor sputter and die. The void was immediately filled with speculative murmurs.

An hour later Spencer found his stepfather and March conversing quietly in the den.

"I don't know why you refuse . . ." March quit speaking the second she spotted Spencer standing in the doorway. Although her expression gave no hint of tension, her knitting needles clicked like castanets.

August was another matter. Whatever they'd been discussing had obviously distressed him. His color was unnatural, almost as red as the chair in which he sat. Strain etched deep grooves in his forehead, around his mouth and eyes.

Intuitively, Spencer sensed the conversation had had something to do with April. Disquiet clacked inside his head in tune to the speedy needles. "How's April?"

"She's fine," August answered, seeming to stress

the point for his sister's sake. "Cynthia's still with her."

If April was fine, Spencer wondered, why did he sense he'd stirred an already agitated hornet's nest? He strode to the couch and eased his long frame into the deep cushions to face August. "The tree took a nasty gouge, but I think it will survive," he reported, bracing his elbows on his thighs and leaning forward. "The Caddy took a few hits, but the nothing that can't be pounded out and painted over."

"Insurance'll cover the repairs. I thank God April wasn't injured."

The knitting needles fell silent. "Were any of the garage doors locked?"

"March," August growled. "I'm warning you."

Spencer gazed from one to the other, trying to figure out the problem, vaguely recalling April had mentioned locked doors. A nameless fear seized him. "As far as I know, none of the doors were locked. Hell, the doors dividing each garage can't be locked. What's going on?"

But March didn't bother to answer him. She sat straighter in her chair. "I knew it!"

"March, you're trying my patience."

"August, the girl tried to kill herself."

"What?" Spencer exploded off the couch as though he'd been shot. The two continued to ignore him.

"Be still March. April did no such thing."

The elderly woman's features grew as tight as one of her stitches, and the needles started anew. "You bought that car when she was five years old," she droned softly. "Lily's limousine. Seeing it again, sitting inside it, bound to bring back memories."

All color fled August's face.

Spencer's heart raced. He felt like an unwilling spectator at a medieval witch hunt. According to March, April was branded and condemned on the face of events. She was wrong! Wasn't she? The nameless fear no longer hid in the shadows of his wary mind. It stood before him, loathsome. Was April still ill? Could she actually wish herself harm?

"We can only guess at the devils that haunt her." The elderly woman rambled on, oblivious to the fury mounting in her brother's eyes, oblivious to Spencer's pain.

Frost iced his heart. Reality seemed fragile, beyond his grasp. Reason was called for, but none present could supply it. "Maybe Dr. Merritt—"

"No!" August shook his head. "This is absurd. April didn't even know how to start that car."

"Humph!" March quit knitting, and shook a needle at her brother. *July* could start that car with the switch you put in it."

"But April knew nothing about the switch," August argued. "She hadn't even heard of the damned thing until she came into the boathouse while I was . . ."

". . . Installing one in the boat." March shook her head, pity evident in her widened eyes. "You're too stubborn to admit the truth when it's staring you right in the face. She's unstable, I tell you. Just like her mother."

"No! I don't believe it. And no one is to call Dr. Merritt behind my back. Is that understood?"

Spencer and March exchanged worried glances, but neither argued.

"I'm going to help Karl clear the wood off the road. Spencer, your assistance would be appreciated."

For the next several days April was leery of everyone. It resolved nothing. She still had no idea who wanted her dead. Or why. The very fact was more than she could comprehend, swamping her with rage and hurt and fear. These people weren't strangers. They were her family, for God's sake. Sadly, the only one of them she now trusted completely was July.

April smiled at the child running ahead of her on the cliff path. "Don't get too near the edge. The ground might be too soft for your weight."

July glanced back over her shoulder. "I know. It's warm out here. Can I take my coat off?"

"Sure. Give it here." April unzipped her own coat and let it flop open. Sun beat down on her, warm and welcome, exactly she realized with a sudden shiver, like the day on which someone had tried to kill her. *No. Don't think about it,* she warned herself. *Don't let the ugliness spoil this time with July.* In the distance she spotted Turtle Rock, their destination. Like a loyal friend it stood in wait for her, ready to lift her burdens, to take on her pain. Her spirits lightened.

April draped the child's jacket over the basket she carried. It contained a picnic lunch, and the aromas of Helga's fried chicken and potato salad had had her mouth watering all the way from the house. "I hope you're hungry."

"Starving!" July raced ahead and took up position in the center of the humpy backed boulder, reminding April of herself in a long ago past.

The girl chattered on about school and friends and the engagement party while gulls squawked overhead as though anticipating the scraps of food that would soon be theirs. Listening with half an ear, April spread a blanket on the ground, comforted by the sanity of seven-year-old logic, sea washed air, and hungry birds. "Which part of the chicken do you like?"

"The leg." July jumped from the rock. "And a pickle, too, please." Hitting the blanket with her knees, she picked up the plate April had filled for her, but instead of digging in, she gazed at April with round, questioning eyes. "Why did you smash the garage? Did you really try to hurt yourself?"

The question took April aback. Gaping at her young sister, she spoke haltingly, "Where did you get the idea that I wanted to hurt myself?"

"I heard Aunt March and Momma talking about it this morning."

Drawing a slow breath, April sank back on her heels and continued putting food on her plate, but her hand was shaking, hard. She released the serving spoon, set her plate aside, rose, and strode to the rock. As her gaze fixed on a seal playing in the tide-tossed swells of Haro Strait, she braced her palms on the boulder's flat surface. So her aunt and step-mother thought she'd tried to kill herself. That meant the whole household must believe it. The real-ization made her numb. It seemed her tormentor had won a victory of sorts after all. She might be alive, but the family was definitely questioning her sanity.

"April?" July sounded distressed. "Aren't you gonna eat?"

"In a minute, sweetheart." April gave her a reas-suring smile, but she doubted the smallest bite would make it by the lump in her throat. She needed to phone Dr. Merritt, perhaps return to Arizona and attempt to trigger her memory some other way. That was the sensible, logical, and safe thing to do. Her fists balled in anger. And let the unknown tormentor win? No way. Others had always controlled her life. If she left Calendar House now her hope for a sane future was all but lost.

With fierce determination, April forced the worries from her mind. Soon July had her laughing and eating and watching the romping seals from their vantage point on Turtle Rock. The difference in their ages seemed to vanish as the day stretched into a pleasant afternoon.

By contrast, dinner that night was an exercise in tension. April spent more time staring at her food than tasting it, and immediately after dessert she sought the comfort of her cozy room. For the first time, its isolated location along the hallway gave her qualms. She lodged the rung-backed chair beneath the knob and sat propped against the pillows long into the night. When sleep came it was like a drug, more powerful than her fears.

Late the next morning she awoke to the sound of rain hitting the window. Grabbing her bathrobe, she went to the kitchen. Only one person occupied the room. Spencer sat at the table, reading a newspaper, sipping coffee from a mug. Her pulsebeat sharpened.

He glanced at her. A quick smile touched his wonderful mouth, but she could see the watchful glint in his eyes. *Even Spencer.* The betrayal, although not unexpected, stung to her toes. She headed for the coffeepot and filled a mug.

"You just get up, sleepyhead?" he teased, failing to keep his tone light.

"Yep." She hated the tremor in her voice, hated

her suspicion of him and his of her. His chair scraped back. She spun around. He was standing close, too close. Panic squeezed her chest.

"If you want breakfast," Spence said softly, "you'll have to fix your own."

Aren't you afraid I might poison myself? she wanted to shout at him. Instead she managed, "Coffee will do." To emphasize the point, she drank from her mug.

Spencer detested this unnatural politeness. If only he had the right to hold her, to reassure her. But he'd given up that right twelve years ago.

April gazed beyond him and around the room. "Where is everyone?"

"Here and there." He could tell she was jumpy. Was it his doing? Had she remembered? Or was she simply unstable as March claimed? The puzzle had him fearful, confused, and pitching all sorts of theories. It was possible that, as March had suggested, sitting in Lily's car might have triggered something shocking enough to account for her smashing the garage door. It could even allow for her anger at him afterward. It didn't explain her claim of locked doors. "April, what happened the other day in the garage?"

"Didn't you get the family version?"

"I want your version."

"Why? You won't believe it."

"Try me."

Oh, how she would love an in-house ally. Too bad his uncertainty stood between them like a brick wall. Besides, how did she know Spencer wasn't the enemy? The notion turned her stomach, but she couldn't risk trusting anyone at this point. "I guess I panicked and did a stupid thing," she lied.

"You're right." Spencer sighed. "I do find that hard to believe."

"Well, that's what happened," she insisted. *Lies, and more lies.* Knowing this one was necessary did little to ease her distress. "Excuse me. I'm going to my room."

Spencer stared after her, frowning so hard it hurt. He felt certain she was lying. The question was—why? Learning the truth suddenly became a major priority.

Two more days passed without threat or incident. April decided her tormentor had gotten the message. She wouldn't be chased from Calendar House. However her memory seemed loath to return, and she began to despair of ever getting it back.

Thank goodness for the impending party, she thought, walking from her bedroom toward the foyer staircase. The family was so busy with preparations that they had stopped watching her like hawks after a field mouse.

As she strode past the double doors leading into the west wing a muffled creak aborted her progress. A shaft of light reached into the hallway, and she realized the doors stood ajar. Curious, she edged forward and slipped through the opening. Before her were three broad stairs leading up into a long, wide hallway with an oval-shaped, stained-glass window at its farthest end.

Gray light slithered down the hall, shadowed, unfriendly, eerie. Blinking in the dimness, April searched for a light switch, but the bulb in the cobweb-riddled fixture overhead must have long ago burned out or been removed. Cold enveloped her,

86

but she barely noticed as her eyes adjusted to the dull light.

The air tasted musty. Dust had deadened the winy hue of the carpet, but its density remained intact. And that wasn't all. No one had redecorated this section of the house. Even the velvet-striped wallpaper endured. April felt as though she'd stepped into the past.

To the left were ornate glass doors set into each end of the corridor. They led into the ballroom. Footsteps resounded from inside.

Keeping in mind her experience in the garage, April proceeded with caution into the vast room. Here the light flooded, wondrously brilliant, through the leaded windows gracing one entire wall. Spotting the intruder, April smiled. Déja vu crept over her. Vanessa was twirling across the floor as though in the arms of some imaginary partner, something she herself had often done as a teenager.

Spotting her, Vanessa froze, then laughed. "Thank goodness it's you. I didn't know if I was supposed to be in here, but I couldn't stand not exploring." The look on her face was that of a naughty child caught on some forbidden adventure. But her artless smile spoke volumes. If she had shared the family's suspicions about April's "suicide attempt" she wouldn't be this affable.

Relieved, April joined her at the windows. Below was Haro Strait, churning, white capped, above, as if in some endless relay race, clouds plunged across the sky in rapid succession. A brewing storm. Weather and nature held their attention, and for a long moment neither woman spoke.

Vanessa broke the silence. "This view takes my breath. I wish we could have our party here." She sighed. "But I don't suppose there'd be any place else to put all this furniture."

"Furniture?"

She pointed to the far end of the room. "Over there . . . under Lily's portrait."

April whirled in that direction. The first thing that snagged her gaze was a life-size portrait of her mother, depicting her role as Mary Queen of Scots. The actress's favorite part. It dominated the wall much as Lily had dominated everything in her restricted kingdom.

"Imagine the parties they had here. . . ."

April had no problem there. Just gazing at her mother's picture dredged up the memories. But these were not the things she wanted to remember. Stifling the sudden shaft of pain, she forced her gaze to the sheet-draped objects beneath the picture. They took up a fair portion of hardwood floor. Before she could move, Vanessa had crossed the room and started tossing the covers aside with an eager expression on her face.

"Isn't this stuff great?"

Unaware she'd moved, April found herself standing next to all the antique oak tables and overstuffed sofas and chairs of her childhood days.

"It would look so good in this house," Vanessa gushed. "Why do you suppose Cynthia has it stored up here?" Almost as soon as the question left her mouth a look of dawning entered her green eyes. "Oh, I'll bet it was Lily's, wasn't it?"

Absently fingering a white chintz sofa arm, April nodded. "I assumed this had all been sold when they redecorated." Why hadn't it?

"Ha!" Vanessa grimaced. "Whoever Cynthia hired to redecorate should be stripped of their license."

She plunked onto a sofa and curled her legs beneath her, appearing thoroughly at home. "Even if I had been wife number two, I would've kept this. It suits the house better and it's still like new."

April agreed that the furniture was too good to be stored away. And even Vanessa seemed to take for granted her future mother-in-law's reason for redecorating had been jealousy of Lily. But it couldn't have been easy to step into Lily Cordell's shoes. After twelve years her presence lingered in Calendar House like a guest who refused to accept all hints to leave.

"I'm surprised you didn't want to be an actress, too." Vanessa's statement seemed to come from nowhere. "Not that the work you do isn't wonderful."

The sudden switch of topic bewildered April. She couldn't imagine anything wonderful about serving food in a college cafeteria. "The work . . . ?"

"Yes, missionary stuff. Although I have to confess, you look nothing like my idea of a woman missionary. I mean, where's the long straight hair, the makeup-free face, the chaste clothing?"

April felt her cheeks flame. Lying to Spence had been necessary. *This* lie was both senseless and easily exposed. Not to mention that it made her blood boil. Couldn't the family see what an injustice they were doing to both Vanessa and her? It would be so simple to set the record straight. April was sorely tempted. But if Vanessa called off the wedding because Thane had lied to her, she knew she would feel responsible.

Resigned to furthering the lie, she plopped to the sofa on the opposite end as Vanessa. Dust spiraled upward. "Missionaries, like everyone else, come in all kinds of packages. I've seen the type you're referring to, but I'm not one of them."

That was as close to the truth as she dare get.

Vanessa caught a strand of her pale hair between her fingers and twisted it absently. "May I ask you something about Spence?"

This was a subject April did not want to think about much less discuss. But refusing might draw unwelcome speculation. "Okay."

"I've tried to fix him up with a couple of my girlfriends, and every time has been disastrous."

Secretly the knowledge pleased April, but she struggled not to show it.

"He's such a catch, I couldn't figure out the problem." Vanessa grinned slyly. "But I think I have now."

April's heart grabbed and flexed. Her cheeks heated uncomfortably. "And what is that?"

"It's you."

Dust danced about the room as wildly as her pulse. "Me?" She shook her head adamantly.

Vanessa nodded hers. "Do you know he watches you when you aren't looking, and that his eyes light up whenever you're near? Has he always had a thing for you, or is this something new?"

Or was it my mother Spencer had the "thing" for? The old sorrow came over April. "Until two weeks ago, I hadn't even seen Spencer for twelve years."

"That's no answer." Vanessa's angled hair came dangerously close to catching in her open mouth. "Deny it all you want, but I can see he makes you light up, too."

The joyous thought of Spencer loving her all these years was more than her heart could hold. But it wasn't true. And hoping so was surefire agony. "I think the stars in your eyes are feeding your imagination."

"Noooo."

Uncomfortable, and out of answers, April lurched from the sofa and crossed to the windowed wall. Clouds were now jammed together as tightly as her confused emotions. Vanessa was too observant for her liking. But maybe that was good.

She turned from the window and peered at the woman still nestled on the couch. Had she noticed someone watching her in some odd or evil way? She needed to ask without explaining her motives. *Step carefully,* she warned herself, opting for a general approach. "Well, what do you think about this family you're taking on?"

Vanessa pushed her head against the sofa and shifted her feet to the floor. "Your father is great." Her tone held a note of caution. She studied her entwined fingers a moment, then glanced up. "I'm not sure what to make of Cynthia. I haven't said anything to Thane, but I've noticed she's not particularly kind to you. I mean she's been extremely nice to me, almost too nice. Know what I mean?"

April nodded. Good, Vanessa hadn't missed the sugarcoated innuendos. As quickly as it had budded, her satisfaction wilted. Would a tormentor be so obvious?

"Normally, I never trust someone who gushes over me like she does. But gripes, she is Thane's mother. What can I do?"

As April started to reply, a voice overrode hers.

"Goodness, what are y'all doin' in here?"

Seven

Cynthia's gaze flicked from the portrait to the furniture and across both women. "Did y'all hear me?" What are you two doin' in here?"

April opened her mouth to answer. Lightning flashed near the windows at her back, extinguishing her reply, and illuminating the ballroom with psychedelic clarity.

As if in slow motion, Vanessa heaved to her feet and faced the woman whose integrity she had been questioning.

The light faded. Cold embraced April. How long *had* Cynthia been there? How much had she overheard? Vanessa's scarlet cheeks said *she* thought Thane's mother had gotten an earful.

"I'm afraid it's my fault." Vanessa flinched as a thunder clap resounded, but diplomacy was second nature to her. Her voice was smooth and level. "I wanted to see this section of the house. I hope you don't mind?"

"Of course not, sugah." Cynthia twiddled her gold cross. "I saw the doors ajar and heard voices. Naturally, I was curious."

Raindrops plinked against the windows.

"Vanessa and I were getting to know each other better," April offered.

Cynthia paled. "That's nice."

She's worried I'll tell Vanessa about my illness, April realized. *Or that I already have.* Obviously Cynthia hadn't eavesdropped on Vanessa and her for long. The knowledge was small comfort.

Cynthia appeared to recover her composure fast enough, but her smile looked forced. Indeed, it eluded her eyes. "I wonder if y'all would fetch a few items from the attic? Things for the party."

"We'd be glad to." At this point April would have gladly done anything to escape this tension.

Cynthia withdrew a slip of paper from her pocket and extended it to Vanessa. "Here's the list Helga made out. Just bring everything to the kitchen. I'm sure most of it will need washin'."

As April and Vanessa strode toward the attic, Vanessa whispered, "I nearly died. My heart is still whumping too hard. Do you suppose Thane's mother heard those awful things I was saying about her?"

"Naw." April didn't believe a word of her assurance to Vanessa, but she knew the woman needed to hear it. Cynthia had overheard. How much, was the question. "I don't think she would've called you 'sugah' if she had."

Wind soughed across the attic rooftop, leaving an eerie silence in its wake. Then a shattering trumpet of raindrops landed like pellets against the weathered shakes as though nature were orchestrating a bizarre symphony with Calendar House as the drum section.

April flinched at the unnerving instrumentation.

Vanessa seemed to suffer none of her qualms. "Ooh, how spooky—like a ghostly warning to stay out of here."

To kill the unsavory notion, April hit the light switch. Dust motes came alive in the dull yellow haze offered by the shadeless bulb suspended from the ceiling. The air smelled as old as some of the pieces of furniture hung from the rafters.

"No ghosts," April said. "Only the usual cobwebs, clutter, and dead bugs."

Vanessa skirted by her into the crowded attic. Her green eyes were as round as grapes. "Calendar House has so many secrets. If only these walls could talk . . ."

The wind and rain replayed their jarring caterwaul. April looked around uneasily. "That would certainly make things simpler. . . ."

"Simpler? What an odd thing to say." Vanessa snatched a nineteenth century woman's hat from a nail and plopped the ponderous contraption onto her head. She turned to April with a mystified expression. "What things?"

Just ghosts of my own to lay to rest, April thought, tempted for the second time this day to tell Vanessa about her illness. But her reasons for not doing so hadn't changed. She pointed to the hat. "Oh, you know, things like—which of my notorious ancestors owned that wonderful hat?"

Vanessa grinned. "It is grand, isn't it? Perhaps she was a slave, smuggled in through one of the tunnels."

"And I thought I had a big imagination," said April, laughing.

But Vanessa was deadly serious. "Have you ever been in the caverns?"

"No. They were strictly off limits to us kids."

Putting the hat back on the nail, Vanessa sighed. "Well, you're not a kid any more. I'm going to make Thane show them to me while I'm here."

"I'm not sure they're even accessible. You heard my father say no one's been in them for years."

"Where there's a will . . ." Vanessa spun away from April, obviously expecting and not wanting any argument, and continued to prowl the attic. Almost immediately, she squatted beside a brass bed frame, examining a cardboard case. "Voila! The punch bowl. Now there's supposed to be a box of extra cups somewhere."

By the time the two women had unearthed and carted to the kitchen various candlesticks, baskets, and boxes, the rain had slowed to a steady thrum.

Looking around the attic, April said, "That's everything but the extra punch bowl cups. You search this end, I'll check the corner by the windows."

She headed toward a chest-high wall of cardboard cartons, shuffled through the first stack and moved to the next. Lifting the top box, she stopped cold. Behind it was an old steamer trunk. Goosebumps sprang across her flesh.

"Aha!" Vanessa shouted from the other end of the attic. A second later she stood next to April with an oblong box cradled in her arms. Cobwebs stuck to her pale hair and her forest green sweater, dust to her slacks. "The extra punch bowl cups."

April paid her no mind. Her attention was riveted to the trunk. Would something inside it trigger her memory? The prospect had her shoving aside crates. Excitement clogged her throat and her voice came out strangled. "Help me get these boxes out of the way."

"Sure." Vanessa set the cups near the door, then hurried back. "What did you find?"

"Something I'd forgotten all about." Anticipation drew a cold film across her skin.

With dispatch, they had the trunk in the center of the room. Using her sweatshirt sleeve, April wiped a layer of dust from the lid.

"Ooh, it's beautiful." Vanessa ran her fingers lightly across the brass hinges and the wooden staves, stopping on the raised initials. "L.W.C. It was your mother's?"

"Yes." Her voice quavered.

"Do you know what's in it?"

Possibly, her past and her future. "No . . ."

"Is it locked?"

April shook her head. Even now as she reached for the leather straps, unbuckled them, she could hear Lily complaining about the lost key. With trembling fingers she unclasped the latch and lifted the lid.

A stale scent of lilies of the valley wafted from the trunk and dropped April to her knees. It was the fragrance Lily doused herself in, made meek by the years of encapsulation in the steamer trunk, yet still powerful enough to assail her daughter with myriad memories.

A sudden panic hit her. All at once, the attic seemed suffocating, the trunk lid too heavy to lift. For the second time since she'd left Phoenix, she wanted to run and hide, let the past stay buried, but her lethargic limbs ignored every command to action she gave.

Vanessa knelt and shoved the lid back until it

rested on its hinges.

Startled, April blinked at the other woman, suddenly too aware of her surroundings, and the fact she wasn't alone. In her zeal to see inside the trunk, she'd pretended it didn't matter who shared the experience. But it did.

The eagerness on Vanessa's pretty face struck her as distasteful. This was just another adventure to Thane's fiancée, but it could mean April's whole future. And it was private. Not for the scrutiny of some avid fan of the movie star her mother had been.

Then why didn't she ask her to leave? The answer was simple. *Fear.* The intense panic she'd experienced only minutes before had stripped her confidence for taking a solo stroll down memory lane.

Besides, the thrill of discovery rife in Vanessa's eyes said wild horses couldn't drag her away. "Wow! Look at these."

Shoving her hair from her eyes, April let her gaze loose on the contents of the trunk. A mélange of vibrantly colored papers stared up at them—posters of Lily's movies. At one time these had covered the walls of the master bedroom; constant reassurance to her mother that the life of glamour and fame and adoration she so coveted had actually been hers, not some fantasy imagined by her sick mind.

April stared at the face so similar to her own. "It's like seeing myself in another era, in strange clothes and peculiar hair styles."

She hadn't meant to say this out loud, but Vanessa was nodding in agreement as she lifted a couple of the posters and held each toward April, comparing the two faces.

"You are very like her—same golden hair, same shaped face, same aqua eyes."

"I've been told that all my life."

"I can imagine, but—and I hope you won't take offense—there's a definite difference, something in her eyes that's lacking in yours. You can almost hear her saying, 'To hell with the world and all its conventions. I'm Lily Cordell and I make my own rules. See? It's in all the pictures. You can see it on the screen, too. That's the quality that set her apart from other great actresses."

What a pity that insouciance hadn't been an act, April mused. She smiled at Vanessa. "I'm not offended. My aspirations don't run to captivating audiences or gaining worldwide acclaim."

"Really? I can't say the same. Bad press isn't any fun, but there are a lot of perks that go with fame, too. I love attending parties important people attend. Having a governor for an uncle has been great! That's what I want for Thane and me. Don't be surprised if you're invited to visit us in the governor's mansion some day." She settled back on her heels and snatched up a couple more posters.

What would it be like, April wondered feeling a twinge of envy, to actually be able to plan a future?

"Do you suppose the whole trunk is filled with movie mementos?" Vanessa asked.

This possibility cast a pall over April's expectant mood. It was doubtful Lily's treasured memorabilia would give her what she was after. Stifling the urge to shove the other woman aside and start plowing through the trunk, she schooled her control to move slowly. "We won't know until we look."

One by one, they transferred the playbills to the floor while Vanessa exclaimed over the movies she had seen and over some she hadn't. Beneath the posters they discovered bundles of paper trussed together with white ribbons. "Fan letters," April exclaimed, upon closer inspection.

"There must be hundreds of them."

"At one time there were thousands." And Lily had known them all by heart. A vision of her mother seated at her dressing table, reading and rereading these accolades, flashed into April's brain, dragging with it the resentment she'd felt for the faceless people who seemed the only recipients of her mother's affection.

With a swish and a rustle, the bundles landed quickly atop the posters.

Bent at the waist, Vanessa dug into the trunk and came up with a fistful of tissue paper. Excitement hovered about her like a visible aura as she propped the package on her lap, and carefully uncovered a comb and hairbrush. "Look at these! My God, are they real silver?"

Nodding, April reached for the tarnished handle of the brush, but couldn't bring herself to touch it. Instead, she rubbed her clammy palms on her jeans. "Nothing but the best for Lily Cordell."

"I feel like a queen," Vanessa trilled, lifting the brush to her sleek hair.

Dismayed at this presumptuous action, April caught her by the wrist. "Please don't."

"Oh, I'm sorry." Looking contrite, but slightly puzzled, Vanessa laid the brush and comb on the tissue paper and began rewrapping them.

Not knowing quite what to say, April turned back to the trunk and extracted one of several leather-bound scrapbooks. Almost immediately, the other woman followed suit. How long they poured over

99

them, April had no idea. Each contained a hodge-podge of newspaper clippings and magazine articles of Lily's exploits. The few snapshots had been taken at celebrity events or royal functions. There wasn't a single picture of her family. She knew Thane's fiancée must have noticed this oddity and was grateful she hadn't mentioned it.

Looking up from the open scrapbook on her lap, Vanessa asked, "How could your mother give up such a wonderful life, the travel, the glitz, the exciting people, to stay on quiet little Farraday Island? Didn't she feel confined? I know I would."

Although, the question shouldn't have been unexpected, it caught April unprepared. Did this fall into the same off-limits category as her illness? she wondered, trying to decide how to respond. She was certain what Spencer would say: leave the past alone. But that was his way, not hers, and the intolerable thought of more lies dissolved all indecision. "I don't know what story was given out to the press or the public at the time—I hadn't been born. But when Lily was thirty-two, she was stricken with agoraphobia; an abnormal fear of being in an open space."

Bewilderment stole across Vanessa's face. "I don't understand. How was she stricken with a phobia?"

"Agoraphobia is hereditary. Her grandfather had it all of his life. And it can come on at any time . . . right out of the blue."

Silence hung heavy in the attic as Vanessa seemed to mull this over. When she finally spoke her voice was almost a whisper. "Aren't you afraid of getting it?"

"I can't live my life worrying about what might or might not happen in the future." The words were flippantly spoken, but the truth was until she dealt with the past the future was too uncertain to ponder. "At least the medical profession has a greater understanding of the disease now. There's medicine and therapy to assist those afflicted in lessening anxiety attacks to manageable levels. There was no such help for Lily."

"It must have been devastating for her to lose her independence."

The suggestion brought April up short. For so many years she had hated her mother for never showing her the tiniest of affection, but not once had she considered Lily in terms of a woman suffering, only one who enjoyed making others suffer. The twinge of compassion inside her felt alien. "I guess it was. I remember she couldn't stand to be alone in a room. And I suppose it explains why the entertaining never seemed to stop."

"Speaking of which — I'd better get those punch bowl cups down to Cynthia before she sends a search party." Vanessa rose and swiped at her dusty knees. "Thanks for indulging my curiosity about your mother. I swear every time I mention Lily's name the rest of the family either changes the subject or acts like they haven't heard me. I was starting to wonder if there was some deep, dark family secret I wasn't to be told."

"Oh, I doubt it." April cringed inwardly. *She* was the secret, but couldn't her family see their efforts to avoid the past were adding to its mystery and allure. If only the trunk had proved as interesting, she thought, turning back to it as Vanessa departed.

She raised from her sore knees to a squat and found her cramped muscles welcomed the switch. From here she also had a better vantage into the chest. A band of sunlight stabbed through the dirty

101

window, glinted off something shiny and gold and into her eyes. Blinking, she reached for the offending object. The quiet inside the attic seemed to creep in on her as her fingers coiled about the cool metal and dredged the weighty statue from the depths of the trunk.

Lily's Oscar. Surprise arrowed through April. It had once retained a look-but-don't-touch prominence on the mantel in the living room. And now it was relegated to the belly of a steamer trunk, buried as soundly as its owner. There was something incongruous, April thought, when a symbol of accomplishment many aspired to and few attained, a trophy whose bestowal proclaimed exceptional artistic achievement, was hidden away like some shameful deed.

Shaking her head, she set the statue on the floor. The trunk was nearly empty. All that remained was another packet of envelopes bound by a navy blue satin ribbon. More fan letters, she presumed, half-heartedly catching hold of the bow.

As the packet cleared the rim of the chest, the tie gave. Envelopes slewed free and spilled across April's lap, alighting in a haphazard array around her Nikes.

"Ohhh." She rolled her eyes and plopped her bottom squarely on the hard wooden floor. Tingles stung her flesh from thigh to toe as the circulation in her legs restarted. This whole thing had been a waste of time and now she had a couple dozen letters to round up before she could repack the trunk.

Sighing, she seized a handful of the loose envelopes and started to pat them into a semblance of order. The other fan letters had been mailed to Lily in care of her studio in California, but these, she noted, displayed addresses in various cities around the world. And they were all written in the same hand. Her father's.

At random, and feeling like an interloper, she extracted one of the letters and spread it open on her lap. The paper was slightly discolored, but the penmanship and the sentiment were as bold and unique as one of August's inventions. She read only enough to know it was a love letter. A quick glimpse at others told her they were all of the same vein and had been written during the early years of the marriage, before Lily's illness.

The simple declarations of love washed an emotional tide through April. As a smile tugged her mouth a lone tear trickled down her cheek. Although he'd managed to convey the seriousness of his affections, typically, her father's messages were succinct, precisely two pages each. But the thing which staggered her was this evidence that Lily had at one time not been the heartless creature she had known. Her mother had loved August Farraday. There could be no other reason for her to have kept these letters and bound them together in a bow the exact color of his eyes.

She scooped up the last envelope and frowned. It was noticeably thicker than the rest. Why, she wondered, would so methodical a man suddenly vary his routine? Concluding there was only one way to find out, April plucked the pages free, disinterring four sheets this time instead of the usual two. She spread the papers on her lap, and ironed them smooth with her palms.

The first two pages were quintessential take-offs of the other love letters written by her father to Lily. But a prickling ran across her flesh as she scanned the third and fourth sheets. Poems. These too were written to Lily, but not by August Farraday. The passionate phrases, the crude immature composition, both suggested the author was a much younger man. And, God help her, the handwriting looked familiar.

Without warning, a memory took possession of her. Thirteen years slipped away. The coolness of the attic became the warmth of that summer day, blowing around her like the soft breeze coming through the French doors in the den. The house was unusually quiet. Her father was in his workshop, Helga and Karl at their cottage, Aunt March weeding in the garden, and Jesse had taken Cynthia into Friday Harbor. The twins were nowhere to be found, and April was bored.

Hushed voices drew her to the den. Unaware of any effort on her part to conceal her approach, she'd surprised them nonetheless. Her mother and one of the twins, sitting close, touching, so engrossed in one another she was nearly to the couch before they heard her. Like startled birds, they'd jerked apart.

Whether it had been Spencer or Thane with her mother, she hadn't known, still couldn't say. Without looking her way again, he'd departed in a cloud of embarrassment, darting out the French doors seconds after releasing Lily.

Her mother had smiled at her with practiced innocence in her lovely eyes and said, "Don't look so shocked, Baby. He was just getting something out of my eye."

Baby, Lily's pet name for her, had been calculated to make her feel and act like an eternal child. And it had worked well that day. Naively, she'd accepted her mother's explanation. But now the truth lay in her hands, and it felt as heavy as the Oscar had.

"April?" Spencer's deep voice went through her like an electric shock.

The jolt lifted her an inch off the floor and stripped away her breath. She rounded on him, fury oozing from every pore. "What's the matter with you—sneaking up on a person like that? You nearly gave me heart failure."

His dark brown brows lifted in amusement. He strode across the attic until he stood less than four feet in front of her. "I called your name three times."

Three times. How long had he been there? Gazing up at him, she clutched the poems against her slamming heart. "I—I didn't hear you."

Squatting, he absently fingered the edge of the papers she clutched. "I noticed. Whatever you were reading here had you completely absorbed." The same way his thoughts were absorbed by her. It was crazy, but she looked damned irresistible with her nose smudged with dust, and her satiny gold hair as mussed as though she'd just awakened. God, how he wanted to touch her, kiss her. Struggling to keep his voice level, he stated, "Vanessa thought you might still be up here. Lunch is almost ready. . . ."

The movement of his fingers touching the edge of the paper rattled April. It was all she could do to swallow an hysterical giggle before it reached her open mouth. If ever she needed composure it was now, but that commodity seemed in short supply. His eyes held her a willing captive, and suddenly it didn't matter that she'd been discovered delving into the forbidden past, or that he literally had his hand on evidence which could potentially alter both their futures. Unable to look away from his intense gaze, she nodded toward the helter skelter items piled next to the trunk. "I'll be down to the kitchen as soon as I

105

put these things back."

Letting go of the papers, he caught a strand of her hair between his thumb and forefinger, savored the feel for a whole second, then let it fall back against her cheek as he watched her eyes darken from aqua to turquoise. He swallowed hard. The compulsion to hold her struck him again, this time so strongly the wind felt knocked from him. It took every ounce of willpower he had to straighten to his full six feet and step away from her. He forced a smile. "You know if you squeeze those papers just a wee bit tighter they'll make great spit balls."

"What?" Bewildered, she glanced at the poems and realized in her agitation she'd tweaked them like an accordion fan. "Oh, my." Immediately flattening the papers over her thigh, she pressed them with her palms, managing to ease the largest of the wrinkles.

"What are those spellbinding documents anyway?" Spencer asked.

Indecision drummed inside her head like a ticking bomb. Should she confront him with the poems now and let the chips fly, or just play it by ear? But Spencer hadn't waited for her answer or her decision. He was too busy eying the trunk, the scrapbooks, the posters, and Lily's Oscar. Scrambling to her feet, she braced for the forthcoming battle.

Instead of the anger she expected to see, his expression was pensive. "What do you suppose it says about a person when their whole life can fit into a trunk?"

Surprised by his question, April floundered for a reply. "I don't know, but then mine wouldn't take up that much space."

His gaze flicked to hers. In that second, she could have sworn she saw a flash of guilt in his eyes, which had changed from dove to pewter, but it happened so rapidly she couldn't be sure.

He waved a hand at the trunk and its disgorged contents. "Are you going to take this stuff back to Phoenix with you?"

Growing more perplexed by the minute, she asked, "What, no lectures on leaving the past alone?"

"No. You have every right in the world to your mother's things. All I ask is that you don't drag the rest of the family down any nostalgic alleyways."

Anger flared anew inside her. "And why exactly is that? Lily is dead! She can't reach out from the grave and hurt anyone." The papers in her hand suddenly felt they were burning her fingertips. She stared down at them, then back at Spencer, with a sinking heart. "Or can she? You wrote these poems to my mother, didn't you? And you're afraid your precious career will be ruined if someone finds out about you and Lily?"

"What?" He looked incredulous. "What are you talking about?"

God, she wanted to believe him innocent, but worry was written all over his face. She waved the papers under his nose. "These . . ."

Snatching the pages from her, Spencer hastily scanned the crude prose. The warmth drained from his face. Damn! Why hadn't these been destroyed with the others? He weighed his options quickly. His years in the political arena had taught him a politician could sweet-talk his way out of most sticky situations, but he despised himself for playing fast and loose with April. Still, there was the flip side of the coin to consider. Adopting a forthright expression and a placating tone, he said, "I'm no poet. I didn't write these and I don't know who did."

But the tips of his ears glowed red with the lie, leaving April only one conclusion. Spencer *had* been the twin with Lily in the den that long ago summer day. The certainty left her feeling oddly bereft.

"Really?" She barely forced the word from her cottony mouth and completely failed to keep the sarcasm from her tone.

His face was so close to hers his exasperated sigh ruffled her hair. This time he waved the papers under her nose. "Now you see why I didn't want you digging up ancient history. If *you're* this worked up about some archaic sentiments penned by some adolescent Romeo—imagine what the gossip hungry press would do with it. Are you willing to put the family through that kind of harassment, through a barrage of suspicion and innuendo? Not to mention August. Have you even considered how these might hurt him?"

So that was what was bothering him. The smoke screen he kept throwing up about the press suddenly made sense. Spencer wasn't worried about his career, but of the inevitable, irreparable rift in the family if her father discovered one of his present wife's sons had carried on an affair with his first wife. Not to mention the loss of August's affection and respect, both of which she'd observed were important to Spencer. She couldn't help feeling sorry for him, even though the dilemma was of his own making.

But he needn't fear her. She just wanted to restore her lost memory. Surely the only Pandora's Box *that* would open was her own. "Daddy is shrewder than you give him credit for. I don't remember my mother showing him much love. What makes you think he doesn't already know about Lily and . . . and . . . these poems?"

Spencer blanched. "On the off chance that he doesn't, I want your promise to put these poems away and forget you ever saw them."

"And if I don't?"

For a full ten seconds they had a stare-down, then finally Spencer blinked and turned his gaze to the floor. His voice was so low when he spoke, she had to strain to hear. "April, there may be things about your mother you don't want to know."

Isn't that for me to decide? she felt like shouting at him. But she feared she already knew more than she wanted to. Without any explanation, she plucked the papers from his grasp and jammed them into the envelope. At the moment she was sick to death of Lily, and the memories she evoked. "Well, don't just stand there. Help me get this stuff back into the trunk."

Puzzled by her sudden change of heart, but grateful for it, he decided not to question it or comment on it. He bent his knees and gathered an armful of scrapbooks.

In no time, they had the lid closed and the leather straps buckled. He maneuvered her to the stairs, insisting they hurry to the kitchen and feed his growling stomach.

They started down the narrow stairwell with April in the lead. Abruptly she rammed to a halt. All of a sudden it seemed she was peering into a dark, bottomless abyss, and if they took one step more they would both plunge to their deaths.

"What is it?" Spencer asked, spying her frightened expression.

To his complete surprise, instead of a verbal reply, she leaned against him, snaked her arm around his back and clutched him at the side. Then pulling him

109

to her as she might a young child needing assistance, she guided him downward. When he protested, she said, "Shhhh. You'll be all right this time. I'll keep you safe."

The dazed look in her eyes and the singsong in her voice alarmed him. It was like talking to a zombie, he thought, as his voice raised a notch. "April, what's going on?"

Without answering, she led him on, careful to secure each shallow step before proceeding to the next.

"April, what's wrong with you? What the hell do you think you're doing?"

Eight

Inside April's head, time had shifted backward twelve years to the fateful afternoon of her mother's death. To her, Lily was about to descend the treacherous basement steps. But this day, she would protect her mother, hold her securely, and deliver her safely to the bottom of the stairs.

April's tightening hold on his middle dismayed Spencer as much as his inability to get through to her. Resignedly, he wrapped his arm about her and let himself be led down the narrow attic stairwell. However, the second they were in the hallway, he ground to a halt and refused to budge.

She blinked and looked around. The fog of confusion lifted, but any hope of relief drowned in a backwash of familiar guilt. Lily was still dead.

Spencer could see the clouds abandon her eyes. His immovable stance had penetrated her stupor as surely as his raised voice had failed.

Befuddled, April released her awkward grip on Spencer and stepped out of his embrace. She didn't recall leaving the attic, much less arriving in the upstairs hall. Reading his equally perplexed expression, she detected an underlying trace of worry.

He caught her gently by both upper arms. "Are you all right now?"

"Now?" The blood in her veins flowed icy cold. *A blackout.* It was the only explanation for the lost minutes. Although, she'd never before experienced one, Dr. Merritt had warned her that unless she could remember her mother's fall and recall it at will, she would be susceptible to them.

Spencer could see she was as frightened and confused as he felt. Had she suffered some sort of relapse? God, if he'd in any way caused this, he'd never forgive himself. Guilt and concern twisted his gut tighter than a sailor's knot, and the only thing he could think to ease her distress was humor.

"You know, what?" His hold on her freed as his hands flailed the air for emphasis. "I finally understand how old lady Flannigan felt when I dragged her through four lanes of traffic to the opposite side of a street she didn't want to cross in order to earn my Boy Scout merit badge."

Somehow, he managed to look adorable and funny and vulnerable all at the same time. The tension inside April spilled out in a burst of laughter. "I remember that. Mrs. Flannigan was so mad she insisted your scoutmaster take the badge back after it had been awarded to you."

He chuckled. "He did, too. Resourcefulness called for better manners in his book."

She laughed again. "I'm sorry I did something to rouse such an unpleasant memory."

The helpless look on her face nearly undid him. Spencer pulled April into his arms, held her trembling body securely to his own, and laid his chin atop her silken hair. "Don't apologize. It does a guy good to occasionally be reminded of his shortcomings."

Shortcomings? At this moment none of his mattered. He must have many questions, and the fact that he hadn't voiced a single one endeared him to her all the more. She clung to him as much from gratitude as from fear, finding in his embrace a measure of comfort that otherwise eluded her.

The feel of April's body molded to his, taxed Spencer's willpower to the limit. A frustrated sigh slipped from his lips. Hell! Why did everything have to be so complicated? Holding the woman he loved in his arms should be a joyful experience, instead of one that left his soul in shreds.

Concentrating on the soothing beat of Spencer's heart, the comforting caress of his hands on her back, April gave rein to her thoughts. As she understood it, in order to protect her from an incident too painful to deal with her brain had tucked the memory of it away in a sort of subconscious closet. One with a swinging door. Any unaccountable thing, at any unaccountable time, might bump against the hinge and pop open that door, setting loose a barrage of weird reactions—usually a reenactment such as had just occurred.

A shiver raced through her. She felt Spencer's arms tighten, but willed herself to relax. The problem wasn't insoluble. According to Nancy, the underlying cause was the helplessness experienced during the traumatic event. An "If only I'd done this or that" feeling caused the victim to relive the incident again and again, in an effort to change the outcome. Getting her memory back would give her the power to deal with it.

Sensing the return of her composure, Spencer

eased his hold on her. He tilted her chin and gazed into her eyes, noting that a trace of wariness remained. "Aren't you getting tired of listening to my stomach growl?"

Despite a lingering disquiet, she did feel better. She grinned. "Now that you mention it . . ."

Determination roared through his veins. He'd be damned if she'd suffer another incident like this. As soon as everyone had gone to bed that night, he'd recover those infernal poems and destroy them. "Come on then. I think I could eat a bear."

She grimaced. "Ugh! And to think I was hoping for soup and a sandwich. First, though, I need to clean up. I'll be there in a jiffy."

April assessed her appearance in the bathroom mirror. Her face was unnaturally pale, but the ordeal had left her more determined than ever to break through her memory blockage, using whatever means were at her disposal. One ride on the reenactment merry-go-round was enough to last her a lifetime. She wanted off that carousel and off now.

A determined urgency ushered her back to the attic. Within minutes, she'd recovered the two sheets of paper from their envelope, tucked them into her jeans pocket and taken her place at the kitchen table.

Acknowledging her arrival with a nod of his head, Spencer wondered at the twin dots of color on April's cheeks. When he'd left her in the hallway, she'd looked downright pale. Probably rouge, he decided, giving his attention to his food before Thane or anyone else noticed his undue interest in April.

During lunch she caught Spencer looking at her. The feeling he knew what she'd done grew with every bite of sandwich, every sip of soup, as though the incriminating pages were somehow visible through her heavy denim pants. Yet why she felt guilty about taking the poems was beyond her. She hadn't made him any promises, and she wasn't the one with the affair to hide.

From across the table, she caught a glimpse of him. His hair was appealingly disheveled and his white sweatshirt now sported a dab of tomato soup in precisely the same spot where she'd so recently listened to his heart.

The sudden lump in her throat was unrelated to food. Perhaps if she'd inherited some of her mother's worldliness it wouldn't matter to her that Spencer and Lily had been lovers. But she hadn't an ounce of sophistication in her, and it did matter. Terribly.

An hour after lunch, she spotted Aunt March outdoors. Alone. Quickly donning her red parka, April left the house via the laundry room. The crisp air was a refreshing change after the stuffiness of the attic. She made her way to the vegetable garden at the side of the house and came upon her aunt gazing at the mulched mounds that would sprout anew in the spring.

The muted crunch of the Nikes on the gravelly ground brought the elderly woman turning around. Her aunt peered down at her through half closed lids, squinted against the harsh sunlight. "What do you want?"

Standing with her broad back arched against the mild breeze, her aunt seemed more a part of the bleak setting than a separate and vital entity. She'd always been a tall woman, well over six feet, and still retained much of that lofty stature, which at the moment intimidated the poise out of April. "I . . . uh . . . I . . ."

"Well, spit it out, girl. I don't have all afternoon to play Charades."

The woman was as ornery as the tenacious seedlings lying dormant beneath the cold earth, but April knew if she voiced her opinion, this interview would end before it started.

Clenching her fists inside her coat pockets, she regarded her aunt with a level gaze. "I want to ask you some questions about my mother."

Surprise was apparent in March's lifted brows. "Like what, for instance?"

Realizing her aunt would immediately recognize and call her on any subterfuge, April cut to the chase. "I know there was no love lost between you and my mother. And I don't remember much affection between my parents, either."

"Anyone in the household could tell you that. Why come to me?"

Butterflies collided in her stomach. "Because I suspect you're the only one with the nerve to tell me the truth."

April could have sworn a glint of respect registered in her aunt's steely blue eyes.

"Most people think it's rude to be frank. Which is why I prefer my garden to most people."

Encouraged, April dug her hand into her pants pocket and caught hold of the envelope. She extracted the two papers in question. "Quite by chance, I happened on these poems. They appear to have been written to Lily by a young man. Would you know who?"

The elderly woman eyed the envelope and then April. "Where'd you get these?"

"From a trunk in the attic."

Scowling, March pulled her reading glasses from her cardigan pocket and studied the pages.

The sudden urge to leave before her aunt confirmed the name of the poet befell April. She shifted anxiously from one foot to the other, attempting to check the cowardly impulse.

After what seemed an interminable time, the gruff voice sounded. "Umph. Can't say I recognize the hand . . ."

Surely, March would know the twins' writing. Hope cultivated the valley of April's heart. Perhaps, she'd leaped to the wrong conclusion, perhaps the author was someone more obvious. "It seemed to me that mother was constantly entertaining. Do you suppose the man could possibly have been the husband of one of her friends?"

March peered down at her from over the top of her half moon glasses. The tiniest bit of pity touched the wizened expression. "You asked for the truth, so I won't mince words."

The breath slid out of April and her lungs refused to pull in more.

"Your mother was what was termed a floozy in my day, but self-preservation was her bread and butter. She thrived on the company those parties afforded. Can't imagine she'd risk offending any of her so-called friends by acting on advances one of their husbands made."

April let herself inhale, but the clear oxygen felt as fortifying as smog.

Pulling off the glasses, March continued, "Besides, women with Lily's terror of growing old seek

117

out the young ones. Supposed to make 'em *feel* young by osmosis or some such folderol." Handing back the poems, her aunt returned her glasses to the sweater pocket. "No, you'd have better luck looking for the author of that drivel among the maintenance men your father employed after Jesse died. Say, there's an idea. Maybe Jesse wrote them. The prose is crude enough."

"What?"

"Good, the idea shocks you. Now take my advice and destroy that garbage before someone's hurt by the damn things. You can't change the past, but you can let it be."

Let it be? That was something she couldn't do, April thought, heading into the house, not if she intended to get her memory back.

The only other person she felt comfortable approaching on the subject was Helga. However, the bluntness she'd used with March wouldn't work for the housekeeper. This called for a subtle opening. As a self-proclaimed fan of Lily's, Helga might consider it disloyal to indulge in the kind of gossip April wanted to hear.

After a brief search, she came across Helga in the living room. Although the housekeeper was one hundred percent American, born and bred, she might've been plucked from the pages of *The Farmer's Daughter*.

Watching her apply spray polish and a cloth to the coffee and end tables prompted the memory of other times she'd seen Helga clean this room. Back then, waxing the wide pine tables, fluffing the deep cushioned white chintz furniture, or rubbing down the Dutch blue porcelain pieces which had once graced this room, she looked more like one envisioned the mistress of this oversized hunting lodge to look than had the actual one. Now, she looked as inappropriate as the furnishings.

For a fleeting moment April thought of the old furniture in the ballroom. Why hadn't it been sold?

The austere sunlight angling through the plate glass windows mocked Helga's efforts to make the black lacquer table tops dustless.

"Hi." Stirring yet more dust, April sank to the nearest couch. She scrutinized Haro Strait in the distance as though the view would yield an opening line for the subject she wanted to delve.

"You look glum this afternoon. Something the matter?"

Pulling her gaze from the window, April asked, "Where is everyone?"

"Scattered about. The twins and Ms. O'Brien went to Friday Harbor to do some shopping and pick up your little sister. I expect your pa's in his workshop. As for the others, I couldn't say."

Relieved that Spencer wouldn't walk in on them, she leaned forward with her elbows on her knees and asked, "How many times do you suppose you've cleaned this room over the years?"

"Whew—now that's a question. Too many to count." Helga balanced the spray can on her ample hip and smiled a smile of remembrance. "Your folks ain't much for entertaining these days. Ah, but your ma, now that was a different story. I expect you remember that, don't you?"

Nodding, April snatched a floral throw pillow from the stack beside her and hugged it to her middle. "I remember almost everything."

"Yes, well,"—the housekeeper gave the table another swipe—"they say what a body don't know can't hurt 'em."

Whoever wrote that old saw, thought April disparagingly, *didn't know a thing about posttraumatic stress disorder.* Keeping her voice low, she plunged ahead. "Even so, I know I'd feel better if I could clear up some questions I have regarding one of my mother's . . . er . . . admirers."

Noticing the woman's white-knuckled hold on the can, April suspected she'd trod sacred ground too soon. Helga asked, "What would I know about that?"

"I've noticed people tend to treat servants like . . . like electricity. It's always there, but as long as it works when you want to use it, who thinks about it?"

"Ain't that the truth."

"I imagine you've observed lots of things without actually being observed, if you know what I mean."

"I see." Helga moved to an end table and squirted liquid wax across its black surface, then furiously wiped until the top gleamed. Seeming to be satisfied with her effort, she finally raised her gaze to April. "That was a long time ago. My memory ain't as good as it once was. Still, I noticed a few things."

"And . . . ?"

"And, your ma had lots of admirers. Which particular one you asking about?"

"I was hoping *you* could tell me that."

The housekeeper's defensive stance eased, but didn't altogether disappear.

April once again withdrew the envelope from her jeans pocket, extracted the poems, and held them out for inspection. "Would you happen to know who might have written these to Lily?"

Helga's rosy cheeks paled, and a film of sweat appeared on her upper lip.

"Well?" April asked, after several seconds, impatient for Helga to finish reading. The eyes that lifted to hers held a glint of distaste. "I know," April said. "They're rather crude."

"Where did you find these?"

"In the attic. In a trunk full of Lily's things." She waved the envelope offhandedly. "Stuck in with some love letters."

"Love letters . . . ? What love letters?"

"Oh, the letters aren't important. I know who wrote them." She stuffed the empty envelope back into her jeans. "I want to know about these poems."

Sighing, Helga dropped to the sofa beside April. She kept her head bowed, her gaze fixed on the can of spray wax and the rag in her lap. Her voice was low as though she were ashamed of revealing something she'd promised to keep secret. "I don't expect your ma set out to cause anyone harm. Least of all your pa. But the mister, he never has had a mind for much but his inventions.

"Lily, she was lonely is all — in a real desperate way. And, believe it or not, jealous, I think — of the marriages her friends had." She glanced sideways at April, a touch of pity in her expression.

None of this was news to April, nor did hearing yet another person tell her what a tramp her mother had been resolve the question she most wanted answered. She couldn't contain her impatience a second longer. "Do you know who composed those poems?"

"Yeah. But it ain't fair to blame the men. Why, they could no more help wanting her, than Lily could help being such a . . . beauty."

For crying out loud, did she have to drag it out of

121

the woman? "Who wrote the poems?"

"Definitely one of the twins. The handwriting looks like Spencer's." Helga handed her the poems and struggled to her feet. " 'Course, it could be Thane's."

"Thanks." Shakily, April rose and headed into the foyer. *It could be Thane's.* Wasn't that exactly the doubt she'd hoped to raise? Then why did her heart feel run over by a steam roller? She returned the poems to the envelope, then to her pocket and started up the stairs. She'd gained but a few steps when the front door swung open.

Through the gaping portal, she could see Thane and Vanessa at the open car trunk, but it was Spencer who held her unerring attention as he guided July over the threshold. The very sight of him quickened her pulse. He'd exchanged the soup stained sweatshirt for a black sweater, she noted, the dusty jeans and sneakers, for black Levis and leather Reeboks.

"April!" July's lightly freckled cheeks glowed pink from the cold weather, and her dark blue eyes were as round as quarters. "I bought you a surprise!"

Making straight for her, the little girl struggled to wriggle out of her coat and at the same time retain possession of a small gift-wrapped package. The effort proved too much for her tiny hands to manage. Together, jacket and box spilled onto the Oriental rug.

April hastened down the stairs and met her sister on the last one.

"Don't worry," July said, holding forth the yellow ribboned package. "It can't break."

"It can't?" Accepting the present, April sank to the bottom step. The slight jewelry sized box settled into her palm like a bar of precious gold. "What is it?"

"You're s'pose' to open it and see."

"Oh." Smiling, she removed the bow and slowly pried at the Scotch Tape.

"Faster," July urged.

Ripping away the last edge of striped paper, April set the wrapping aside and lifted the lid. Nestled in tissue paper were two clunky green objects with a cluster of gaudy rhinestones in their centers. She lifted one by its silver hook. The light caught the faux gem and glinted at her. "Earrings."

"Spence said they'd be right 'cause you have pursed ears."

"Pierced," he corrected, softly.

Her gaze flicked over July's head to Spencer. Why did it have to matter so much that he'd noticed her ears were pierced?

"July picked them out herself," he explained, wondering at the pain he noticed in her beautiful aqua eyes, hoping he wasn't somehow the cause of it.

Coughing away the lump forming in her throat, she returned her gaze to the gift, then looked at July. "What's this design on the earrings?"

"Turtles. Like your Turtle Rock. See the sparkly eyes."

In that instant, April realized it wasn't her heart that felt flattened. It was her spirit. Before she came here she'd looked forward to returning to her structured, if somewhat sterile, existence in Phoenix, but these two people had made a difference in her she hadn't counted on. And now her future stretched before her in Technicolored loneliness.

At eleven-twenty that night Spencer was still dressed, sitting on his bed, working a crossword puzzle. His thoughts were as fretful as the breezes railing the house. After ten minutes trying to come up with a word for sixteen down, he decided, the strain was too much. Sleep would be the best cure for what ailed him.

Setting pencil and paper on the chenille spread, he reached for a shoelace. A knock at the door stayed his hand. "Who the devil . . ." But as he strode to the door, he figured he knew who it was. And he was right.

Wearing brown striped pajamas, a brown and white robe, and brown leather slippers, Thane didn't wait for an invitation. He shoved into the room and immediately began to pace.

Spencer shut the door, leaned against it, and watched his brother traipse the length of the bedroom like a cuckoo counting ten. It was ironic. Usually Thane was the one with the cool head in a hot situation. Tonight, their roles were reversed. "Why don't you calm down before you wear a path in the carpet? We know April has the poems. We'll get them tomorrow when she's out of her room."

The wind complained against the rooftop, groaning with all the irascibility visible on Thane's face as he ground to a halt and pinned Spencer with an angry glare. "Tomorrow? I don't intend to give her chance enough to flash those poems around. We're getting the damned things tonight."

Shaking his head, Spencer tried to reason with his twin. "I know it was a shock to discover any of those poems still exist. I felt the same way this afternoon. But you're not thinking straight. What if she wakes up and catches us searching her room? That'd make her even more suspicious."

Raking his hands through his hair, Thane growled,

"I don't care."

"Of course you do. Think about Vanessa."

"I *am* thinking about Vanessa. Not to mention her family. They'll freak out if any of this crap comes to the surface."

Spencer let out a heartfelt sigh. The situation kept growing uglier; all these lies and deceptions. He hated it. The longer he put off telling April the truth, the more rotten he felt. But as his brother had just pointed out, he wasn't the only one who'd be hurt by such a confession. Damn!

"Look, I couldn't very well take them away from her this afternoon. And it's too risky to do it now."

Thane shook his head, as though he pitied Spencer. "Never mind. I'll do it myself."

The thought of another man, even his brother, pawing through April's personal things raised his hackles. As Thane started for the door, Spencer caught him by the arm. "Like hell you will. If anyone searches her room tonight, it'll be me."

For six whole seconds the twins glared at one another. Thane blinked first and jerked his arm free. Pulling a large flashlight from the deep pocket of his robe, he slapped it in Spencer's palm. "Then get going. I won't rest until those poems are ashes."

With that, Spencer found himself standing in the hall, his back to the closed door, wondering how in blue blazes he was supposed to pull this off. He glanced anxiously at his watch. 11:45. At least she should be asleep.

As he started down the hallway, the lights suddenly dimmed, then burned brighter. Realizing the power might go out at anytime, he was glad to have the flashlight.

* * *

April stared at the luminous bedside clock. Nearly midnight. By now the rest of the family would be fast asleep. Maybe she should wait another hour to be certain. *No.* There would be no better time to go to the basement, to confront her memories without chance of outside distractions. Besides, she couldn't bear to wait a minute more. Every day her memory stayed blocked the more painful it would be to leave Calendar House.

Sitting up, she turned on the table lamp. Soft white light bathed the hardcover version of LaVyrle Spencer's latest novel, situated within easy reach atop the nightstand. Earlier, she'd tucked the envelope containing the poems between the book's pages. Quickly double checking, she assured herself it was still there.

Tossing off her covers, she climbed out of bed and donned her robe and slippers. Armed with a purse-size flashlight, she cracked the door and scanned the hallway. Nothing but the wind creaking through the old bones of the house. Then why was she shaking?

Fighting the fear building inside, she forced herself into the dimly lighted passage and shut the door behind her. *You can do it,* she whispered, but she had to repeat it three times before her knees no longer felt wobbly. As she turned toward the back stairs, she heard footsteps coming along the adjoining hall from the opposite direction. Her pulse braked, then shifted into overdrive. She hurried to the stairwell.

A trickle of sweat dampened Spencer's upper lip. He felt like a cat burglar, slinking down the hallway. Although the muted snores interplaying with the soughing wind convinced him that the rest of the household was asleep, every time a floorboard creaked his pulse tripled.

As he rounded the corner into April's wing of the house, he spotted her slipping stealthily into the back stairwell. She must be going to the kitchen for a glass of water or something to eat. He'd have the room to himself for a few minutes. The tightness in his chest eased, but the film of sweat covering his nervous body increased as he ran down the hall and into her room.

Pressing the flashlight into service, April tiptoed down the stairs. The lingering odor of fried chicken hung in the darkened kitchen and permeated the laundry room, but the cellar smelled of dust, gunny-sacks, ripening onions—and her own fear. Swallowing hard, she flicked on the light switch, and let out an uneasy breath as the vivid illumination careened into the room and chased away scary shadows, imagined spooks.

Glancing across the room, she was surprised to find the door into the basement standing open.

From inside the belly of the house, the lamenting wind sounded more like an eerie murmur. Trying not to notice, April stepped across the threshold and caught another unexpected sound. Stealthy movement. Rats? The fine hairs on her neck prickled as she flailed the narrow beam of her flashlight into the dark room. She was suddenly too aware of the flimsy protection her gown and robe and her open-toed mules offered, should one of the vile creatures decide to attack. A shudder chilled her middle. Maybe she should leave this until daylight. Her churning insides attested to the idea's merits.

No! Before her courage deserted altogether, April flicked on the wall switch. Dull light issued from the ceiling fixture, inadequate for the vast room, causing more shadows than it erased. Ignoring the disquiet riding her nerves, she shuffled past her father's shrouded, abandoned inventions to the spot where the stairs had once stood.

Cold seeped through her lacy clothing and raised goose bumps across her flesh. As she lifted her gaze to the shelf that had been the landing, she had the unnerving sensation of being watched. Overhead, the bulb dimmed. April shivered and glanced nervously around.

The lights went out so suddenly that she jolted, flinging the flashlight into the darkness. Helplessly, she listened to it skid across the floor.

Nine

The wind seemed louder now, a daunting sigh. Shaking with fright, April fell to her knees and frantically patted the floor in all directions, trying to find the flashlight. A noise to her right stilled her groping hands. Holding her breath, she strained to hear the sound again.

Were the rats coming after her, drawn to the scent of her fear? Panic climbed up her throat. *Stop it!* she berated herself. The rats were probably as scared of her as she was of them.

"Shoo!" she shouted. "Get away from me!"

A soft skittering ensued, satisfying her that the bluster had the hairy, long-tailed, would-be assailants scurrying back into their hiding places. With her courage battered, but intact, she resumed her search for the flashlight.

"Aprillll . . ." It was no more than a whisper, but it pinned her like a snagged moth.

Blindly, her gaze arrowed the blackness. "Who's there?"

"Aprillll . . ." The disembodied voice floated out of the dark, seeming to come at once from no direction and all directions.

Terrified, she scooted backward and bumped

against something rough and cold. The wall. Planting her spine to the cold, coarse concrete, she inched higher and higher until she stood erect. The cellar was less than forty feet away. With her heart beating so loudly she could hear it, she took a sideways step.

"Are you still sorry, April . . . ?" The hideous whisper grew louder, bolder, and this time she was certain it had come from near the cellar door. "Sorry, you killed me . . . ?"

With surgical precision, the words laid open her worst fear. She couldn't bear to listen. Clamping her hands over her ears, she wailed, "No! Nooooooo."

Spencer discovered the fear of being caught snooping magnified every noise. Drawers creaked louder, floorboards groaned louder, hell, even his breathing sounded louder. But the wind took first prize. It whined across his nerve endings like misplayed violin chords.

What would his campaign people think if they could see him now, completing phase one on his way to becoming a real life second story man? The imagined uproar soured his stomach.

Shutting the last drawer in the chest, he strode to the nightstand. He caught hold of the spine of the novel lying next to the bedside clock.

The table lamp flickered and went out, pitching him into total blackness. Cursing, he released the book and shined the flashlight on his watch. Holy . . . He'd been here too long. April would be back any second. Unless . . . unless she was stuck somewhere below floors. He hadn't seen a flashlight in her hand. As a child, she'd been afraid of the dark.

He swung out of the room and headed down the

back stairs. Guided by the strong flashlight beam, he hastened through the dark house, and shortly had covered the entire first floor without turning up a trace of her.

There was only one place more to check. The thought sent a chill through him as he descended the stairs to the cellar, suddenly, inexplicably convinced he'd find her in the basement.

"What the hell is the little fool up to?" Spencer grumbled.

Worry slapped against him like the driven slap of his Reeboks on the wooden steps. In the best of conditions the basement was an obstacle course, now . . . He shuddered at the thought of what could happen to her in the dark.

From somewhere below, he heard a muffled whimper. A vision of her tender flesh crushed and broken beneath one of August's monstrous metal hulks made his blood run cold. Frantic, he picked up his pace, calling, "April?"

Too frightened to move, April huddled against the dank wall with her hands hugged to her ears. Still, the sound of someone whimpering reached her, a sound she'd often heard at the sanitarium, a sound usually allotted to her nightmares. Who was making the offending noise? Why didn't somebody make them stop?

Out of the darkness a light appeared, growing brighter as it neared, illuminating the way to safety. It was like a lifeline to April. Lowering her hands, she stumbled toward it, swiping at the tears on her cheeks. Almost at once the blinding light was fanning her face.

She was so relieved to hear Spencer's deep voice, it didn't matter that he was shouting at her. She ducked past the flashlight and slammed against him, effectively cutting off his tirade.

The wind burst from Spencer's lungs, and for a split second, he swayed precariously off balance. But as April's arms locked around his middle, he forgot the worry of minutes before, he forgot the poems, he forgot everything except the sweet feel of her trembling body crushed to his.

To rid himself of the unwieldy flashlight, he slid it onto the storage shelf next to them, then gently lowered his arms around her and gradually strengthened his hold. "It's all right, Angel. I'm not going to let anything happen to you."

The tenderness of his declaration skimmed the frayed edges of her nerves, smoothing, soothing, as effectively as his fingertips smoothed and soothed the planes and valleys of her back. The chill inside her melted, then evaporated in the wake of a delicious warmth. April tipped her head to see the face of the man who possessed this magic touch, and beheld a glimmer of flame in his molten silver gaze.

Too aware of the effect she was having on him, Spencer tried to ignore her quickened breath, the intensified rhythm of her heart beneath his palms, the rise and fall of her breasts against his chest. But the desire he read in her innocent gaze sent his pulse careening wildly, his self-control to the four winds. Need rose in him with such force and such speed it rocked him to his toes. The next thing he knew, his lips were on hers, tasting, exploring, arousing.

Entranced by the bedevilment he conjured inside her, April moaned and arched into him, kissing him back with dangerous abandon. His mouth was now the master of the magic. Everywhere it touched, alarming blazes kindled. On her mouth, on her cheeks, on her neck. Was this the way it was between all men and women? The wondrous joys exploding inside her body said no. But before she could decide what made this so special, Spencer raised his hands to her shoulders and gently pried a space between them.

"I'm sorry." His voice came out in a croak. "I promised nothing would hurt you and I meant it. Not even me."

In the dim light of the flash she could see his eyes had darkened. She reached to straighten a lock of his chocolate hair, and whispered, "You weren't hurting me."

God, didn't she realize what she was doing to him? He was only human. And she was such sweet temptation. Once more, he cupped her face in both hands, only this time under extreme duress, he confined his kiss to her forehead. "Not yet, but it was inevitable."

Inevitable? The hypnotic rapture cracked and fell away like broken glass. Yes, she thought, one of them would end up being hurt, but her greatest fear was it would be Spencer.

Without warning, the overhead lights came on. Blinking beneath the harsh glow, Spencer cried, "Voila!"

"Spencer? Is that you down there?" August shouted from somewhere on the stairwell.

Dropping his hold on her completely, Spencer retreated three steps and snatched the flashlight from the shelf. "Yes, down here."

Wearing a plaid robe and moccasins, her father

emerged into the cellar. At the sight of her, his eyebrows shot up. "April?"

Suddenly aware of her disheveled clothing, her swollen lips, her mussed hair, April gathered her loosened robe back into place, tightening the belt. But she couldn't conceal a blush.

August's gaze went from one to the other. "Whatever are the two of you doing down here?"

The question took April aback. She glanced at Spencer. Until this very moment, she hadn't thought a thing of his auspicious arrival in the cellar, but on reflection, it seemed a little too convenient.

Ignoring the burning look of accusation in her eyes, Spencer said, "I was reading when the lights went out. I came down to see if it was a breaker, but after finding the whole house dark, I figured the storm blew the transformer. As I started up the backstairs I heard someone in the basement and I found April."

A tinge of red colored his eartips. He was lying. What had really brought him down here? A qualm twisted her middle. Both men were staring at her, waiting for *her* explanation. And as much as she hated to, she was forced to tell a lie of her own. "I was in the kitchen getting a drink of water. I thought I heard something crash in the basement — a box or some such. I came to investigate and the lights went out."

Almost imperceptibly Spencer's brow lifted. Obviously, he didn't believe her, but her father appeared to accept her story. He said, "Probably just rats. Every now and then, a couple'll gnaw through the boarded-up tunnels and get in."

April shuddered. She hadn't seen any beady yellow eyes, but she'd heard the scudding feet. Or had the sound been created by a stealthier kind of "rodent"? The notion fired an instant need to escape to her cheery, vermin-free room. She kissed her father on the cheek. "I don't know about you two, but I'm going to bed. See you in the morning."

As April started up the stairs, August nodded. "Yeah, guess we'd better all get to bed. Must be after one."

After one? Cripes, Thane might have come looking for him by now. Spencer turned off the light in the basement, then closed the door. Dogging the older man through the stairwell, he asked, "What brought you down here, August?"

"Helga, actually. Seems the wind caused several restless souls. She noticed the usual night lights were off over here and called."

They'd reached the laundry room and were now facing one another. Perplexed, Spencer frowned. "Are you saying Helga's electricity was still on?"

"Yep. And she was having a conniption about the frozen canapés. As if they'd thaw by morning in this weather. Women." He chuckled, then checked the back doorlock. "Strange thing though. The main switch was thrown. Never known that to happen. We'd better get an electrician out to examine that box."

Dismayed, Spencer winged his gaze to the metal box stuck in the wall opposite the washer-dryer. Was there a short somewhere in the system? Or . . . A chill tracked his flesh as the image of April whimpering in the dark basement replayed his mind. Had someone deliberately tried to scare her? The idea was unthinkable. And yet . . . it would explain a lot.

He clapped August on the shoulder and steered him toward the kitchen. "Listen, I'll take care of getting an electrician over here first thing tomorrow."

"Good. Then I won't bother Karl about it."

Without bothering to remove her robe or slippers, April dropped to her bed, flung her arm over her head, and stared at the ceiling. Her emotions felt gridlocked, jammed together so fiercely she couldn't tell what she was feeling. Had Spencer heard the voice in the basement, too? Or had he been the one taunting her? A shiver zigzagged up her spine, but she couldn't quite accept the picture of Spence as a Jekyll and Hyde.

Sighing, she closed her eyes and skimmed a fingertip over still-tender lips. What kind of picture *could* she accept of him? A young man caught in a torrid affair with an older woman—her mother? That image disheartened her, but it hadn't kept her safe from his wiles. Whenever he so much as looked at her, touched her, she turned to putty for his molding. Her mouth compressed in annoyance. God, when she pondered the easy way she'd surrendered to his polish, his proficiency—both obviously attained through their years of separation—it was laughable.

She was definitely too naive for her own good. Rolling to her side, she kicked off her slippers. There was a time they'd both been naive, a time when his kiss . . . The half-finished thought startled April. She sat up and stared at the opposite wall, consumed by a memory. Since she'd returned to Calendar House, Spencer had kissed her twice, but somewhere in the past he had kissed her before. Strange, she hadn't recalled sooner, but remembered it now . . . vividly.

Dropping back to her pillow, she closed her eyes

again. She'd been fourteen, he eighteen. And she could see the mixture of eagerness and shyness on his face as clearly as though they were once again standing beneath the basement stairs.

Spencer had held her hands in both of his. Staring at their twined fingers, he'd said, "In four months I'll be graduating. At the end of summer, I'm going to college. Every day the thought of being away from you eats at me. But my feelings for you are way out of line. You're young enough to be hurt by me and that's the last thing I want. I love you, April. And I'm willing to wait for you—if you'll just say the word." Only then did his eyes seek hers, pleading for understanding, praying for affirmation.

She felt as though her heart might burst with joy. "I love you too, Spence. Please wait. I'll grow up as fast as I can."

His face lit up. Holding her only by the hands, he lowered his mouth to hers. The kiss was as light and golden as the morning sun stroking the glistening waters of Haro Strait, sealing the promises of their tender love.

But fate had had other plans in store for them. Regret brought a sting of tears to April's eyes. She swallowed hard and swiped at her cheeks. At least no one could ever again take this sweet memory from her.

Clandestine. Her eyes flew open. Why did that word hover about a recollection of one harmless kiss? What wasn't she remembering? Lily. It had to be. Everything always came back to Lily. A frustrated sigh shoved through her pursed lips. Clamping her eyes shut, she struggled to hold onto the memory, expand her recall past the kiss to whatever had occurred next. For once her subconscious cooperated.

Lost in the aftermath of their kiss, they hadn't noticed the kitchen door creak open. But the tap tap of high heels on the landing above made them jump apart.

A sultry voice drifted down to them. The person was humming noisily like someone walking in the woods at night, trying to scare away any frightening animals. April's eyes widened in horror. Her mother. If Lily so much as suspected about Spencer and her, the woman would do her best to ruin everything. Frantic, April implored in a whisper, "She mustn't find us like this. Oh, please, Spence. Do something."

"Wait here. I'll go up and see if I can get her into the living room. Then you can go up the back stairs."

Nodding silently, she retreated into the shadows and listened to the clump of his shoes ascending the risers. When he was halfway up, she heard her mother say, "Oh darling, you startled me. I need a little winy-poo for my empty glass. Lord, I didn't know how I was going to manage that scary wine cellar alone, but as you can see, I'm desperate. Come along, darling."

"Don't you think you've had enough, Lily?"

"Well, maybe you're right, darling. What do you suggest instead?"

There was a rustle of fabric and then silence. April crept from her hiding place. The scene that met her eyes set her back on her heels. Spencer was kissing her mother.

Slowly opening her eyes, April returned to the present, wrenched to a sitting position and threw her legs over the side of the bed. Her heart was hammering like a riveter's gun. Confused and hurt, she shook her head, trying to understand. How could he

138

have professed such love for her one minute, then immediately thrown himself at Lily?

Suddenly, Jekyll and Hyde didn't seem so far-fetched. The more she learned, the more it looked like Spencer was the poet in the Garrick family. With a heavy heart, she reached for the book on the bedside table.

The author's smiling countenance stared up at her. Odd. Hadn't she left the novel lying other side up? A chill slithered across her flesh as she pulled the book into her lap and began flipping through the pages. Where were they? Gripping the spine, she shook the book. No poems.

The slam of the novel hitting the table exploded in the small room. Spencer. So, he'd been reading when the lights went out and gone to check the switches, had he? Hah! More likely, he knew he'd find her in the basement because he'd been the one she'd heard coming down the hall. He must have seen her slip into the back stairwell and taken advantage of her absence to steal the poems. Well, wasn't it fortunate she no longer needed the stupid things to confirm his affair with Lily? Instead, she had her own precious memories to recount. This time the tears at the back of her eyes evaporated in anger.

Male voices sounded in the hallway outside her room, and April realized her father and Spencer were passing by. She sprang from the bed and flung open the door. Both men stopped and cast curious looks over their shoulders in her direction.

As calmly as possible, she said, "Spence, could I have a word with you?"

The expression on her face told him she was waging some kind of inner struggle, but the glint of anger in her lovely aqua eyes said it was nothing like the battle going on inside himself. The worry he'd felt since August's strange news about the breaker switch continued to churn his gut, while April looked simply angry. And he figured he knew why. Although he'd tried not to disturb anything, she'd probably discovered her room had been searched. Still, she couldn't know by whom.

"Good night, you two," said August, already heading along the hall. "Oh, and Spence, be sure you take care of that little matter we discussed first thing tomorrow."

"You bet. Good night."

" 'Night, Daddy."

In three short strides, Spencer covered the distance to April, braced his palm against the jamb and smiled into her upturned face. Knowing full well what her answer would be, he asked anyway, "Now, what couldn't wait until morning?"

April motioned him inside, then shut the door and stood with her back propped against its solid core. As though the feel of the cold knob against her hand would keep her in tune with the cold reality of the situation, she clung to it. But there was something unnerving about being alone with Spencer in this intimate space, something about his lazy smile that had her desperately clutching to her anger. "You were in here—going through my things while I was downstairs, weren't you?"

The bitterness in her accusation set his conscience squirming. He licked his dry tongue across drier lips. She'd offered no evidence of his guilt and until she did, he intended to deny it. Gently slapping the flashlight against his palm, he said, "I don't know what you're talking about."

Her gaze flicked from the flashlight to his face. "I

140

imagine that innocent look wins you all kinds of votes, but you forget I'm not one of your constituents."

Spencer winced inwardly. Nothing better than a deserved insult to make a man really feel like a heel. If only his priorities started with telling her the truth. But they didn't. "April, I'm very tired. . . ."

"So am I. Tired of this runaround." She drew a shaky breath and tightened her grip on the door knob. "You searched my room, didn't you?"

"Why would I do that?" He managed to sound genuinely perplexed.

For one split second, her confidence wavered. Maybe he didn't know she'd taken the poems from the trunk, and she was walking into a trap of her own setting. Then she noticed the scarlet tinge on his eartips. Damn. He was lying again. "You did it to find and take the poems. They're mine and I want them back. Now."

"What?" The flashlight froze above his palm as his mouth gaped and his eyes widened in disbelief. "Are you saying someone stole the poems from this room?" His voice had risen unnervingly louder with each word.

April was less impressed with this new act than she'd been with the previous one. The only way he could be certain the poems were in her possession was if he'd gone back to the trunk to get them himself. Smug sarcasm vibrated from her narrowed eyes, the tilt of her head. "And we both know who has them now."

The one thing he knew was that April was wrong. "I swear I did not take those poems from this room."

Rolling her eyes, she jerked open the door. "First

you lied about writing them, now this. Good night, Spence."

As much as he hated letting her think him a complete cad, what could he say in his own defense? He had acted like a jerk, pawing through her clothes, violating her possessions with his uninvited touch. Hating himself, he mumbled good night and escaped into the hall. Thane. When he got his hands on him . . . Gripping the flashlight as though it were his brother's neck, he stalked to his bedroom.

Thane stopped pacing the moment Spencer entered the room, but Spencer gave his twin no chance to speak. "I told you to stay away from April's room."

"What the hell are you crabbing about?"

Trying to school his anger, he tightened his strangle hold on the flashlight, and spoke through clenched teeth. "The poems!"

The mystified look on Thane's face pricked an uneasy path over Spencer's nerve endings. "You went to her room and found them — right?"

"Exactly how would I have managed that? The lights went out right after you left." He threw his arms up in a gesture of frustration. "And you have my flashlight."

For a whole five seconds the two men stared at each other as reality sank in. A lead weight seemed to settle on Spencer's shoulders. He dropped to the bed. The flashlight rolled from his slack hand. "Well, if you don't have the poems and I don't have the poems . . ."

Thane's face was ashen. "Then who does?"

Ten

Pulling up a chair, Thane collapsed into it, and repeated, "Who could have taken the poems?"

Spencer fixed his gaze on the face so similar to his own, suspecting his complexion matched the pasty shade he saw on his twin. "I think a better question is who else knew that the poems had been found?"

Thane's eyes flashed wide, exuding sudden comprehension. "You mean—who did she talk to about them?" His head bobbed. "But of course, she must have. Lord, you don't suppose she told August?"

The thought had occurred to Spencer for no more than seconds before he'd discarded it. "I doubt it. She loves her father. Telling him would only be cruel. Besides, August was too normal just now. No man with his lack of guile could hide that kind of disappointment, or disgust." His mouth felt dry with self-loathing.

The strained voice that came out of Thane sounded unfamiliar. "Then who did she tell?"

Spencer released a loud, frustrated sigh. "The only way to find that out would be to ask her. And, frankly bro', after the scene we just played, I don't think she'd tell me the truth. You didn't see the look on her face. She was furious. She accused me of lying and threw me out of her room. Hell, she thinks *I* took the poems."

"We can't do anything about that now."

Scowling, Spencer started to protest, but Thane pushed ahead before he had the chance to interject a word. "If either of us broaches the subject to her, even once more, Lord knows what kind of suspicions will occur to her — or how she'll act on them."

The logic of this brought Spencer to his feet. He stalked to the window, threw aside the drapes and stared unseeingly at his reflection. The odors of wet glass and dusty cloth were lost on him, as was the muted howl of the wind against the pane. The only thing he could relate to was the fly struggling to free itself from a spiderweb angled against the sill. He too was caught in a web, a web of his own making. "If we hadn't been so intent on keeping this whole mess a secret, we wouldn't have woven ourselves into this trap."

"Hindsight is a waste of time."

"True." Spencer dropped the curtain and spun around. "Why would someone else be interested enough in those poems to steal them? What purpose could they have in mind?"

Thane lurched to his feet. "You think the person who stole the poems intends to show them to Vanessa and tell her about Lily's penchant for young men, don't you?"

"You'd better beat the person to it."

"How can I?" Thane groaned.

He'd rarely seen his brother show so much emotion. Struggling to keep his own wits, he reasoned with him. "I don't think you're giving your fiancée enough credit. Vanessa is a modern woman. And given her background, she's not likely to air the family's dirty linen in public."

Pacing, Thane seemed to mull this over. Finally, he ground to a halt in front of Spencer. "But, what if she calls off the wedding? I'll, I'll, I don't know what I'll do. I love her."

Clapping his brother on the shoulder, Spencer said, "I know, but what if — down the road — she discovers your marriage is based on half truths . . . ?"

Pain registered in Thane's eyes as he tugged his fingers through his mussed hair. "You're right. She deserves to know what she's getting into. I'll have to find the right opportunity . . . tomorrow . . ."

Relief and dismay twisted in Spencer's gut. How nice it would be to unload his own burden of guilt, but he couldn't take the same route as his brother. Thanks in large part to himself, April wasn't a modern, worldly woman. He couldn't see her accepting the twins' duplicity as easily as Vanessa or accepting a young man's first experience with lust. Not when it involved her mother.

Intuitively, Thane said, "Don't worry about April. She'll come around."

For a fleeting moment, Spencer considered imparting his worry about the lights being put out on purpose, but decided he was probably jumping to erroneous conclusions. The thought of one of his family deliberately trying to harm another struck him as downright unbelievable. Anyway, his brother had enough to sleep on for one night. There was no sense stirring up trouble. He'd keep his suspicions to himself, at least until he heard the electrician's report.

It was nearly noon when April entered the kitchen. Two days remained until the engagement party, and activities abounded in a noisy frenzy. The tantalizing smell of baking bread permeated the room. Helga punched at a bowl of rising dough and July, with flour dusting her arms to the elbows and an apron shielding her clothes, assisted. Karl was sharpening knives. The metal scraping against metal pulled a shiver down April's spine. Cynthia and her father were going over the wines to be served, while Thane and Vanessa painstakingly lettered place cards. Spencer was on the telephone.

"Good morning," April murmured, feeling self-conscious as all heads turned toward her and responded in kind.

Only one person in the room forced the greeting, barely managing to mask shock and agitation behind a cheery smile. That person presumed April's absence this morning was a direct result of the scare she'd undergone in the basement less than twelve hours ago. That person took for granted she'd been found, cowering and whimpering like she had when Lily died.

What the hell had gone wrong this time? the person wondered, breathing slightly faster than regular, studying April with an appraising glance. Except for the flush coloring her cheeks, she looked extremely normal. One hundred percent sane. Damn.

The person returned to the task at hand, broodingly. April had been such a meek, submissive child, one assumed she would be even more malleable after her years of catatonia. Anger gave way to mounting fear. Selling short the young woman's mental strength had proven a major mistake, a blatant breaking of the first rule of the hunter: underestimate the quarry and you become the prey.

Stricken eyes swept the room as panic swelled in the anxious heart. Time was running out. Day after tomorrow guests would start arriving, buffering April with the safety of their numbers. If she remembered — all would be lost. Only a fatal accident would insure permanent silence.

April poured herself a cup of coffee and escaped to

her father's den. Relishing the quiet, she stared through the French doors at the overcast day. This morning her body felt as battered as the sea-ravaged rocks buttressing the cliff just beyond the way.

The coffee's strong aroma beckoned from the steaming mug in her hands. She took a drink and heat flowed into her queasy stomach like a soothing salve. Taking another gulp, she willed the caffeine to kick in and lift the lethargy claiming her limbs and her mind.

All night she'd tossed and turned, plagued with nightmares. In her sleep, she'd acted out one scene after another, all with similar themes inspired by the petrifying experience in the dark basement, and further fueled by the memory of Spencer's betrayal twelve years ago.

Could the horrid dreams have contained snatches of the truth? Had she killed Lily in a fit of jealousy? The thought made her skin crawl.

"April, about last night . . ." Spencer's voice burst her reverie.

She jumped. Hot coffee spurted from the cup and scalded her hands. Swallowing a yelp, she bit back the pain and slowly spun around to face him. At the sight of his contrite expression, the fury she'd felt last night returned full force, but she didn't know if she was more angry because Spence had searched her room or because he'd lied to her about it afterward. "Don't tell me you've decided to confess?"

Her effrontery wavered beneath the scowl he sent her. Quickly recovering, she straightened her shoulders and raised her chin, hoping she didn't look as awful as she felt. An extra layer of makeup cloaked the dark circles underscoring her eyes, but someone who knew her as well as he might not be fooled by a bit of female camouflage.

Spencer studied her with a discerning eye. Detecting

147

a haggard edge to her composure, he tamped down the urge to pull her into his arms and kiss the anger and hurt from her eyes. She wanted answers he couldn't give and he had questions he wouldn't ask — not until he got the electrician's report. "On second thought, enough's already been said about last night. I just wish you'd forget those poems. They aren't important. At least not to you. I was wondering if you'd accompany July to school?"

Evidently, he intended to shove the dirty subject under the carpet. Well, she had no such compunction. "Since it's already past noon, I can only suppose you want me out of the house so you can search my room again — just in case you left something untouched."

He opened his mouth, then slammed it shut. How could he blame her for suspecting his motives? God, he wished he was free to confess. But that would only ease his conscience. No telling what it would do to April's fragile well-being. "Since she'll be missing classes for the next few days her teacher has agreed to let her do her lessons at home. But someone needs to pick them up. I'm expecting a repairman at any time now. I can't leave."

And everyone else, she realized, was obviously busy with last minute party preparations. She took another swallow of coffee. At least getting angry had chased off her fatigue, but peering at him over the rim of the mug, she could see any further discussion of the poems or his search of her room would be a waste of energy. And she had little to squander.

She reined in her ire, and caught herself staring at his mouth, remembering. Pulling her gaze from his face, she turned back to the windows. The sudden intense feeling that she had to get away from him before she did something foolish made a boat ride in the cool salt air sound absolutely irresistible. "Of course, I'll

148

take her. I've been wanting a chance to visit Friday Harbor."

"I'll show you around," July exclaimed, bounding into the room. The child was already wearing her coat.

April smiled. "All right. I'll get my jacket."

"Goody. I know the ferry's back 'cause there's a man here asking to see Spence."

"Where is he, twerp?" Spencer moved toward the little girl and caught her affectionately by both shoulders.

"In the entry."

"Thanks." He kissed her cheek, then glanced at April. There was fire in his eyes. "See you later."

"Sure." The sudden dryness in her mouth annoyed her. Darn him anyway. As angry as she was at Spence, she *would* look forward to later. She pulled her gaze from his departing back and told July, "Could you put this dirty cup in the kitchen and then meet me in the foyer?"

"Sure. Hey, you're wearing your turtle earrings."

"Yes. I love them. Now hurry along, I'll only be a minute."

Her parka was not on the hall tree and April realized she'd left it in her room. She hastened up the stairs and down the long corridor. As she rushed by the west wing, the doors creaked open. The unexpected sound startled April. She stopped abruptly. Her heart hammered too hard. She glared at the doors. Everything seemed bent on unraveling her frayed nerves, she decided, grasping hold of both doorknobs.

From deep inside she heard someone call her name.

April froze. A cold sweat broke across her flesh. "I'm not going in there," she muttered. It could be a trap . . . like last night.

The call came again.

Reason-stealing anger overtook April, wiped out

her better judgment, and compelled her into the west wing. The musty air irritated her nose, and the thick carpet buffeted her footsteps. The hallway was gloomy and shadowed, but not pitch black, as the basement had been last night.

She pushed ahead, straining to hear the call when it came again. Nothing. Not even a breeze against the house. Her stomach clenched. She hadn't imagined the voice, had she?

Suddenly it was imperative she prove to herself whether or not someone was in this section of the house, deliberately trying to frighten her. She tiptoed into the ballroom. Reassuring daylight occupied every corner and crevice. Only one place anyone could hide in here. With her pulse thudding in her ears, she eyed the old furniture.

To her surprise, the dust covers littered the floor. Before leaving this room the other day Vanessa and she had replaced all the sheets. She shuffled nearer. Shock arched through her. Every sofa and chair cushion sat askew, the fabric gouged and shredded as though someone had taken a knife to it. The oak tables were mutilated, their lovely grained tops chipped, scratched and grooved.

Numb, April noticed the table shoved against the wall beneath Lily's portrait. Slowly her gaze lifted. The horror had not stopped with the furniture. Long jagged slashes crisscrossed the painting from Lily's shoulder to the hem of her gown. Ruined. Senseless vandalism. Who had done this? Why?

Forgotten was the need to prove she'd heard a voice. She forced her leaden legs to carry her out of the room, down the darkened corridor and into the main hallway. The only thing moving with any speed was the panic swirling inside her. She must tell her father. Where would he be at this moment? In his workshop?

Stumbling like a drunk, she made for the back stair-well. Near her room an awful thought stopped her cold. What if the family believed *she* had vandalized the furniture? Slashed Lily's painting? With chilling certainty, she concluded the damage had been wrought with that exact purpose in mind.

April slumped against the wall. She felt like scream-ing, but getting hysterical was definitely not a good idea. The best course, she realized resignedly, was to ignore the whole thing, pretend she hadn't discovered the destruction. Several deep breaths later, she gath-ered her wits and went for her coat.

By the time she returned to the foyer, July was half-way up the stairs. "What took you so long?"

"I couldn't find my coat," she invented. "Come on, let's get going. Karl is probably wondering where we are."

The trip to Friday Harbor kept April's mind occu-pied with the past and the changes that had occurred in her absence. But too soon they were boarding the ferry to head back to Calendar House.

The deck swayed beneath her feet as she stepped from her rented compact parked near the aft railing. July was already out of the car helping Karl wedge chunks of wood beneath the rear tires.

Although the temperature hovered in the low fifties, Karl wore no coat or cap, and the sleeves of his flannel shirt were rolled to the elbows revealing strong, golden-furred forearms. The plaid fabric strained against his well-muscled shoulders and chest. Evidently he spent hours lifting weights or otherwise toning his body and expected to see his efforts applauded with admiring glances, a concession April, embarrassingly, found herself yielding to.

"Got hot coffee in a thermos, if you're interested." He nodded toward the wheelhouse, causing one blond lock to fall attractively across his forehead. There was an eager glint in his ice-blue eyes.

April suppressed a grimace. The one thing she couldn't take right now was verbal handball with Karl. "Thanks, but I'd really like some fresh air."

"Suit yourself." He made it sound like she'd passed up some delicious confection. Shrugging, he departed for the stern of the boat.

"I'm going to help cast off," July informed her, and scurried after Karl on the heels of April's warning to be careful.

Absently listening to her sister's excited chatter, April moved toward the railing and glanced at the cloud-riddled sky. The smell of rain hung in the briny air. She drew a breath and let out a heartfelt sigh. Behind her, the wheelhouse door opened and closed, and July's voice was suddenly lost to her, supplanted by the lap of water against the hull and the shriek of gulls overhead. The motor roared to life.

As the ferry edged away from the dock, a lone gull swooped and landed on the rail nearby, setting off a creaky protest and an almost imperceptible wobble all along the weatherworn balustrade.

April waved her hands and shooed at the bird.

It squawked and flapped its wings, but made no attempt to leave. Settling back down, it eyed her with eerie disdain, as though it had more right to be there than she. Perhaps it did, April thought, wondering if she would ever really belong at Calendar House again. She shoved her hands into her parka and glanced away from the bird, out over Friday Harbor.

She knew she was clinging as tightly to the hope of proving herself innocent of her mother's death as the gull clung to the railing, but she also knew the bird could fly free if the structure beneath it collapsed. There was no such easy way out for her.

The ferry gained speed, creating a breeze that lifted April's hair and flattened it against the sides of her head. Unbalanced, the gull screaked, abandoned its perch and winged skyward. The railing shuddered, then stilled.

Lost in thought, April sidled along the deck, heedless of the gusts batting her ears and the growl of the noisy engine. It struck her that the water looked depthless, deadly. And dark . . . as dark as the basement last night. She shuddered.

Her recollection of last night's ordeal in the basement was as choppy as the icy waves. Logic told her no one could have known she would go there at that hour. Only Spencer had had the opportunity to guess what she was up to, but he'd been busily searching her room at the time the voice was making its accusations.

She stepped closer to the rail and stared at the ferry's wake, conjuring the disembodied voice inside her head. Had she been victimized by another person? Or had the voice been of her own making, risen from her fear of the dark, her fear of the basement, her fear of remembering?

Without warning, a blow struck her in the back. April slammed against the rail. Wood cracked and fell away, pitching her toward the icy water.

July screamed.

Terrified, April made a desperate grab for the balustrade braces on either side of her. Her knees buckled and smashed against the deck. Pain spiraled outward from each kneecap. She whipped forward, then back like a human slingshot.

The braces held.

Gasping, she sank onto her haunches and tried to catch her breath.

Seeing the horror on July's face, April realized what had happened before the girl started to explain. "I'm sorry," she cried. "Spencer and I always play that game. He pretends he's pushing me in the water. It's . . . s-s-so funny. But I couldn't catch you like he does me. I didn't know the rail would break. I didn't know you could really go in the water."

Only too aware of the pain throbbing in her limbs, April pulled the weeping girl into her arms and began wiping at her tears with the palm of her hand. "I know, sweetheart. Don't worry. No harm has been done. Only a little smudge on my slacks, but that'll come right out."

"Are you sure?"

"Absolutely. We'll tell Karl. He'll see that the railings are repaired." Remembering the pride Jesse Winston had taken in his work, she decided his son had not inherited the trait. "And as soon as we get back I'll speak to Daddy about having the whole ferry given a good going over."

"Okay. Here." Uncurling her fist, July extended it toward her. "One of your turtles came off."

Smiling, April released the child, then slipped the gaudy, rhinestoned earring through her earlobe, reminding herself to figure out a way to better secure them. "Thank goodness you found it. I'd feel terrible if I'd lost it." She felt bad enough as it was. Distraught, jumpy, her nerves at their rawest — she would cause herself one accident after another if this kept on. Her tormentor had won another round.

"Do you need help up?" July asked.

"Nope. I can manage." April stood, and brushed at her soiled clothing.

"I'm gonna tell Karl what happened," the child exclaimed and scrambled for the wheelhouse.

The ferry continued to plow through the water, its steady course giving April an inner balance. Stiff-legged, she hobbled to her car and slumped against the front fender. Behind her the wheelhouse door slammed shut.

Her gaze drifted, but not her thoughts. Absently eying the passing beach houses and cabins along this side of San Juan Island, she determined not to give in to the mind games being played on her. She needed to differentiate between real and imaginary. For instance, the voice. Spencer hadn't heard anyone. He'd have mentioned it otherwise. But it had sounded so real. Well, she hadn't imagined the incident in the garage, or the vandalized furniture in the ballroom.

It added up to an odd equation. An anonymous note, a beheaded doll, and mutilated furniture pointed to a sick mind. But what about the attempt in the garage? Had it been any more life-threatening? After all, as long as the car was turned on, it had always been a means of escape. She nodded. Her reasoning made perfect sense. Most likely, the incident in the garage had been just another way of making her appear unstable.

The first real sense of calm she'd felt in hours sluiced through April. Knowing the rules to any game was the best means of winning it. She would have to keep on her toes, but as long as she expected to be trapped, she wouldn't be.

The electrician snapped shut the hinges on the lid of his tool box. Rising, he gazed up at Spencer. "Nothing wrong with the wiring. That box is as sound as the day I installed it."

"Then there's no way the main switch could have been thrown, by say, an overload?"

"An overload? At midnight? Naw." He hoisted the metal box with one beefy hand. "It'd take more than last night's little squall to put out the power. Either someone hit the switch by accident, or some jokester in the house did it on purpose."

On purpose. The words sent a chill through Spencer. Until now, he'd clung to the hope that August had somehow confused the facts. He couldn't believe someone in this household was vicious enough to prey on April's fear of the dark. It was unthinkable. And yet, what else was he supposed to conclude after this?

"I'd take you back to the Harbor in the speed launch," Spencer said, leading the stocky man into the kitchen. "But Mr. Farraday has it in dry-dock, doing a few modifications to the engine or the running gear or something."

The man chuckled. "Yeah, he's one lucky guy—making money at his tinkering."

Spencer poured the electrician a cup of coffee, then joined him at the dinette while they awaited the return of the working ferry. As the man rambled on about a recent fishing trip, Spencer mentally retraced his journey of the night before from April's room until he found her near hysteria in the basement. This attempt to detect something he might have missed left him frustrated.

Anyone passing him would've been captured in the sweeping beam of his flashlight. If his subconscious had registered a sense of another being in the cellar while he and April were there, it refused to release the detail. Nor could he recall so much as one unexplained sound.

With a start, Spencer realized the man was staring at him as though he expected some kind of response. Spencer knew just how he felt. The minute April returned from town, he was going to get some answers.

Eleven

At Karl's insistence, April spent the remainder of the journey to Calendar House inside the wheelhouse, being plied with equal doses of coffee and concern. As much as she appreciated both, she couldn't wait to escape. Five minutes after docking she was driving her car up the ramp, past one of the twins, July, and a stocky man she didn't recognize, to the garages.

Moments later, inside her assigned parking stall, April shut off the motor and drew a deep breath. She still felt a little shaky. Of course, exhaustion and too much caffeine were hardly calm-inducing, she thought, gathering July's homework and stepping from her car.

The garage was eerily quiet. Unable to suppress thoughts being trapped here, she hastened toward the open door.

A shadow fell across it. April froze.

One of the twins appeared, and skidded to a stop. He was breathing heavily and his cheeks were flushed as though from running. His gaze swept her, paused briefly at the smudges on each knee of her slacks, then returned to her face. "Are you all right?"

Spencer! April felt as if her stomach had crawled

into her throat. She swallowed hard and, wishing her nerves would settle to a controllable level, gave him a weak smile. "I'll have to avoid knee-revealing skirts for a few weeks. No big loss. Please don't raise a fuss. It was an accident."

"Yeah, I examined the broken railing. Weather rot. We're going to speak to August as soon as Karl returns."

She nodded, hugging July's books and Pee Chees against her thudding heart, wishing she could seek the comfort of Spencer's embrace instead. Unwittingly, she moved toward him. "Who was that man with you at the dock?"

"Tom Jacks." Spencer took a step toward her. "He's an electrician."

"Oh?" This morning when he'd mentioned a repairman, she hadn't bothered to ask, or even wonder, for what. Now myriad notions flooded her mind. Had Tom Jacks's visit something to do with last night's blackout? Her stomach pinched at the possibility, and yet, she reminded herself, there might be a more mundane reason. "Don't tell me Helga's oven quit?"

"No." Spencer had the oddest feeling that April was holding her breath. "Jacks was checking the main panel box."

April's heart beat crazily. "Why?"

"August thought a short might have caused the electrical failure last night."

"Did it?"

"Not according to Jacks."

Was he saying that someone had deliberately turned off the main switch? That didn't come as much of a surprise. The whole household knew her fear of the dark. Once again the garage walls seemed to close in on her. Someone besides Spencer must have known she'd gone to the basement. Who? She shifted the heavy books to her other arm, wishing she could ease the weight of her worries as easily.

"April, I realize it was too dark to see anything, but did you *hear* anything unusual before I found you last night?"

"Unusual?" *Like Lily's whispering, accusing voice?* She bit back an hysterical laugh. How could she tell him about the voice? If he'd heard it he wouldn't be asking generalities. The watchful glint in his dove-gray eyes sparked an awful thought. Did he think *she* had turned off the power? She squared her shoulders defensively. "Unusual? In what way?"

"I don't know — noises. Breathing . . . Footsteps . . ." Spencer shrugged. "Noises . . ." He stepped closer, approaching her as cautiously as he approached the subject. He didn't want a repeat of the incident on the attic stairs. But anger wasn't good either. If she got mad she'd close him out in a heartbeat. From the wariness in her eyes and the set of her shoulders it might already be too late.

April couldn't forget he had believed the worst about her after the car incident. Why would this time be any different? "Did *you* hear any of those things?"

"Well, no . . . I —"

"Neither did I."

Frustrated, Spencer cut the distance between them to inches. He was bungling this. Either she was telling him the truth, or she didn't trust him. Hell, why should she trust him? When had he been supportive? Right from the first, he'd told she'd been selfish to come at this time. And why? Because he couldn't bear to look at her without remembering, without wanting to touch her and love her. He caught hold of a strand of her hair. "Oh, April . . ."

April's pulse thrummed, and she knew without doubt that the sudden influx was due to the nearness of the man, not their conversation nor her displeasure at being stuck in the garage. All her intentions to keep up her guard deserted. God help her. When Spence looked at her with such need in his darkening eyes, she couldn't believe he meant her harm.

He tilted her chin and lowered his mouth to hers. The kiss was tender, fragile, breath-stealingly sweet. Heat surged in the pit of April's stomach as she leaned into Spence, urging him to deepen his possession.

Spencer obliged. He slipped his arms about her, pulling her against him as close as her armload of books allowed. His tongue seemed to have a mind of its own, plunging, tasting, delighting as his fingers stroked her back and tangled in her silken hair.

April moaned, and murmured his name.

Spencer gazed lovingly at her flushed face, her glazed aqua eyes, and realized she wanted him as much as he wanted her. Shame and guilt sobered him. He had no right to do what he was doing, no right to draw these feeling from this woman.

He pulled away. "I'm sorry. I shouldn't . . ." Shouldn't what? Love her? Desire her? How could he explain? Once she remembered she would hate him forever.

"Sorry . . . ?" April clutched the books to her thundering heart.

"It's not you," he said feebly. "It's me."

What was that supposed to mean? Only a blind person wouldn't see that he wanted her. Or was it Lily he wanted? Confusion, shame and anger tangled inside her. With tears threatening, she brushed past Spencer and ran all the way to the house. In her room, she threw herself on the bed and gave vent to her self-pity.

Spent, she fell asleep.

Two hours later, she awoke, surprisingly refreshed, and more than a little embarrassed at her outburst.

What must Spencer be thinking? He'd initiated a simple kiss, not a marriage proposal. She was the one who'd wanted more from it. For a woman who was normally even-tempered, around Spence she seemed as touchy as nitroglycerin.

She changed clothes, washed her face, brushed her hair and went downstairs. In the kitchen, she came across one of the twins. Readying an apology, she was relieved to realize it was Thane and not Spencer standing at the counter with his head bent over a paper. He seemed engrossed in its contents and didn't look up until April asked, "What are you reading?"

Thane flinched. He glanced around with a half-dazed expression as though he'd been miles away in some other land or time. "Pardon? Oh, you mean this?"

For an anxious second she wondered if it was one of the poems, but he quickly quelled the notion.

"The wine list for the party. Guess I was thinking about something else. Have you seen Vanessa? We haven't had a moment alone all day and I really need to discuss something with her."

"Well, now's your chance. I just saw her go into her room upstairs."

"Now, huh?" He swallowed as though there were a lump the size of a baseball in his throat. "I suppose I should take care of getting these wines from the cellar first."

April had the distinct impression that Thane was looking for an excuse not to go and have that talk with his fiancée, and yet she sensed it was also important to him that he not put it off. The solution was obvious. And it would give her an excuse to spend unchallenged time in the basement. But did she have the nerve?

As soon as the thought filled her mind, she knew she had to find the nerve. What was that old adage about getting right back on a horse? If she put off going to the basement, she might never recover her memory. "I'm not doing anything at the moment. Why don't you go and talk with Vanessa? I'll see to the wines."

He hesitated, flicking his gaze from the sheet of paper in his hand back to April. "Are you sure you can handle it alone?"

The uncertainty in his voice made her ponder how much Spencer had told him about the night before. Probably everything. She felt heat slide into her cheeks. "Just how many bottles are we talking about?"

"A dozen."

A dozen. The thought of repeated trips to and from the wine cellar shook her resolve. This might prove more than she'd bargained for. Perhaps she should have help. "Where's Helga?"

"I think she's gone to her cottage, to rest before starting dinner."

April nodded. "She's really been working her legs off." The housekeeper didn't need more work to do, and besides, how could she confront her past if she didn't do it alone? She plucked the list from Thane's grip before he could protest further or she could change her mind, then propelled her hand into the small of his back. "Look, I'll manage. Even if it takes twelve trips."

"Thanks. I really appreciate it."

Armed with the list, a pen, and a cloth rag, April tried to ignore the fissure of anxiety grazing her insides as she descended the narrow stairwell to the larder. Nothing attained easily was ever appreciated, she reminded herself, and breaking through her fears to recover her memory would be no exception.

Before she was partway down the stairs, the familiar odors of dry earth and stored foodstuffs reached her and revived her flagging confidence. She felt even better a moment later as she gazed around the little room. Although the overhead light cast several shadows, only a vivid imagination could make any of them into something sinister.

She crossed to the basement doorway and halted for a second on the spot where Spencer had held her and kissed her the night before. A warm glow raced through her bloodstream, conjured heated images, and brought a tingle to her flesh. But her heart ached with confusion. How could she harbor these feelings for him in light of the knowledge of his affair with her mother, in light of the experience this afternoon in the garage? She had no answers. Nor would she get any, standing here brooding about the situation. She moved across the threshold.

The basement was spookily silent. Although she tried not to let it, disquiet pinged through her mind and painfully squeezed her chest. Her gaze zipped across the room. Seeking what? Ghosts? She gave herself a shake, and took several slow calming breaths. Granted, the clutter might be considered dangerous, but it certainly wasn't hiding any ghouls.

Her gaze shifted to the spot where the staircase had stood. She closed her eyes and pictured it there. It was amazing what the mind could do. She could almost see it, almost smell her mother's Lily of the Valley perfume. April leaned against the larder doorframe, letting the image come.

Voices.

On the landing overhead.

Her mother . . .

April's breath lodged in her throat. She recognized the other voice.

Cynthia.

April was fourteen years old again, and flushed with guilt. Why? The memory flooded back. She'd been trying to pry the boards from one of the cavern accesses. Karl and she had been taking turns whenever they could chance it. The caverns were off limits to them, but two teenagers stuck on an island the size of Farraday had more energy and curiosity than nine cats. The plan was to gradually loosen the nails holding each board, then remove the barrier altogether in one quiet operation, enter and explore to their heart's content.

Now she'd been caught.

Stealthily, she set the pry bar on the cement floor. The metallic plink seemed to explode in the open room. On tiptoe, she ducked beneath the stairs and crouched in the farthest corner, dreading the certain discovery.

It took her a moment to realize the voices hadn't faltered at the sound of the pry bar hitting the floor. In fact, they hadn't seemed to notice it at all, she realized, listening to the tense exchange going on overhead.

"I assure you I have never made advances toward Mr. Farraday." The angry, defensive note in Cynthia's usually soft voice was unmistakable. "He's kind to me, but completely devoted to you."

Lily's cruel laughter rang through the basement. "But of course he is. I simply wanted to make you aware that simpery Southern belle charm you exude whenever he's around is wasted. Dear, sweet Augie, he's a bit preoccupied, but not stupid. The act is just too-too hokey."

"Hokey . . . ?" The word sounded choked off.

"Seriously, darling, you should drop it. You never got farther south than Dallas. And for the past fourteen years you've been here. Maybe you're missing Texas, is that it? I could talk to Augie about getting another secretary."

"You know better than that."

"I'm just saying that if you wanted to go, I wouldn't stand in your way."

"I'll leave Farraday the day you do."

"Hmph!" Footsteps started downward. The scent of Lily's perfume grew stronger with every swish of her ruffled petticoats. April put her hand against her mouth to block out the cloying smell.

Two legs appeared between the risers. April inhaled raggedly.

"You and your sister are so different." Lily's tone was creamy without a hint of malice. "Davina is such a breath of fresh air. I'll never understand how John Garrick left her standing at the altar to run off with you."

"Really, Lily . . ." Indulgence laced Cynthia's voice.

"Oh, but then you were with child as they say." Lily didn't miss a beat. "In this case children, weren't you?"

"You know that's not the way it was. Furthermore, Davina and I have worked through that long ago. It's water under the bridge."

"If you say so, darling."

The two women had reached the basement floor. April could see their faces between the open risers. Her mother wore an innocent expression she'd popularized on the big screen. "I must admit though, until lately, I never could understand why Davina grieved so for the loss of that man. John was so crude, so earthy." She said the last word as though the person it described was something to be held by finger and thumb and shaken until clean.

"I won't argue the virtues of my late husband with you, Lily." Cynthia's face was crimson.

Lily clutched her by the elbow and led her in the direction of the wine cellar. "Did John ever mention that time he made a pass at me? No?"

As they moved away from her, April breathed easier.

She considered attempting a hasty retreat up the stairs, but her nerve failed her.

"It was shortly after he'd given Davina that pathetic little engagement ring. I set him straight and fast. After all, Davina was my dearest friend." Lily laughed again. "She'd probably get a hoot out of that story. Perhaps I'll tell her about it at the party this evening. Oh, by the way, darling, you won't be attending tonight. Chas left a message that he's bringing a date, so we don't need an extra girl. Now let's get the wine, shall we? Do you have your list handy?"

April's fingers curled around the wine list in her own hand as the image vanished. Paper crumpling startled her. For a full second, she blinked looking about the basement in the confused aftermath of the forgotten memory. The staircase was gone. Her father's discarded inventions cluttered the room. She was no longer fourteen, and she was quite alone.

The memory, although interesting, was not the one she coveted. However, she consoled herself, it was a step in the right direction. Bearing that in mind, she glanced down at the wrinkled wine list, smoothed it as best she could, then made for the wine cellar door, a rustic unit of heavy planks and handmade wrought iron fixtures like something from an old English pub.

Gripping the latch, she pulled it toward her, surprised at how easily and silently it slid open. Evidently someone had oiled the hinges since the other day. She felt for and found the light switch. Dust motes skittered in the instant glare of illumination.

The pungency of earth and dust and wine-soaked wood rushed at her from every corner of the vast chamber, which had been carved out of the rocky ground sometime after Octavius had had the house built. In fact, if she recalled correctly, there was an access into the tunnels from this room. Idly, she wondered if Karl ever succeeded in getting into the tunnels. She would have to check their spot, she decided. Not now, but soon.

In spite of her reborn bravery, she braced the door open with a cardboard box. Wine racks crowded the room in a haphazard pattern. Each was six-tiered and towered over her like top heavy bookshelves, filled with dusty bottles reposed in downward slants.

She'd had no idea her father had such an extensive collection of wines. As she moved between the racks, she noted there were selections from France, Italy, Germany, California, and even Washington State. Some of the racks appeared too flimsy for the precious charge they tended, and it struck her that repairs were needed here as well as the ferry.

A muted noise sounded behind her, near the doorway. She flinched and spun around. A chill shot through her before she could stop it. Damn. She was doing it again. This foolishness had to end.

Concentrating on the wines, she located a Chablis from California and checked it off the list, then gathered a Washington Reisling and did the same. She took the two bottles to the kitchen and returned.

On a rack near the back wall, full of very old, very dusty bottles, she found the requested French Bordeaux. She lifted the bottle. The ancient framework creaked, alarmingly. With widening eyes, April backed away from the decrepit structure. How solid were these racks? It looked as if this one could collapse at any minute. God, the weight of all those bottles, the flying glass — could badly injure, even kill someone.

Shivering, she hastened to the wine cellar door, gave the bottle a swipe with the cloth and set it on the floor. Out of the corner of her eye, April caught a movement. Her imagination? Rats? Or . . . ?

"Is someone here?"

No answer.

Calm down, April. Don't do this to yourself! Forcing herself to continue, she moved between the racks, hunting for another bottle of Washington wine. A zinfandel.

After an extensive search, she finally found it on a bottom shelf of another unstable-looking wine holder. Gingerly, she hoisted the bottle. The rack vibrated and screaked.

To her right she heard a different sound. Somebody else's breathing? Her head snapped around. She caught a movement of shadow on the wall. This wasn't her imagination. Her pulse zinged. Clutching the bottle to her trembling heart, she started to rise.

"Thane, is that you? July? Are you playing games again?"

She could have sworn she heard a grunt. A second later the full-packed wine rack came crashing toward her.

Twelve

Loud, tinny clanks rattled the walls of August's workshop as Karl and Spencer entered. The place reeked of wood smoke, grease, and boiled coffee. The latter came from a blackened pot atop the old fashioned airtight stove in the far right corner, the sole source of heat. The shop was usually either too warm or too cold; Spencer suspected August only fed the rumbly, black contraption whenever the chill reached him. Three steps into the room, he started to sweat.

August sat on a tall, metal stool, hammering a length of pipe that was wedged in the vice attached to his worktable. Catching sight of them, he stopped and laid the hammer aside. A puzzled frown crinkled his freckled brow. "Is something wrong?"

As Karl rapidly explained the incident on the ferry, the color drained from August's face. "Dear Lord, my daughter could've been killed." The realization of this seemed to hit him hard. His face reddened in an odd splotchy pattern. He leaped off the stool and shouted at Karl. "Why didn't you let me know the barge was in such a state of disrepair?"

Spencer had never before heard August raise his voice in anger. Obviously, Karl was equally stunned by the outburst. He took a defensive backward step as though expecting to be struck. "Johansen told you about the ferry before he retired last month."

"He did not!"

Karl's tan face went ashen and his blue eyes widened in disbelief. His head bobbed on his shoulders like a velvety dog in the rear window of a car. "Man, you're such a space-case you can't remember what day it is, let alone what you're told. Johansen gave you a whole list of things that need repairs."

August blinked, clearly taken aback. "Then why didn't you follow up on it, son?"

Crimson charged up Karl's neck. "Don't call me 'son'. *My* pa is dead," he growled defensively as though being fatherless explained being derelict.

Instead of August laughing it off as he expected, Spencer saw a flicker of guilt steel through the wizened navy blue eyes. Did August feel somehow responsible for the defective jack that had caused Lily's sports car to crush Jesse Winston's chest?

But, of course. That would explain why August had financed Karl's two failed attempts at college, why he'd given him this job, and why he tolerated his negligence. Lord, could he empathize with feeling responsible for another's death, but until this moment, he hadn't considered the trauma August must have endured; first with Jesse, then Lily, then April.

How dare Karl play on it now in order to save his own butt! Without a thought to the man's superior strength, Spencer grabbed Karl by the collar and pulled him close, intending to smash his perfect nose unless he apologized.

"Don't touch me!" Karl smacked Spencer's hand away, and stepped out of his reach. For five whole seconds, he glared at both men, breathing hard, then wheeled around, and stormed to the workshop door. "All this family's ever given mine is grief!" He hollered and slammed out.

Caught in the wake of his own anger, Spencer mumbled, "Of all the ungrateful, insolent . . ."

"I shouldn't have called him a liar." August's expression wavered between flustered and embarrassed.

Spencer couldn't believe it. August was apologizing for Karl. "That guy's always been a spoiled brat. And he's gotten worse since Jesse died."

"Well, you can't blame Helga for indulging him overmuch these past twelve years. Hell, I've been guilty of it, too. Perhaps, we've made him a bit lazy, but Karl's young. He'll grow up."

Spencer considered reminding August that Karl was twenty-eight and should have outgrown such immature conduct by now. But why waste his breath? "We inspected the ferry railings before we came up here to tell you about them. Actually, they're in better condition than it first appeared. April had the unfortunate luck to crash against one of the few weak points."

"I thank God she wasn't hurt." August wiped his brow on the sleeve of his blue flannel shirt. "But I'm worried about the rest of Calendar House. Now that I think about it, Karl was right. I seem to remember Johansen giving me a list, but I was in the midst of redoing the speed launch. One project at a time keeps the mind clear."

August threw his hands in the air. "God only knows where I put the list, or how many dozens of things need repairing. What in hell am I going to do?" His voice dwindled to a whisper, and the sudden slackness in his face said the undertaking was more than he thought he could execute.

A tight band squeezed Spencer's heart. Frowning, he contemplated the mortality of this man who'd been the only father figure he'd ever known. Granted, August exuded a fitness and health few his age did, but he was nearly seventy, and just as susceptible to the strength-zapping effects of time and nature as the next person.

Spencer had already had to juggle his schedule to be here for the engagement party, somehow, he'd find a few more days. He pressed his palms to the worn surface of August's worktable.

"Look, I'll help Karl compile a new list and take care of getting estimates on the jobs he can't handle."

August's expression brightened, but he shook his head. "I appreciate the offer, Spence. However, I won't ask you to take more time away from your campaign."

"You didn't ask. I offered. And I won't take no for an answer. Besides, we could probably do most of it in a couple of days."

"Really?"

"Yes. Now that's settled." He glanced at his watch. "We'd better get up to the house. Helga told me dinner was ready fifteen minutes ago."

By the time Spencer and August arrived at the house large raindrops were falling. In the kitchen, they found the counter spread with a little smorgasbord of cold cuts, condiments, and salads. The attractively arranged platters showed signs of violation and, indeed, only four unused plates remained.

Helga sat alone at the table, eating. Her greeting was polite, but strained. Spencer concluded Karl had run directly to his mother after the blowup in the workshop. Although she would never voice her irritation, it was as plain as August's freckles that she resented his treatment of her son.

Trying to keep his own voice level, Spencer asked, "Where is everyone?"

The housekeeper glanced up from her position at the end of the table, chewed faster on her sandwich, then washed it down with a swallow of milk. "July's already eaten. Your mother's seeing to her bath. Thane and Vanessa took their plates upstairs.

"And April?" August queried. He seemed totally oblivious to the housekeeper's mood as he reached for a plate and began layering it with ham and cheese slices.

"Don't know. Maybe in her room." Helga took another sip of milk, then filled her fork with potato salad. "I figured she'd come eat when she got hungry."

August nodded, but disquiet chattered in the recesses of Spencer's brain. He could no more define the feeling than its source, except to say it had its root in the discovery that the electricity had been turned off on purpose. He tried to shove the worry aside. Probably, she was just taking a nap—she had looked beat earlier—and would not appreciate being disturbed.

He reached for a plate but suddenly realized he was no longer hungry. To hell with it. Let her get mad. He'd rather be chastised than sorry. "I'll go check on her."

Three knocks on her door brought no response from April. The prospect of being caught snooping in her room again had Spencer grimacing as he turned the knob and silently slid the door inward. The room was empty, the bedspread smooth. He reshut the door, then trekked down the hall away from the back stairs.

The bathroom door stood wide open. Bright light and the boisterous whirl of a hair dryer spilled into the hallway. He stopped in the doorframe, and wedged his shoulder into the jamb.

Dressed in flannel Minnie Mouse pajamas, July stood with her neck bent forward as their mother kneaded her wet tresses with one hand and plied the drier with the other. Cynthia's red skirt had damp patches as though his young sister had shaken her dripping hair across it. She smiled at him. "Hello

173

darlin'. What're you up to?"

July peeked from beneath the damp tangle of fiery hair. "Hi, Spencer!"

"Hi, twerp. Have either of you seen April?" He had to shout to be heard above the noisy dryer.

Cynthia cut the motor. "Not since July and she returned from Friday Harbor. Is it somethin' important?" There was more than curiosity in his mother's eyes. He sensed she suspected his true feeling for April, but he wasn't sure she approved.

"Not really."

"Well, if you happen upon my gold cross let me know. I seem to have misplaced the thing."

"Sure." He threw July a kiss, and continued toward the front stairs. Thane's door was ajar. The murmur of a low, intense-sounding discussion drifted to him. He hesitated, his arm raised to knock, then decided not to bother them. Maybe April was in the living room or her father's den.

Sprawled on the earthen floor with her cheek pressed to the dank ground, April drew a constricted breath, and tried again to buck the weight from her back. Something sharp dug into her shoulder. She winced with pain and abandoned the effort to free herself.

God, how long had she been here, trapped beneath the heavy wine rack? Long enough for the stench of wine to gag her, long enough for her voice to grow hoarse from hollering for help. Another attempt produced only a dry croak.

Surely someone would be wondering where she was by now. She closed her eyes and strained to hear possible footsteps coming down the stairs, a voice calling her name. Instead, she heard the squeak of a rat. Ter-

174

ror shot through her. She twisted her neck, peering in the direction of the unwelcome noise. From amid the rubble of broken glass and shattered wood came the flash of four beady eyes.

Within five minutes Spencer had searched the main level and was standing in the otherwise unoccupied den. Frustration deepened his worry. Where was she?

Wind rattled the French windows, startling him. He stared at the flickering lace curtains, contemplating the bizarre notion that some greater force might be trying to tell him she'd gone outside. What the hell? At this point he'd accept help from any source. He threw open the glass doors and was immediately sorry. Rain slashed against him in sheets, wetting his clothes, his face, his hair.

He yanked the panels back together and wiped his face across his damp sweater sleeve. Even if she'd started for a walk before the rain began, she'd have been back by now.

He returned to the kitchen. Karl and Helga sat at the table, talking over steaming mugs. There was no sign of August.

"Karl, have you seen April this evening?"

Having ignored his entrance into the room, Karl now slowly raised his head. Contempt glinted from his ice blue eyes. "Maybe I have and maybe I haven't. What's it to you?"

Spencer's boiling point lowered two degrees. Barely managing to keep the lid on, he flexed his fists at his sides. "She missed dinner, and I can't find her anywhere in the house."

"You ain't eaten yet neither," Helga said in a voice slightly higher than normal. "I can't keep this food sitting out much longer."

"Go ahead and put it away. I'll help myself to something from the fridge later." He eyed Karl pointedly, still waiting for an answer to his question about April.

Karl ignored the look. He took a lazy pull on his mug and returned Spencer's stare with scoffing indifference.

Fed up with this game, Spencer headed for the stairs.

Karl scraped back his chair and caught up with him. "You act like April's your personal property. Is she?"

Spencer could see Helga was listening to the exchange, otherwise he would have lied. "No." The small word and its big meaning left his heart feeling bruised.

"Good. Then she's fair game."

Itching to smack the delighted look off Karl's handsome face, but not wanting to deal with the aftermath, he wheeled around and charged up the steps two at a time.

After assuring himself April wasn't in her room, he started down the hall to Thane's. The door was still ajar. He rapped and shoved it open without waiting for an invitation. Thane and Vanessa sat on the floor, using the bed as a backrest. Half-full dinner plates balanced on their laps.

At the intrusion, Thane's head snapped up. The fork he'd been tugging through his salad stilled. A scowl creased his brow. "Do you mind? This is a private conversation."

"Sorry. I'm looking for April."

"Well, as you can see, she's not in here." Thane motioned with his head for his twin to leave, indicating with overt eye movements that haste would be appreciated.

"Have either of you seen her since she returned from Friday Harbor?"

Vanessa shook her head, and it struck Spencer she

wasn't her usual exuberant self. In fact, she seemed almost somber. Thane, on the other hand, exhibited signs of being downright exasperated.

With dawning realization, he knew exactly what he'd interrupted. Dear God, Thane must have been telling Vanessa about the past, about Lily and April.

He apologized and turned to leave.

Thane said, "I talked to April in the kitchen a couple of hours ago."

Spencer halted and rounded on his twin. At last a starting point. "Did she say where she was going?"

"As a matter of fact, she insisted on fetching the wine August and Mother want for the party."

Insisted on going to the wine cellar? Alone? The memory of April whimpering in the basement the night before flashed through Spencer's brain and sped the chattering inside his head. What was the little fool trying to prove? Lord, let the conclusions he was jumping to be wrong. "You said that was two hours ago?"

"Yeah, about that."

"And you haven't seen her since?"

"No, but I haven't looked for her either. Maybe she went for a walk."

"I thought of that, but I can't imagine she'd take on this storm."

Apparently unaware of the rain until this moment, Thane tossed a puzzled glance toward the window. He dropped his plate to the floor and scrambled to his feet. "Why are you assuming something's happened to her? She didn't go down there in the dark, and the electricity is still operating."

"I'm not assuming anything." For some reason he couldn't bring himself to confide in Thane about this. Even feeling that a rift was developing between them, perhaps one of his own making, didn't compel him to open up. "I'll just feel better when I know for certain she's all right."

Thane followed him to the door. "Well, it's easy enough to check. There were twelve wines on the list I gave her. If they're all in the kitchen, then she probably went out for a walk and got stuck in the storm." He clapped his twin on the shoulder. "Come on. Let's go see."

"Thanks, but I can manage alone." Spencer wasn't sure he wanted his brother's assistance, and the alien emotion stunned him. "Besides, it appears I've interrupted an important discussion."

"You did, but I've told Van all there is to tell." Thane glanced over his shoulder and studied his fiancée.

"Really, Thane. You can lose the hang-dog expression." Vanessa had gathered both dinner plates and was standing right behind them. "I won't hold your past against you, if you don't hold mine against me."

The two men pivoted toward her.

She looked from one to the other. "My concern is for the damage the gossip mills could do to your career, to our future, if this story leaked. No, neither of you needs to worry that I'd ever tell anyone."

Thane beamed. "I love you, babe."

"Yeah? Well, I love you, too, big guy. Now be a gentleman and carry these plates for me."

"Shoo!" April's voice cracked.

The rats advanced, pausing only to take occasional laps of the cloying wine. They were so thin their rib cages protruded through their matted fur.

Bile rose in her throat. "Scat!" She tried to squirm backward, but the jagged pain in her shoulder ended the attempt. Something wet and sticky trickled down her neck to her collarbone. Probably blood, she worried.

Glass tinkled nearby. Her eyes widened in horror. "Leave me alone," she begged.

The two rodents halted, cowered on their haunches with their gnarled ears perked high as though awaiting further instructions, and for one insane moment, she thought the whispered plea had actually gotten through to them. Then she caught the sound. The rodents split apart, darting into separate recesses as several pairs of footsteps thudded her way.

Thane and Vanessa collided as Spencer froze in the doorway.

"Dear God!" Spencer cried, appalled at the sight before them. Two of the wine racks had toppled; the first was cantilevered against the second. Broken bottles and chips of glass littered the floor. Wine was splattered everywhere. The acrid stench burned his nostrils. "April, where are you? Answer me!"

"Here." Her reply was feeble, but it sent a whirlwind of relief through him.

Glass crunched beneath his feet, and sticky, disgorged wine that had run together into rose-hued puddles sucked at his shoes. Despite this, he was beside her in seconds, squatting, asking, "Are you hurt?"

Even from her awkward position, she could see the fear in his eyes. It took three tries before her voice rallied and sounded stronger than a squeak. "Something's stabbing my shoulder, otherwise, I don't know. I'm too numb too tell."

Alarm spread a layer of ice across his heart. Had she damaged her spine? Please God, don't let that be the case. He eyed the trickle of blood oozing from somewhere on her shoulder. Fighting back panic, he told himself it could be worse. The blood could be pumping out. Anxiously, he grabbed the wine rack that held her pinned.

"Careful, Spence," Thane grasped his arm, staying

his attempt to hoist the damned thing off her. "If you dislodge that rack the other will crash down on her, too. Vanessa's gone to get August and Karl."

Stifling his impatience, Spencer surveyed the situation more fully. Thane was right. The two racks had locked tight and lifting one without supporting the other could cause April further harm. He hunkered down again and took her hand. "Hang in there, sweetheart. It'll just be a few more minutes."

She nodded and closed her eyes. In the comfort of his concern it seemed like no time before she heard her father and Karl arrive, along with Cynthia, Vanessa, and Helga.

Between shouts of dismay and exclamations of worry, the wine racks were righted. Spencer immediately knelt beside April. "Stay still another minute. There's a sliver of glass stuck in your shoulder."

Actually the wedge of glass was the size of his thumb. He wrapped his handkerchief around the blunted end. "Mother, squeeze her hand. Real hard. This will only hurt for a minute, April."

Wincing, he jerked. The glass came smoothly out, spewing forth a fresh stream of blood.

Cynthia took the hankie from Spencer and pressed it against the inch-wide gash. "Can you sit up, sugah?"

April tested her limbs and found them in perfect working order. Gingerly, she rose to a sitting position, feeling her circulation sting with the movement, and noticing for the first time that her face, her hands and her clothes were tacky with partially dried wine.

Directly, she was aware of the pale faces and widened eyes watching her. Was one of them disappointed she hadn't been crushed by the heavy wine rack? Suspiciously, she gazed from one to the other. "I'm fine. Look, I can stand. And walk."

"It's a damned good thing you can." Her father patted her hand. "There's no excuse for these racks being in such shameful condition."

Karl's face flushed as red as the blood seeping into Cynthia's hankie. He pointed his finger at August and his ice blue eyes were constricted to twin orbs of indignation. "Hey man, you were told!" He dropped his arm and stormed out with his mother on his heels.

The outburst surprised April so much she forgot about the pain in her back. But before she could ask what had brought it on, Cynthia pressed harder on the wound and instantly received her rapt attention. "Sugah, we'd best get you upstairs and see to this nasty cut."

"Lordy, girl," March grumbled. "I never knew anyone to be so much trouble—one crazy stunt after another. It's a good thing July was spared this. She's had enough scares for one day."

"Why, Aunt March—it was an accident." Incredulity swam in Vanessa's green eyes. She shrugged. "Anyone can have an accident."

But was it an accident? Spencer wondered, as he followed the others upstairs.

An hour later, April was still wondering the same thing. Clean, and sporting numerous bandages in varying sizes, she leaned against the stacked pillows of her bed, picking at the delicious array of salads and meat slices Helga had provided for her.

Cynthia had pronounced her injuries minor, except for the gash on her shoulder, and even that had been subdued with a giant butterfly bandage. Professing relief, the rest of the family had headed to their own rooms for the night, all but her stepmother.

She hovered about as though she had something to say, but wasn't certain how to begin.

181

Finally April could stand the weighted silence no longer. "Would you like to sit down a minute and visit?"

Nodding, Cynthia seemed relieved. She pulled up the room's single pine, straight-backed chair, sat, and folded her hands in her lap. For several more seconds she watched April eat, then at last said, "I think we got off on the wrong foot, sugah, and I'd like to try and clear the muddy waters between us."

The statement surprised April. Somehow she managed to swallow the wedge of cheddar in her mouth as though her throat hadn't constricted. Was Cynthia actually trying to apologize for her less than cordial treatment of April since her return to Calendar House? As amazing as that seemed, April felt she might be. It was a pity that a few sessions nursing someone's injuries didn't wash away distrust.

"Tonight's accident made me admit somethin' to myself. I'm ashamed to say, I've been a tad bit jealous of you."

"Jealous—of me?" Not wanting to appear too eager to hear this explanation, April concentrated on folding a piece of Swiss cheese with a slice of turkey. Slowly, she glanced at her. "Why?"

Cynthia drew a deep breath. Her fingers automatically sought the ever-present gold cross. Inexplicably it was not there. She made a self-conscious gesture and dropped the hand back into her lap. "Your daddy loves you very much and I'm afraid I saw that as a threat—to July and me—especially since you look so awfully much like Lily."

Adding this admission to the memory she'd had in the basement earlier, April concluded she'd been right about Cynthia's feelings for Lily. "I may look like Lily, but I'm not *like* her."

"I know that. You were nothing like her as a child. I

should have remembered . . ." Tears stood in Cynthia's eyes. "I've watched you with July. Honestly, those awful earrings she picked out — and you wear them every chance . . . just to please her. You're kind and lovin' and generous to a fault. I haven't been the least bit fair. I hope you'll accept my apology."

At a loss for words, April bit into the turkey and cheese, but the unexpected lump in her throat made swallowing impossible.

Her stepmother continued. "I'm not expectin' instant approval. But, I love your daddy very much. I hope someday you and I might be friends — for the sakes of the loved ones we share."

It was quite a speech, April allowed, one she would dearly love to believe. However, at this stage, she didn't trust her own judgment enough to be certain she wasn't being naively drawn into the wrong web. Every internal sensor she owned had to be set on alert and kept there until her memory block was penetrated. The incidents in the garage, the basement and the wine cellar could not be shrugged off. Someone had been trying to get rid of her.

At the moment, all she could offer Cynthia was a nod and a smile.

"Sugah, might I ask you a large favor?"

A favor? Was that what this was all about, Cynthia wanting something from her? There was an odd twitch in her stomach. Disappointment? "What favor?"

"Please don't be angry, hon. March told me you'd found some old poems?"

"What about them?" She braced herself for whatever was coming.

"I'm askin' you not to mention them to anyone else. If certain people — like your daddy — found out about 'em, they'd be ever so hurt."

"You know who wrote those poems, don't you?"

Cynthia's hand went for the missing cross again, came up empty again, and went instead to her dark brown hair. She loosened a pin from her chignon, re-anchored it, then bent her head and stared at her folded hands. "Yes, yes, I do know who authored those dreadful verses." There was a genuine touch of shame in her voice.

April's pulse surged unsteadily. "Tell me."

Her stepmother's head lifted with aching slowness until their eyes were on a level. "Only if you promise to forget they ever existed."

Put like that April knew it was a promise she couldn't make, let alone keep. However, she could agree not to mention the poems again to another soul. "I can promise that daddy will never learn of their existence from me."

Cynthia studied her face for a moment, then nodded. "Yes, I believe I can trust you."

April's mouth felt as dry as ashes. Somehow she managed to ask, "Which one of the twins wrote them?"

Thirteen

Cynthia's deep set eyes widened. "So, you know that much, do you?"

And more, April thought, but didn't say it. "Yes, I know that much."

"Then may I assume you also know a little somethin' about your mama?"

April nodded. The dryness in her mouth worsened. "I won't be shocked by whatever you have to tell me, if that's what you're worried about."

For a long moment Cynthia studied her with appraising eyes. "No, I don't suppose you would after all the truths you've had to face. I was terribly wrong to ask you to lie to July about the sanitarium. My reasons were purely selfish, and considerin' my background, not well thought out, but I swear I won't put that kind of burden on you again."

"Thank you." April took a swallow of water from the glass on her bed tray, then tried to steer Cynthia back to the subject. "About the poems . . ."

"Before I explain about those, I think there are a few other things that need clarifyin'." She leaned into the chair's back, locked her arms across her chest, and sighed. "My sister Davina had been friends with your mama in the years before Lily became famous. They'd stayed close even afterward, and when Lily realized the nature of her illness, Davina was one of the few people who told the truth. That's how I came to be at Calendar House, through Davina's recommendation. At the time, I'd been widowed less than a year—my boys were three years old—and I'd nearly depleted the piddly insurance compensation awarded by their father's death. I was desperate for anythin' that would give the boys and myself a home."

"I know all that." Impatience slithered through April and into her voice.

Cynthia unlocked her arms, hunkered forward and swiped her palms on her red skirt. "And I dare say you believed I was only your mama's social secretary."

Taking a bite of potato salad, April nodded.

"Well, it wasn't the whole truth."

April continued chewing, grateful that the food gave her an excuse not to talk.

"I was in fact, a registered nurse hired to look after Lily and later, you."

Surprise brought April's full attention to the woman seated across from her. A registered nurse? How easily the pieces of a puzzle fell into place when you held the right framework. She'd been a fool not to see it herself considering how often in the past few weeks she'd been subjected to Cynthia's gentle nursing, her knowledge of first aid.

And a woman with Lily's debilitating illness, a woman emotionally incapable of caring for her child had definitely needed the services of a nurse. Thinking back, April realized what a good cover the social secretary guise had been. Lily hadn't needed constant watching or nursing, but she had thrown loads of parties, sent tons of invitations and answered all fan letters.

She finished the bite of salad without tasting it.

How strange it felt to view someone in a whole new light, to have everything you thought you knew about them wiped away in one sweep. "I didn't know."

"Few did, hon. The greatest role your mama ever played was pretendin' she'd chosen to retire at the peak of her success rather than fade into obscurity portraying agin' matriarchs as other film legends had. It couldn't've been easy—makin' like Farraday Island was her idea of heaven on earth when it must've felt like a prison, one she couldn't even fake the courage to escape. Eventually, it got to the point where she couldn't step outside the door. Do you remember?"

April nodded. The twinge of sympathy she'd felt for her mother the other day in the attic came again, harder. "I'm only starting to appreciate the horror of it. Do you know how restrictive even a house this size would seem?"

Cynthia nodded. Her smile was mirthless. "It was why both wings of the house were kept open, although there was no need for all that space. And, lordy, how she came to resent others' ability to come and go as they pleased. I will give her credit though—she was sly enough not to take her anger at her sickness out on her friends. They wouldn't have returned. Instead, Lily vented her spleen on you and me."

She reached to touch April. April flinched and Cynthia pulled back. Lacing her fingers together, she laid them in her lap. "Oh, how I pitied you. I was an adult with some good ole Southern steel in my spine. Your mama couldn't bend, much less break me, but you were a different matter, sugah."

Anger as old as her childhood and as fresh as her memories flooded through April, washing away every ounce of compassion. Why didn't realizing her mother was ill alleviate the impotent rage she felt whenever she thought about the way Lily had treated her? Her stomach contracted. The savory aromas rising from the food on the bed tray suddenly sickened her. April grimaced, and attempted to lift the tray from her lap.

Leaping to her aid, Cynthia placed the tray on the dresser, then returned to the chair. This time there was no hesitancy when she reached for April's hand, and April made no attempt to pull free from the comforting touch. The three people she loved best in the world adored this woman. So why hadn't she even looked for any redeeming quality in Cynthia, instead of automatically condemning her like some jealous fourteen-year-old who'd lost her father to his new wife . . . ?

The thought gave April serious pause, and as she studied Cynthia's concerned expression, she realized her stepmother wasn't solely responsible for their getting off on the wrong foot. She also had been jealous, jealous of all the years Cynthia had had with her father and Spencer. Years she could never retrieve.

Cynthia said, "I can only guess at the emotional scars your mama inflicted on you, but surely in therapy you discovered what a sick woman she was?"

Until this moment she had discussed this aspect of her past with no one but Dr. Merritt. The thought of opening herself up to someone else felt alien, and yet the time seemed right. "I tried to be so good, to do everything she wanted me to do, thinking that would make her love me. But I was never quite good enough, or smart enough, or pretty enough."

"Sugah, you're wrong. You succeeded and then some. That was the problem. Lily didn't just suffer from agoraphobia you know, she also had the actor's disease: fear of growin' old. To Lily, every candle on your birthday cake was like a nail in her coffin, an annual party in honor of her dead reign as queen of the cinema. As you entered your teens and your potential beauty began to emerge, Lily grew obsessively jealous of you. Why do you think she insisted you wear those silly clothes that were years too young for you?"

And undermined my confidence at every turn? And brainwashed me into thinking you—who had probably changed my diapers and rocked me to sleep—were worthy of nothing but my scorn? April was stung with self-contempt.

"Don't blame yourself, hon. Can't do anythin' but pity an actress who believes she'll forever be able to play ingenues." Cynthia patted her hand, then brushed an errant strand of hair from April's eyes. "Once, I actually screwed up the courage to confront your daddy about the way she was treatin' you, but he—well, you know how he is. He spent every possible minute in that workshop of his. In his own way he was in as severe a state of denial as Lily."

For some unfathomable reason, April couldn't stir up any anger at her father. Perhaps because he'd been as much a victim as she, or perhaps because even in his normal preoccupied state he'd always managed to convey his love for her. Tears stung the back of her eyes, but she willed them not to fall.

"August has lived to regret his inaction more than you know, hon. In one fell swoop, he lost both Lily and you. He blames himself for your illness. And deep down inside I can't say he's wrong. Perhaps you might have withstood the shock of your mama's death if you'd had your daddy to lean on."

April felt the heat drain from her face. If she'd killed Lily, all the support in the world wouldn't have helped. She sank back on her pillows and stared at the ceiling. She could hardly tell Cynthia that. However, if she kept on indulging this new found vulnerability she might divulge more than was wise. "Could we get back to the poems?"

"Certainly, I didn't mean to get so carried away."

189

Cynthia sounded hurt.

April instantly regretted her bluntness and the necessity of it, but offered no excuses or apologies. She didn't dare.

Her stepmother was once again seeking and not finding the gold cross. More than ever, it struck April that she relied on the thing for emotional support.

Twin dots of color stained Cynthia's cheeks. "Agoraphobia is extremely destructive on a person's self-confidence. Add to that Lily's fear of agin' and you've got trouble in capital letters. Lily needed constant reassurance of her attractiveness to the opposite sex. At first she encouraged the flirting of her friends' husbands, but then a couple of the women refused invitations to other parties and she smartened up.

"She turned her attention to the men who did the maintenance work Jesse Winston couldn't handle, or the appliance repairmen, and I had my suspicions about a couple of your father's business associates. I don't know how many of these flirtations went beyond the battin' eyelashes stage. I can only speak of one such case with any authority."

The way she said that, April knew she meant one of the twins. Her heart crawled into her throat and dread pressed in on her.

Gazing at the floor, Cynthia seemed to be speaking to herself. Resentment and pain vied for dominance in her deep set gray eyes. "He was only eighteen years old. What young man at that age wouldn't be flattered by the attentions of a beautiful older woman? A movie star, no less! Poor Thane, he never knew what hit him."

Thane, not Spencer. Oddly, knowing the truth did nothing to ease the tightness in April's stomach. After the memory of Spencer's betrayal with Lily, learning he hadn't written the poems felt anticlimactic.

Unexpectedly, Cynthia laughed, a nervous laugh. "Well, you read those sappy poems. I don't need to tell you how hard Thane fell. But after a few weeks of thinkin' with the wrong end of his anatomy, he realized how much August would be hurt by his actions. It shamed him back to his senses. Lily was furious enough to smack him. The ring she was wearing left a tiny crescent shaped scar near his left eye—a permanent reminder of the harm lust can inflict."

"Did you know about the affair while it was going on?"

"No. Thane told me about it afterward."

April shook her head. "I can't believe she had the nerve to carry on right here inside Calendar House. Are you certain Daddy didn't know?"

"About Thane? My husband is a gracious person, but I can't honestly believe any man who held such knowledge about another would treat the offender with the love and respect August shows my sons." Only someone listening as closely as April was would have detected the quaver of worry in Cynthia's confident tone. Cynthia added, "As to any other affairs Lily might have had, well, we've never discussed it."

"Even if there had been others, and even if Daddy had found out, I don't suppose he'd have divorced her?"

"Probably not. With her illness, Lily would've ended up in an asylum. And in those days, society and industry alike would've shunned August for not standin' by a mentally ill wife. Plus, he had you to consider, and I suppose he figured any mother was better than none."

He'd been wrong. April felt certain Cynthia thought the same, although they were both too polite to say it aloud. Weariness seemed to seep into her every pore. She tried and failed to stifle a yawn.

191

"You'd better get some sleep, hon." Rising, Cynthia turned off the bedside lamp, fetched the tray from the dresser and left.

Spencer crossed the basement room slowly, forming impressions, memorizing details. At the wine cellar, he found the door wide open with a box levered against it, the same as when they'd discovered April amid the wreckage a short while ago. The light was still on but cast questionable illumination through the ruby colored wine splatters wreathing it.

Before entering, he considered the cellar with a critical eye born of a calmness that had been absent earlier in his anxiety over April. How had this terrible thing happened? He wanted answers. Accident or negligence or treachery? So unsettled were his thoughts, he barely registered the chill in the earthen room. If someone had deliberately tried to harm April—mightn't they have shut the door, turned out the light? They might. Unless they meant it to look like an accident.

He picked a path across the viscous floor, crunched broken glass with every step, and twice lost his footing on the syrupy spillage before managing to reach the two toppled wine racks, which now lay clumped together looking, Spencer thought, about as harmless as a dismantled gallows.

Squatting, he grasped the fractured two-by-eights and examined them at closer range. Logic told him it was a waste of time; April's rescue would have destroyed any evidence of villainy which might have existed. Still, he had to look.

After inspecting every contorted board, Spencer was more confused than when he started. The wood had aged to the point of rotting, exhibited by the jagged, top to bottom splits in both of the side supports. How long since anyone had taken a bottle from this particular rack? The damned thing must've been a potential deathtrap, awaiting any imbalance in weight that would set it vibrating enough to career, collapse. He uncurled his long body and stepped over the heap of splintered wood. Was it really that simple, that innocent? Lord, he wanted to believe it.

His gaze circled the room. Racks and dust laden bottles alike looked polka dotted from the out-gushing of wine that had taken place. Bending his head forward, Spencer combed his fingers up his chin, across his face and through his hair. The splotches blurred before his tired eyes, but the image of other spots darted into his brain; damp patches on red fabric. Ice grazed his heart. *July sprayed Mother's skirt with her wet hair, didn't she?* God, of course she had! He felt despicable for even entertaining such a notion.

Yet . . . He slumped against the wall, recalling how jealous his mother had been of Lily. Reflecting on it now, he realized she must have been in love with August years before he was widowed. She'd certainly taken every advantage to console him after Lily's death. He frowned, trying to remember if she'd also been the one to suggest the private sanitarium in Arizona for April. But all he could say for certain was how upset she'd been when April accepted her father's invitation to come to Calendar House for the engagement party.

His gut wrenched as though someone had dragged a fish hook through it. For God sakes, had he lost his mind? How could he suspect his own mother of something so unspeakable? No! April's mishap had been an accident. Hell, a damned fool could see the repairs needed in this room—if they'd ever bothered to notice. He glanced around again, uncertain if the standing racks were listing or if his overwrought imagination was making them appear too top heavy. Concluding that he'd lost his objectivity, Spencer decided the best thing was to leave and come back in the morning.

That was where April found him after lunch the next day. It had taken every ounce of courage she could muster to come down here, but she had to see the room, the devastation, the proof that what had happened was no accident. Steeling herself against flashbacks the cloying odors raised, she tucked the box of plastic garbage bags she'd brought beneath her arm and leaned into the heavy door.

Three sides of the cellar and the ceiling were carved from the earth, but the back wall and overhead beams were man-made from rough-hewn pines. Spencer had swept clear an area of the floor and was divesting the standing racks of their precious wares. Already his Levis and sweatshirt displayed dirty smudges from his labors.

In spite of his betrayal with Lily, her pulse sped faster through her veins at the sight of him, and no amount of coaxing could keep a smile from her lips. "How many hundreds of dollars of wine do you suppose was lost?"

Spencer glanced over his shoulder. The frown tugging his brows eased, and his heart gave a leap. God, she was beautiful, even in baggy gray sweats, with her hair pulled back like a horse's tail and a tiny bandage, nearly hidden by her golden bangs, forming an X on her forehead.

"I'm amazed you can joke about it." He knew he didn't find the thought of losing her the least bit humorous. Relegating the bottle in his hands to a place beside the others, he straightened and faced her. "How did it happen, April?"

"I'm not sure." Heat sprang to her cheeks as she moved into the room, debating whether or not to tell him about the noise she'd heard. Or thought she'd heard. Today, she wasn't so certain what to make of it. Had someone pushed the rack over on her or not? At the time she'd been positive, but now she realized her only evidence—another person's breathing—would have been impossible to detect above the clamor her pulse had created in her ears.

Then again, what if she'd been right? The possibility soured her stomach equally as much as the stench lifting from the floor. It would mean someone in the household, a member of her family—or Helga or Karl, whom they all considered family—had deliberately tried to kill her. How could she suggest *that* to Spencer? He'd be furious, and she doubted he'd believe it without proof.

"Well, you must have some idea what happened." Obviously, he wasn't going to quit questioning her until she gave him a satisfactory answer.

"What happened?" Being deliberately evasive, April moved between the wine racks like a cat looking for a place to settle. She meandered toward the back wall, talking as she went. "All I did was lift a wine bottle from the bottom shelf, but you'd have thought the rack was a living thing and I'd just pulled off an arm the way it screaked. The next thing I knew, it came toppling over on me. Unfortunately, I wasn't quick enough to avoid the fallout." The memory sent a shiver through her.

"However I *was* lucky it fell the way it did, otherwise—I wouldn't be here now to help you clean up the . . ." Her voice trailed off as she spied a golden object poking from between shards of glass and wood. Bending, April retrieved the item, realizing what it was the second she lifted the chain from amid the debris. She carried it to Spencer. "Look. Cynthia's cross. I noticed she was missing it last night. The chain is broken.

195

It must have pulled loose when she was helping me."

Spencer stared at the swinging cross as though April were using it to hypnotize him. Disbelief scurried through his brain. His mother hadn't lost the cross when helping April. She'd lost it before they'd found her trapped beneath the wine rack. The implication was unavoidable. "I'll give it to her."

There was an odd flatness in his voice. Puzzling about it, April released the necklace to his extended palm.

Spencer stuffed it into his jeans with uncalled-for speed.

Whatever was the matter with him? she wondered, as he picked up a nearby broom and began sweeping furiously.

Deciding to give him some space, April fished two of the few remaining wine bottles from the last rack, then returned them to the center of the room. The empty space she had created revealed a section of wall behind the rack that had planks nailed crosswise in a haphazard fashion from floor to ceiling — one of the accesses to the smuggling tunnels. If the boards were loose, it could be a means of escape for someone deliberately scaring or otherwise harming someone else. Reaching through the shelves, she gripped a plank and tugged. It gave slightly. No one, she thought disappointedly, had used this access since it had been boarded up.

"What have you found?" Spence asked bearing down on her.

"It's one of the openings into the tunnels, but it's boarded up tight."

He gave the wall a cursory glance as he reached her side. His attention swung to her upturned face. Under his intense gaze, April felt her poise slip. Breath seemed to sputter to and from her lungs. "Have you ever been in the tunnels?"

"Nope." Spence braced his arm against the wall with the flat of his palm, and leaned nearer her face. "August had all the accesses closed off about the time we four hellions started skating in the other room — probably didn't want to chance losing one or all of us in that maze."

The scent of his spicy aftershave filtered through the heavy wine, adding to her discomfiture. "How did the smugglers get into the passageways from the Haro Strait side?"

Spencer felt her warm breath on his mouth and an instant response in his loins. God, how he wanted to pull her into his arms and crush her against his needy body. The air between them seemed to crackle and he knew it had nothing to do with talk of smugglers and secret tunnels. "Rowboats. There were stairs cut into the cliff wall, but I think erosion's probably destroyed them by now."

April saw the desire in his gray eyes, and felt her traitorous body respond in kind. "Vanessa says she'd love to explore in there, but I can't say I've any such temptations."

"Me neither." He lowered his face until their lips were mere inches apart. "I'm a man of simpler temptations."

Swallowing hard, she planted the box of garbage bags against his belly, forcing him to grab it, and skirted around him. Trying to steady her breath, she walked to the center of the room.

Behind her, she heard him chuckle. "If you change your mind, I'll gladly shove this rack aside, rip the planks free and go exploring with you. 'Course, God knows how secure the rafters are in those caverns — not to mention how dark they are, or how full of rats."

"No thanks. I've had a year's worth of rats and darkness in the past couple weeks." She shuddered, recalling.

Spencer extracted a trash bag from the cardboard container and shook it hard, snapping it unfolded. April moved to help him gather the rubbish from the swept-up heap. As he handed her the black vinyl bag, insisting she hold it while he scooped up glass bits and dumped them inside, their fingers bumped, sending disturbing tingles up her arms. Unable to look away, April watched his coffee brown hair swing across his forehead as he bent and lifted, bent and lifted. She saw his eyes seek hers each time he emptied the dustpan into the bag, and she tried to ignore the sweep of his tongue across his sensuous mouth, and the quivering in her middle.

Could she feel this strongly for a man who'd been intimate with her mother? Perhaps she wasn't being fair to Spencer. All she'd remembered was a kiss, and a kiss was hardly reason to condemn a man. Confused, she didn't know if he'd meant the words he'd said to her beneath the stairs moments before Lily intruded, or if he'd meant the kiss to Lily. He deserved a chance to defend his actions as much as she deserved to know the truth.

Nervousness made her tongue feel too thick. "I had a memory the other night about Lily and you — an incident that occurred shortly before she fell."

Spencer's head shot up and his compelling gray eyes seemed to search her face. His odd expression washed away the underpinnings of her resolve. Instead of what she'd intended, she heard herself say, "I remembered she was headed to the wine cellar and that her voice was slurred, as though she'd had too much to drink."

For ten whole seconds, she waited for him to tell her what had happened next, waited for him to explain why he'd been kissing her mother. Disappointment knotted her stomach as it became obvious he wasn't going to say anything. Was this his way of sparing her the truth?

Out of nowhere a thought struck her. "Do you think Lily's drunken condition contributed to her fall?"

Spencer dropped the dustpan and grabbed her by the shoulders. "Dammit, April! Why can't you let that subject alone? No one wants to be reminded of Lily's accident."

No one? Or just him? The anger swimming in his eyes was mingled with a more disturbing emotion. Fear. The realization rocked her to her toes. Did he somehow know what had taken place immediately after he'd left Lily on the landing; that she must have rushed up the stairs and accused her mother of trying to steal him? She could almost remember the argument, hear the words inside her head. Was that what he wanted to keep from her?

She had to know. As she started to ask, Spencer caught her mouth with his own in a rough, bruising kiss. The trash bag slipped from her grasp. April levered her palms flat against his chest and shoved, but her body ignored all brain signals to the contrary and arched against him. The heat spiraling through her melted sensibility and doubt from her mind. She felt Spencer kick the vinyl sack out of the way, felt him drag her tightly to him, felt the pressure of his kiss soften as his tongue invaded her willing mouth.

Need rose hard and fast inside Spencer at April's eager response. He slipped his hands inside her sweatshirt and up, across the silken expanse of her back, around the slender span of her waist to the flat of her midriff and higher. A groan spilled from him as his fingers pushed aside her bra and felt her nipples grow taut beneath his touch. God, how he'd ached for this moment. No woman had ever been able to make up for the loss of April.

Lifting her clothing, he gazed at the wonder his fingers had experienced. Her breasts were full with upturned, bronze-hued tips. He cupped one breast in his palm and stared at it lovingly, then tasted it. She was even sweeter than his dreams.

Want throbbed in his gut. He searched her face. Was this what she wanted, too? The smoldering glaze in her lush aqua eyes said yes. Would it be so wrong? Just once? To hold the memory of her forever in his heart? Yes, it would be if she was as innocent as he suspected. "Have you ever—"

As if she knew exactly what he was asking, April interrupted, "No. I always hoped you'd be the one."

Her answer was everything and nothing Spencer wanted to hear. He was the last man on earth who deserved what she was offering. If April ever remembered what had happened between himself and her mother on the landing, there was no doubt in his mind that she would hate him forever.

No, he couldn't add to her pain, wouldn't make her live with the shame of giving her innocence to the man responsible for her mother's death and her own years in a sanitarium. Wearing his guilt like a suit of armor, he stepped away from April as though her very touch burned his skin. Reaching for the dustpan and vinyl trash bag, he murmured, "Cover yourself up."

Disconcerted and smarting with humiliation, April swung away from him. Her thoughts were in as much disarray as her clothing. Adjusting her bra and her sweatshirt, she stared at a nick in the earthen wall and forced herself to take several calming breaths. Damn him! He'd made her feel as worthless as one of the chips of glass she could hear him depositing in the vinyl bag.

Well, this was the last time he'd ever use her feelings

to distract her from a purpose. She rounded on him, her knuckles curled against her hips and demanded. "Tell me, Spencer, what is it you're so afraid I'll find out?"

Fourteen

Spencer opened his mouth, then shut it. Feeling like a complete heel, he yanked the vinyl drawstring closed and hoisted the full trash bag as easily as he would a pouch of marbles. He was a man whose honesty bordered on bluntness, but on this subject, with this woman, he could no more find the words than look her in the eye. "April, there's nothing to find out," he lied.

The tips of his ears glowed as tellingly as the dying ember of hope in her heart. The truth had been there all along, waiting for her to see, but she'd refused to face it. Now she had no choice. The only reason he was attracted to her, desired her, must be her resemblance to Lily. Always Lily.

Her anger dispersed in a blur of self-pitying tears. Second best. Nothing more than a surrogate, a substitute. The awful thing was a part of her would willingly accept this man who owned her heart and soul on those terms, on any terms. But admitting she was a virgin had spoiled any such possibility. A liaison with a naive, inexperienced lover could never simulate the memories he had of her adept mother.

Never before had April rued her decision to stay chaste until marriage, but in light of Spencer's rejection it suddenly seemed foolish beyond belief. Making to leave, he glanced over his shoulder. "Are you coming?"

"In a second," she managed to choke out the words from her tear-blocked throat.

Spencer set the bag on the floor with a sigh. "April, I'm not leaving you down here alone."

She didn't want to be left down here alone. What she wanted to do was rush past him and up to her room before he witnessed her complete collapse. But he filled the doorway and she couldn't get through without touching him. Feeling her self-control slip another notch, she stubbornly snatched a new plastic sack from the pack and snapped it open. She had to get rid of him before she further humiliated herself.

"I don't need a nursemaid, Spence." Gingerly, she bent and swept glass shards into the dustpan, keeping her back toward him as the tears slid from her brimming eyes. "My therapist says I have to learn to face the things that scare me most. I won't stay here any longer than it takes to fill this trash bag."

"Damned stubborn . . ." The rest of his diatribe was lost to her in the clatter of glass as he hefted his own trash bag. Listening to him leave, she felt her world crash around her ankles in as many broken pieces as the shattered bottles of Bordeaux and Chablis.

Minutes ticked by as April stood there, silently crying, allowing enough time to pass to assure herself that she wouldn't run into Spencer on the way to her room. At length, the dreadful stillness had her wiping her wet cheeks and eying the room uneasily. She was certain she was alone, but the fact did little to quell the goose bumps lifting along her arms and legs.

Moving faster than necessary, she stumbled through the basement room into the cellar, charged to the stairs with the speed and tunnel vision of a race horse wearing blinders, and barely managed to skid to a stop centimeters from being stabbed with the two-by-eight planks Karl was carrying through the larder.

"Whoa!" The boards hit the floor with a muted clatter. Karl caught her by the upper arms to steady her. "Hey, pretty lady, where you headed in such a hurry?"

"Nowhere special," she muttered. Afraid he'd realize she'd been crying and would pry into the reason for it, April purposely kept her head averted.

But that didn't stop Karl. He took hold of her chin with one beefy hand and tilted her face toward his. She meant to pull away, but the look of compassion he gave her changed her mind. He wiped the damp area beneath her eyes with the pads of his thumbs with a gentleness she wouldn't have expected from a man his size. "You get scared—being down here all alone? No, you don't need to explain. Not after what you've been through."

Without knowing exactly why, April allowed Karl to pull her against his muscular body, press her cheek to his shirtfront. He smelled different than Spencer. Sawdust and sweat infiltrated her nostrils, but the musky scents were not unpleasant, and the undemanding strength of his embrace felt as comforting as any offered a younger sister by an older brother.

Listening to his heartbeat accelerate against her ear, she noted another dissimilarity to Spencer. There was no stirring in her blood at Karl's touch, no yearning to expand the hug to anything more intimate, she discovered, as his hands slid across her back, caressingly. In fact, April felt nothing more for him than friendship.

His touch grew bolder, and she realized he was misreading the situation. She wedged a space between them, then stepped from his grasp. "Thanks for the shoulder, but I'm fine now."

"Anytime, honey. Anytime."

April brushed past Karl and hastened up the remaining stairs almost as fast and as carelessly as before. As she rounded the curve in the staircase, she nearly knocked Helga off her feet. A startled gasp flew from her mouth. She slammed to a stop.

Helga reared back. There was a fiery blush on her rotund cheeks.

Touching her sleeve, April said, "I'm sorry. Are you okay?"

"I'll live," Helga grunted. Shrugging off April's hand, she continued her descent to the larder, muttering as she went, "Cripes, everybody's in such a hurry today—a cook ain't safe going to her own root cellar."

Moving at a diminished pace, April proceeded to her bedroom, mulling over both encounters with the Winston family. The furious color in the housekeeper's face hinted at more than a near collision. Had Helga actually needed something from the larder, or had she been eavesdropping on Karl and her?

She entered her bedroom frowning. Karl had definitely wanted some encouragement from her. The irony sapped the calming effect she usually derived from her peach-hued room. She moved to the dresser and withdrew fresh undergarments. Why was it that she couldn't care for the one man she knew didn't give a hoot if she looked like her dead mother?

A quick shower and fresh wool slacks and sweater did little to lift her spirits or clear her mind. Her nerves felt as though they'd been run across a cheese grater. Spying her turtle earrings, she decided a walk to her favorite rock was just the thing she needed. She grabbed her parka and, attaching the earrings, headed downstairs to the kitchen.

There, Helga was bent over a bread board, chopping onions with a wicked-looking butcher knife. July sat at the table eating cookies and milk.

Cynthia stood three feet from the child, sizing up an arrangement of flowers perched on the table's center. She glanced at April, taking in her outdoor apparel. "Where you off to, sugah?"

"For a walk. Probably to Turtle Rock."

Expecting an objection, she was surprised when Cynthia said, "Well, the weather seems to be cooperatin' for once."

"Can I go, too?" July scrambled off the chair, but her mother intercepted her.

"Not so fast, missy. You've got a date with a bubble bath. Or did you forget?"

"No." July sighed resignedly.

April bit back a smile. "I'll take you next time. Okay?"

"Okay."

With that, April left the house and set out toward Haro Strait at a fast clip. Pungent sea air climbed the cliffs to meet her. She welcomed its bracing entrance into her lungs and its bite on her cheeks.

Turtle Rock. She sighed. The limbering walk to her special place was just what her confused brain needed. And it was the last chance she'd have for much privacy. Vanessa's family would be arriving for dinner and staying until after the engagement party.

As she made for the trail along the cliff, she heard the loud bangs of a busy hammer coming from the direction of the ferry dock.

"If you hit that nailhead any harder, Spence, you're liable to break that railin' clean in two."

At the sound of his mother's voice Spencer jerked. Remaining squatted, he glanced over his shoulder and let the hammer droop between his bent knees to the ferry deck. "What brings you down here?"

Cynthia moved closer as Spencer sank from his haunches to his rear and gazed up at her. "I wanted to see how the work was comin'. It looks like you're 'bout finished."

He surveyed his efforts. The new lumber he'd used to shore up the unsteady railings was unpainted, ugly even, but it was serviceable. Karl could take care of the weathercoating after the engagement party. For now it would keep all passengers safe.

His mother squatted and lifted a lock of hair from his forehead, as though he were a young boy. "The way you were attackin' that nail a person would of thought it an enemy. You upset about somethin'?"

"Nothing I can't handle." He avoided her gaze and cast his eyes at the waves hitting the ferry hull. The gold cross felt heavy in his pocket. He should give it to her. Ask, no demand, an explanation, instead of torturing himself with speculation. She deserved better. But he was too afraid to do the right thing. His whole world seemed to be spinning out of control.

"I'm not tryin' to pry," she said. "You just look so sad and—confused."

Her concern went straight to his heart. He hated himself more than ever for suspecting his mother could have had any reason to harm April. For the briefest moment, he considered handing her the gold cross, pouring out his troubles to her. But he couldn't figure out where to start. His mother would be deeply wounded by his disloyal thoughts. As to the other, hell, she didn't know what had transpired on the basement landing right before Lily's death. How could he tell her what he couldn't confess to the woman he loved?

When she reached reflexively for the cross that wasn't there, he felt even worse.

Cynthia tilted her head to one side. "Did you and April have an argument?"

Although the question came out of nowhere, it didn't take him totally by surprise. He knew better than to underestimate her where family was concerned. Pushing his hand through his hair, he asked, "How long have you known?"

"How you feel about April? Probably always. You were awfully fond of her before the accident. Later, at college, why, I don't think I've ever even heard of anyone who cracked the books like you." She ran a knuckle lovingly along his unshaven cheek. "You threw yourself into your career just as diligently, never allotin' time for any serious romance. Then when you finally brought home that one girl for us to meet — what was her name, Mary Jane somethin' or other — she looked so much like April — well, it was all March talked about for days afterward."

"I hadn't realized I was so transparent."

She patted his knee. "What you are is a one woman man and that, my darlin' son, is no crime." She cast him a sad smile. "April's not out of the woods yet, you know. Is that what's worryin' you — the hurdles she still has to overcome?"

Feeling the heat drain from his face, Spence cast his gaze over the dark waters. It wasn't April's blocked memory that had him scared, it was what she would learn when the blockage dissolved. "I think April will be well sooner than any of us imagines."

She pressed her lips together, but sympathy telegraphed from her deep-set eyes. After a long moment, she patted his hand. "Just the same, maybe you should give April some space—at least for the time bein'."

"Yeah, maybe you're right." Spencer struggled to his feet and gathered his tools. He'd treated April abominably, all because he couldn't bear the thought of her rejection when she remembered the truth. God only knew what she must be thinking after offering him her virginity. Talk about rejections, he deserved to be crowned for the one he'd handed her. Giving her space shouldn't be too difficult. She'd probably take every opportunity to avoid his company for the remainder of her visit. The prospect dug into him.

Cynthia raised on tiptoe, kissed his cheek, then wrinkled her nose and plucked at the collar of his workshirt. "Don't forget the O'Briens are arrivin' in a couple of hours. I expect you'll want to make an impression befittin' a mayoral candidate."

"Yeah," he muttered absently, only half listening to his mother. April consumed his thoughts. He owed her an apology, an apology he had to try to extend.

As his mother headed up the slope, taking the shortcut to the house, he stowed the tools inside the service shed and secured the padlock. Starting his own trek up the hill, he edited and reedited the apology in his head, until he'd figured out exactly what he wanted to say. Five minutes later, he entered Calendar House via the laundry room, determined to find April and convince her to hear him out.

After all the mayhem of the past few days the house was surprisingly quiet. Helga was nowhere to be seen, but the tantalizing aromas issuing from the oven affirmed dinner was under way. The sweet fragrance of arranged flowers followed him from one unoccupied room to the next on the main level as he searched for April, or someone who knew where she was.

He should have asked his mother, he thought hastening up the back stairs to check April's bedroom. It was empty. The smooth bedspread and general tidiness had the untenanted look of a readied hotel room. He blew a breath through gritted teeth.

Ending up back in the kitchen, he felt his frustration climb. Where the hell had she gone this time? Lord, she wouldn't have been stubborn enough to stay in the wine cellar for two whole hours, would she? Chills shivered his flesh as his mind filled with the sickening image of April sprawled beneath the collapsed wine racks. He headed for the basement at a clip, trying to assure himself with every step that she wouldn't be there.

An arc of yellow light, and strained-sounding, off-key whistling spilled from the wine cellar. Frowning, Spencer slowed his forward momentum and halted in the open doorway. His brows raised in surprise at the sight before him. Karl had wasted no time reconstructing the two destroyed wine racks and looked to be waltzing one of them across the earthen floor, evidently trying to jostle it into some prechosen position.

If he hadn't seen it with his own two eyes, Spencer wouldn't have believed that Helga's son could put his shoulder to the grindstone. Obviously, all Karl needed was the proper motivation. Or perhaps, he'd allowed his jealousy of this handsome rival for April's affections to color his opinion of the man himself.

Karl noticed him for the first time and let loose of the wine rack. "Man, don't just stand there gawking. Help me haul this heavy bugger into that corner."

Moving to assist, Spencer noted the trash bag April had started to fill, lying limp, empty, in the exact spot where she'd obviously abandoned it. She must have left here almost immediately after he had. Damn! He'd seen Karl entering the house as he was stuffing the trash bag into the garbage can. Had he found April down here? Crying? The likelihood fed his self-loathing.

Karl asked, "You finish the railings?"

"Yep. They need weathercoating." Spencer hoisted one end of the wine rack with a grunt.

"Well, that'll have to wait a few days," he replied, walking backward.

Spencer deposited his end on the floor, straightened, and brushed sawdust from his work clothes. Within minutes, they had both racks positioned and had started to replace the expensive bottles in their usual repose, heedless to any specific order. Trying to sound as though the answer meant little to him, Spencer eyed Karl above the end rack. "You haven't seen April by any chance?"

The bonk of glass hitting wood punctuated Karl's amused expression. Spencer squirmed inwardly, but he'd be damned if he'd let the other man see that his knowing look was getting to him. Turning his back to Karl, he snatched a couple of bottles from the floor and set them in place with a care that gnawed at his patience. He needed another battle of wills today like he needed to lose his upcoming election, but Karl seemed set on spoiling for a fight.

"Man, for a guy who eats tact for breakfast, you sure don't know how to woo a woman." Karl laughed derisively, then grinned. "But I guess I should thank you, guy, for sending her straight into my arms."

Heat burned up Spencer's neck and into his face. Never before had he wanted so much to grind another man's nose into a dirt floor, but if April had chosen to turn to Karl after the despicable treatment she'd suffered at *his* hands, how could he blame her?

He dug bloodless fingers into his palms. This visit to Calendar House should have been a happy reunion; instead it had stripped him of the woman he loved and was draining what was left of his self-respect.

With a sinking heart and an ebbing anger, he admitted there was only one way he could undo the mess. He had to tell April about Lily. Knowing April would be lost to him forever afterward didn't sway his decision. She'd been through enough hell at his hands. She deserved to know that nothing she'd done had caused his rejection, that his reasons for keeping his crime a secret had been purely selfish.

He handed Karl the last wine bottle and left the cellar. Now that he'd made up his mind to unburden his conscience, he felt a touch of self-esteem return.

Finding April became imperative.

The descending sun speared through huddled clouds and warmed April's face. The air felt as crisp as an autumn day with none of the dampness of winter. Watching a pleasure boat chug through the whitecapped water, she stood and stretched, then rubbed her sore bottom. Turtle Rock wasn't as comfortable as she'd remembered, nor had sitting on it staring at the glistening waters of Haro Strait cleared her thoughts as it had when she was a teenager. Just more proof that a person couldn't go home again, she decided, gaining the path back along the cliff. Or perhaps it was she who had changed, not Calendar House or Turtle Rock.

She'd lost sight of her objective in coming home—to unblock her locked memory. Her feelings for Spencer had become her top priority and that was a mistake. As much as she loved him, he was lost to her. She had to forget any future they might have. It wasn't to be. Spencer's rejection had hurt to the core, but she supposed she should be grateful he wasn't the sort to take advantage of her inexperience, and that he hadn t let things progress beyond the point of no return.

A rush of fresh sea air into her lungs had a heartening effect. What a beautiful spot this was, with the greenery of the pines to her right, the jagged rock formations on the cliff walls below and the dark waters spraying white foam against them. It made her problems seem insignificant.

She wasn't in the least bit hurried to get back to the house, but the guests would have to be faced, and, if it killed her, she would put on a happy face for Vanessa and Thane's sakes. They didn't deserve anyone ruining their party.

Treading near the steep precipice, she remembered Vanessa's enthusiasm over the history of this island and the pirates who had once weighed anchor in

213

these treacherous waters. In spite of her melancholy mood, she had to smile. The woman would be a nice addition to the family. And she had to admit, the history of Farraday Island fascinated her, too.

What had it been like in Octavius's time? Squinting her eyes, she studied the shoreline trying to imagine. The land curved to and away from Calendar House in an erratic pattern only nature could have designed, and as she continued along the edge of the cliff, she found her gaze scouring those rocky walls visible from this height. She hadn't paid much attention before, but now she noticed a couple of dark areas that even the most unobservant mind would realize were caves.

Curiosity lengthened her strides. As the sun hung above the horizon, beams spotlighted the sheer cliff wall like a stage, seeming to accent one particular dark section way up ahead. If her judgment was on target, and it was a cave, it would be almost directly aligned with the house. As she approached she kept her gaze riveted to the spot, sometimes having to lean out over the precipice in order to do so.

Ten paces away, she decided it was definitely a cave, or at least, what appeared to be an opening. She felt as excited as a scientist discovering a new germ. Contrary to what she'd told Spencer, the subject very much interested her, especially when faced with actual proof. Who wouldn't want to explore?

As she neared the spot, she thought she spied some of those stairs Spencer had pronounced eroded to the point of oblivion. Was it possible he'd been wrong?

Being careful not to smudge her fresh slacks, she squatted to have a better look. A tenacious Douglas fir clung to the cliff and obscured her view. She shuffled to the side slightly and peered over the precipice again. Yes. It looked like a step.

Pebbles skittered from beneath her feet and clattered to the flat surface of stone below. Alarmed, she scooted back an inch, feeling safer.

As a relieved breath slid through April's partially open mouth, something struck her in the back.

She flew forward.

Off the cliff.

Fifteen

Spencer made his way to April's bedroom once again. But she wasn't there, and as far as he could tell, she hadn't been since his earlier attempt to find her. Frustration followed him back into the hallway, sensitizing his muscles, his nerves, convincing him she was purposely avoiding him. Too bad. Calendar House was big, but not so much so he couldn't unearth her.

His gaze fell on the attic access. Would she have returned to Lily's trunk seeking answers to her past? The thought of April regaining the memory of Lily's fall before he could speak to her seemed more than justifiable punishment for his part in the deed. Nonetheless, he hastened up the steep steps and pushed the squeaky door inward. The quiet inside the musty storage space slammed against his ears. Or was that his own pulse?

"April? Are you here?" His words echoed off the open rafters, mocking him. If she was here, she wasn't answering.

In the dim illumination afforded by the single dirty window, he proceeded toward the center of the room. He was paying so much attention to what lay beyond his vision that the crackle of paper beneath his feet startled him. Looking down he realized he was stepping on one of Lily's posters. He moved back. His gaze rolled across the playbill and on to the next, and the next, all scattered about like litter on a roadside.

"What the hell?" The last time he'd seen Lily's trunk was when he'd come back up here to retrieve Thane's poems and discovered April had beaten him to it. Even as upset as he'd been at the time, he'd replaced every item with care. Now the contents were strewn about, the lid flipped open, the trunk empty. The evident disregard to both the age and the worth of Lily's effects implied a hastily conducted search. But for what? Surely not the poems. And yet, although he'd never understood why, someone had stolen them from April's room.

Or had they?

Was this April's doing? God, he didn't want to think so, but worry accompanied him from the attic back into the hallway. Was there actually somebody in this family who wished April harm? No matter how long he chewed on the possibility he couldn't swallow it. It was unthinkable. The only evidence substantiating any foul play was the electricity being turned off on purpose, and that didn't prove who ever had done it knew April was in the basement.

The gold cross in his pocket seemed to burn a reminder into his side. This possibility was even too tough to chew. He couldn't bear to suspect his mother of any wrongdoing. An awful thought occurred to him. Had April stolen the cross from his mother, then handed it to him in the wine cellar as though she'd found it on the floor?

He shut the attic door harder than necessary as his mother's words rushed into his mind. *April's not out of the woods, yet. She still has hurdles to overcome.* Try as he might, Spencer couldn't dispel the unwelcome memory of finding April hysterical in the basement, or the disoriented way she'd ushered him down the attic stairs, or the peculiar action of plonking July's Barbie doll on the breakfast table as though accusing someone of some unclarified crime. And what about her two mishaps? Had her state of mind contributed to her being in the wrong place at the wrong time?

He ran his hand through his hair and headed toward the kitchen. As much as he'd prefer to ignore them, these signs pointed to the instability of her mental condition. Which was all the more reason to find her, tell her the truth, and give her the chance to get well.

This time he found the kitchen full of people and activity and something else: an uneasiness so subtle Spencer half suspected he was imagining it. The sense hovered elusively in the click clack of March's knitting needles, in the copper lids Helga rattled atop cooking pans, in the murmur of conversation between Cynthia, Thane and Vanessa who were hunched around the counter, holding mugs of fragrant coffee. But he couldn't pinpoint its origin.

"Hello, everyone," Spencer said. He paid particular attention to each person's expression as they acknowledged the greeting, yet the source of disquiet remained unknown.

Curious, he steadied his gaze on the cook as she bent over the open oven door basting a huge sirloin tip roast. The slight tremor in her hand spoke volumes, but it was only natural she'd be nervous with the governor's family coming for dinner. Moving toward her, he wondered if he should mention the dark smudge on the crisp white apron shielding her stomach.

He decided instead to try to lessen her distress. "It smells great, Helga." Dropping his arm around her shoulder, he felt her flinch. The baster slipped from her hand and sank in the thick juice at the bottom of the pan.

She glared at him with exasperation. "Now look what you done."

"Oops." Without meaning to he'd managed to upset her more. "Here, I'll get the blasted thing." He reached for the baster.

Helga smacked his hand. "Don't be putting that filthy paw in my food. Liable to poison the whole lot of us."

Throwing his arms wide, palms flat, he backed away. "No problem. I'll stay out of your way."

"Good."

Surprisingly the round of laughter which circled the room did nothing to dispel the aura of tension. Strange, Spence mused. He strode to the counter, grabbed a cup from the mug tree, and filled it with hot coffee. It crossed his mind that it could be his own anxiety — to speak to April — that was disturbing the quietude. Perhaps if he lightened the mood . . . "See what you get for trying to help?"

"Maybe you should help yourself to a bath." Grinning, Thane picked a chip of wood from Spencer's hair and handed it to him. "Unless, of course, you'd rather meet my future in-laws for the first time looking and smelling like a sawdust bin."

"Funny." He quirked the corner of his mouth sarcastically. "I'll shower before they arrive."

Oddly, this warmhearted banter seemed to add to the edginess in the air. Spencer frowned, sipped his hot coffee, and finally plunked the mug to the counter. He was finished playing *who's got the button?*. "Has anyone seen April?"

Cynthia stiffened and lifted an eyebrow, but Spencer ignored the pointed look she sent him. He'd keep his promise to give April a wide berth — after he'd set the record straight.

Although everyone responded negatively, one person in the room could have told Spencer exactly where April was. Dead. Sprawled on the treacherous rocks of

219

Haro Strait as silenced as a slain seagull. Now the truth of how Lily Cordell had actually met her maker would forever remain secret. The thought should have brought release, and peace, at long last peace, but it hadn't.

Pain accelerated behind narrowed eyes. Fear. Still the fear of being caught. Too much to lose. Mustn't let it happen.

Cynthia poked a loose strand into her mussed chignon. "I'm sure April has the good sense to be getting ready." She glanced at the wall clock. "Heavens, the O'Briens will be here in less than an hour. Does anyone know if Karl's gone to pick them up yet?"

"I'm on my way." Karl strode into the room. Obviously, he'd showered, shaved and changed clothes.

Begrudgingly, Spencer admitted to himself that in the form-fitting Levis and hand-knit, sky blue sweater, his rival for April's affections had the leading edge in more ways than one. He raked a hand through his unkempt hair, fingered his whiskered chin. Before he talked to her, he needed every advantage he could muster. Starting with a shower.

His mother caught his arm. "Darlin', you and I don't have much time to make ourselves presentable. We'd best get a move on."

He didn't resist as she ushered him toward the stairs.

Spencer scraped the razor across his face one last time, then rinsed the blade beneath the tap water and dragged a cold washcloth across his cheeks and chin. A strange calmness had settled over him, perhaps from resignation. He felt like a man readying himself for his own funeral as he scanned his appearance in the mirror and grunted dissatisfaction.

Where was that smooth persona he'd spent years

developing, honing? Why couldn't he eliminate the look of despair from his eyes, around his mouth? April. She'd done this to him, shattered his self-protective mode with her pliant body, her passionate kisses, her offers of love. Grumbling, he yanked on his terry cloth robe and trudged to his room. The best he could hope was that the years ahead would dull the pain.

Politics. His career had always been his salvation. He could throw himself into his work even harder than ever, he decided, tossing his robe across the bed. Pulling on briefs, socks, and slacks, he toyed with the idea of aspiring to an office higher than the mayorship of Bellingham, but the thought seemed as dull as the gray polo shirt he'd chosen to wear with none of the warmth of the coordinated pullover sweater.

And suddenly he knew why. It wasn't just his outrageous, outspoken attitude keeping him from attaining the heights in his career that came so easily to Thane. His heart wasn't in politics, or in anything else for that matter. He'd sealed it away in some nether regions twelve years ago when April had looked at him with blank eyes and not known who he was.

The only time in his life he remembered being alive had been these last two weeks, and now he was about to die again. But a major difference had occurred in him. He couldn't go back to political office and carry on with a life he wasn't participating in. The people of Bellingham, not to mention all of his campaign supporters, deserved a candidate who cared about their town and the issues.

His mother's gold cross stared up at him from its position on his dresser. There was nothing to be gained by keeping it, he decided. He plucked it up and stuffed it into his pocket. She'd be glad to have it back.

A knock at his door was followed by Thane's uninvited, but not unwelcome entrance. "You about ready?"

Spencer ran a comb through his hair and peered at his twin's image in the mirror. Thane, too, wore slacks and a sweater, the outfit a striking statement of black and white. Somehow, Thane always managed to merge good taste and up-to-the-minute style while he, on the other hand, yielded to comfort.

Thane moved closer. "Is something wrong?"

"Actually, for a change, something is right." Spencer set the comb aside and faced his brother. "I've made a decision about my life, my future. I'm going to withdraw from the race for mayor." He hadn't known he was going to say that, but it seemed the decision had been made.

"But you're a shoe-in! Have you lost your mind?"

"On the contrary, I think I've finally found it." Spence felt as though an invisible weight had lifted from his shoulders.

"Politics is all you've ever known. What the hell are you going to do?"

Spencer slipped into gray loafers. "I do have a law degree, remember? Surely some big firm needs a lawyer with a political background. If not, hell, there's always private practice. Be happy for me, Thane."

"I would be, if you looked happy about it, but you look like you've been hit by a train."

Striding to the window, Spencer lifted the drape and glimpsed the landscape in the dying sunlight. "I've decided to tell April everything."

"Dear God, why?" Springs squeaked as Thane sank to the bed.

Spencer stared at the darkening scenery. "I would have gone to the grave honoring your confidence, but there's no longer any need of secrets. Vanessa knows about your affair with Lily, and the wedding is going

222

off without a hitch."

Behind him he heard Thane say, "I don't understand what one thing has to do with the other. Why tell April?"

He let loose of the curtain and wheeled around, not certain where to begin. Or if he wanted to. The subject was too personal, too raw. But after all these years of lying to himself and to Thane the need to clear the air was powerful.

He raked his hand through his combed hair, mussing it. "I've made some important discoveries about myself these past few days, bro. When April lost her memory, I built a wall around my heart as high and as dense as the one surrounding that damned sanitarium in Phoenix. Finding her again has released me. From here on out I can start to live life instead of faking it."

And no matter how painful, at least it would be honest, Spencer realized, gleaning a small amount of comfort from the fact. "April has already missed too much of life to build a new start on lies and half-truths. She deserves the same chance she's given me."

Remorse was written on Thane's face. "God, I've been a selfish ass. I didn't even consider what your loyalty to me was costing you." He gained his feet and clasped Spencer by the shoulder. "Would you like me to talk to April for you? I'll tell her about the affair and clear up this mess."

He shook his head. "How are you going to 'clear up' the fact that I killed her mother?"

Thane grabbed his other shoulder and shoved his face so close their noses nearly touched. "Lily's death was an accident. Why can't you accept that?"

The old guilt churned his gut. "Because I shoved her. She wouldn't have fallen otherwise."

Blowing a sigh through pursed lips, Thane stepped back and dropped his arms. "You didn't mean for her to fall. April won't blame you."

"April saw the whole thing. If she realized it was an accident, why do you think she blocked it out?"

"I don't know. But I'm not sure telling her is the right thing to do. Didn't her doctor say she should remember Lily's fall on her own?"

Stepping away from his brother, Spencer threw his hands in the air. "What if she never remembers? Don't you see? I love her too much to keep her tied to a fantasy I want to play out. I have to release her."

The sympathy emanating from his twin melted some of the chill inside Spencer, and reminded him of the damper he was placing on Thane's special evening. "No more serious talk. This is supposed to be a happy occasion." He recombed his hair and plastered on a smile. Yanking open the bedroom door, he motioned for Thane to follow. "Come on, we're keeping your new family waiting."

As they traversed the hall, Spencer's thoughts spun back to April. An anxious twinge traveled his middle. Now that guests had started to arrive, he didn't know when he'd get to speak to her. Before dinner was out of the question, but perhaps he could make an opportunity afterward.

They headed downstairs. Voices rose up to meet them and Spencer heard someone exclaim, "What a glorious sunset. I can't wait to see the view from this window in the morning."

It seemed to him the living room teemed with people, consuming drinks and hors d'oeuvres, exchanging the stilted pleasantries of two families meeting for the first time to celebrate the marriage of their children.

Spencer's eyes automatically scanned the room in search of April. Noting her absence, he breathed easier. As much as he wanted to see her, he dreaded the

224

moment he would confront the pain he'd inflicted on her transmitting from those glorious aqua eyes. Nothing he could say or do would save the most precious gift he'd ever been given, April's love.

He headed straight for the makeshift bar, poured himself a Scotch on the rocks, and got down one bracing swallow before Cynthia caught him by the arm and escorted him around the room like a tugboat leading a lost ship. Keeping an eye on the doorway, he nodded through the introductions of Vanessa's parents, grandmother, and aunt, but he couldn't relate to Thane's joy when his whole world was capsizing.

Without warning, his hand was gripped in a hard, confident manner. Startled, he stowed his dark thoughts and looked at the man shaking his hand. Vanessa's father.

"Call me Walt." Walter O'Brien had the lean-muscled physique of an executive who spent his lunch hour in a gym. There was no question where Vanessa got her looks. Although his was grayed at the temples, her father had the same thick blond hair, and beneath horn-rimmed glasses, the same clear green eyes.

By contrast, her mother, Dee Dee—who stood at Walt's side—had mahogany hair, a button nose and the soft brown eyes of a cow, but nothing about the woman was the least bovine. She couldn't weigh eighty-five pounds dripping wet, Spencer concluded, doubting the three-inch high heels she had on brought her up to an even five feet tall.

"I hear you're running for mayor." Walter beamed.

Spencer blanched inwardly. Announcement of the decision to withdraw from the mayoral race, and politics in general, would have to wait until he could inform his family. In private. He gave Walter a practiced answer, then asked what the man did for a living.

As Walter O'Brien discussed his position at the Boeing Company, Spencer nodded and forced himself to act interested. The anxious knot in his gut was growing to gargantuan proportions, and his face muscles were starting to ache from the effort it took to keep smiling. Although at first he'd welcomed April's absence, he was starting to wonder what was detaining her.

He murmured an "I see" to Vanessa's father and hoped the response was appropriate, for try as he might to participate in the conversation, he couldn't concentrate. Night pressed the plate glass windows and coldly reflected a reverse imagery of the people gathered in the living room. It gave Spencer the eerie impression of watching a similar gathering in some other dimension. What was keeping April?

As his gaze fell on Helga, who was passing around a platter of rolled cheese concoctions, it occurred to him that August had asked Karl to act as bartender for this little soiree. But his stepfather was the one pouring drinks. Where was Karl? With April? The thought drained the moisture from his mouth.

Downing the last of his Scotch, he noticed July sitting all alone on the couch, fidgeting, observing the adults with a polite, if somewhat strained expression. The first genuine smile he'd felt tugged Spencer's lips. Here was an ally. Excusing himself, he made straight for his young sister and claimed the seat beside her. "You sure look pretty in those fancy blue tights and that striped sweater. New?"

"Yeah." July smoothed the hem of the knee-length sweater and crossed her ankles above her white flats. Her sigh tore at his heart.

"What's the matter, twerp?" He patted her head where her wavy hair hugged in a single, tight braid down the center.

July stole a glance at their mother, then said quietly, "I thought parties were supposed to be fun. Not just a bunch of hugging and shaking hands and talking about boring stuff."

He bit back a grin and gave her knee a sympathetic squeeze. "Yeah, well, adult parties can be kind of dull for a kid."

"You're a grown up—so how come you're not having fun?" The question caught him by surprise, although it shouldn't have. Kids, he'd found, were often more perceptive than most adults. Too bad they didn't have the wisdom of experience to offer solutions to problems they could so readily detect.

"What makes you think I'm not having fun?"

"You look sad."

He gave her an exaggeratedly broad smile. "Is this better?"

"You look funny when you show all your teeth like that." July giggled, and crawled into his lap. "Spence, you want to play Nintendo?"

Hugging her fragile body to him, he thanked God for this small person and her enormous love. "Even though we aren't having a great time, we can't leave the party. But I'll probably feel like taking on the Mario Brothers later."

"Promise?"

"Yep."

Hearing footsteps in the foyer, Spencer set July on the sofa and stood. His heart leapt with anticipation as his gaze fled to the arched doorway. Karl entered the room. Alone. If he'd been with April, he wasn't now. Spencer didn't know which he felt strongest, relief or disappointment. Watching Karl make a beeline for August, speak to him in hushed tones, and receive a nod of appreciation, it occurred to him Karl might not have been anywhere near April. Then what was keeping her?

Deciding to find out, he moved toward the foyer, but

Vanessa's grandmother waylaid him. There was a mischievous twinkle in her crinkled, blue eyes. "My, but you're a pair of handsome devils." She tossed a look in Thane's direction, then back at Spencer. "I don't know how my granddaughter tells you apart."

Spencer assured the charming woman that the differences were marked, but her observation triggered the memory of April's adverse reaction to being compared to Lily. Could that be why she hadn't joined them yet? Was she in her bedroom, anxiously delaying the moment when she'd be confronted with strangers, more people who would remember her mother and make comparisons? Great! His rejection of her had probably added insult to injury atop whatever inadequacies she already harbored. Mentally kicking himself for the umpteenth time, he started across the foyer for the stairs. He was probably the last person she would want to see, but the least he could do was try to coax her to join the group for dinner.

Helga was coming out of the kitchen, wringing her apron until it looked as twisted as his stomach felt. Evidently, she still hadn't calmed down. "Dinner's ready," she told him.

"I'm going to tell April now."

She nodded and shuffled past him toward the living room. He made for the stairs. With dinner imminent, he had little time to undo some of the damage he'd done to April's ego. As his foot gained the bottom step, the telephone rang. The cook spun around, staring pointedly at Spencer. He was nearest August's den. "I'll get it," he said, begrudgingly.

Silently cursing the caller's bad timing, he strode to the den and lifted the receiver. "Hello?" he answered irascibly.

The caller hesitated a moment before asking, "Is this Calendar House? The Farradays?"

The voice was female, husky, and unknown to Spencer. It struck him the call could be for one of the O'Briens. With that in mind, he strove for a softer tone. "Yes, it is. To whom do you wish to speak."

"April Farraday."

Of all the people in the house he'd expected the caller to ask for, he'd never even considered April. As far as he knew this was the first call she'd received since she'd arrived here. His brows came together so hard his forehead ached. "May I tell her who's calling?"

"Nancy Merritt."

April's psychiatrist. His mouth went as dry as powder before he realized he was jumping to conclusions. Given April's circumstances it was only natural her doctor would call and check on her progress. "We're just about to sit down to dinner, but I'll round her up for you."

As he set the receiver on August's messy desk, he heard the doctor's voice beckoning him and lifted it to his ear again.

"Pardon?"

"I don't want to interrupt your dinner. April can call me afterward."

"Are you sure?"

A whole ten seconds passed before Nancy replied, "Yes, I'm sure." But she didn't sound like she was sure at all, Spencer thought, as he replaced the receiver and stood staring at it long moments. He had the distinct impression the doctor would have preferred to speak to April immediately. Why? The question conjured myriad possibilities, all of which reenforced his anxiety.

"Who was on the phone?" Cynthia was standing in the doorway of the den.

"It was Dr. Merritt."

"Heavens, whatever did she want?"

He shrugged. "To speak to April. April can call her

229

back after dinner and find out, I guess."

"Speakin' of which, we'd best join the others in the dinin' room. Helga's outdone herself with this dinner." When they entered the dining room, Spencer instantly sought April. But she wasn't present. "Mother, where is April?"

"Why, I don't know." Cynthia's gaze traversed the room and she seemed genuinely surprised not to find April present. Her hand went to her chest, seeking the absent gold cross. Distress pinched her features. "I've been so busy with my hostess duties I didn't realize she hadn't joined us."

"April's a little shy," August explained, to the curious-faced O'Brien family. The tint of red in his cheeks expressed an evident embarrassment at his older daughter's manners. "Would you go fetch her, Spence? I'm sure she's in her room."

"No, she's not." July exclaimed just as Spencer reached the doorway.

He spun around, feeling as though he'd been gut-punched. "How do you know, twerp?"

"I looked before the party."

Spencer felt a shield of ice form on his heart. He moved back into the room and caught Cynthia by the shoulders, rougher than he meant. "Mother, when was the last time you saw her?"

Alarmed confusion showed in her furrowed brow. "This afternoon. She said she was goin' for a walk—out to that Turtle Rock of hers. But I assumed she'd returned hours ago. Heavens, hasn't anyone seen her?"

At the negative answers, March Farraday's ruddy complexion heightened to the color of boiled beets. "Lordy, don't tell me that crazy girl has gone and pulled another lame-brained stunt."

Sixteen

For one death defying micro second, April hung suspended above the killer rocks. Then her stomach flew into her throat as she started to plunge. Flailing the air, she gathered handfuls of nothing.

April screamed.

Prayed.

Cursed.

Dropped.

Prepared to die.

Instead, her feet hit something brushy and pliant and full. It grabbed at her slacks, then poked between her legs and jerked her body, hard. The odor of pine exploded in her nose.

The tenacious fir tree. Its sharp scent defied the stench of certain demise. Hope revived inside her.

Frantically, she clutched at spiky branches. But the boughs slipped through her hands, squashed beneath her belly, and retreated into the cliff wall as if trying to shove her out — toward the water.

Using every ounce of strength, April snaked her arms around a thicker branch and held on tight. Her body rammed to a halt and left her dangling like a snagged kite. Tree limbs trembled and stilled. Coarse bark bit into her palms. Spiny needles stabbed her cheeks and gouged her parka, and each breath burned her lungs.

Nothing had ever felt so wonderful.

The feeling vanished in a twinkling. Her gaze stole to the bank above. This was no accident. What had struck her in the back had been a set of human hands.

Realizing the fir offered no concealment, she felt her mouth go dry. Surely, whoever had pushed her from the cliff would stick around long enough to make certain they'd finished the job. Terrified, she eyed the precipice. Her heart beat so hard her whole chest ached as she waited.

And waited.

The sun sank into the horizon and squelched the spotlight effect along the shoreline. Still no one came. No head peered over the cliff to ascertain whether or not the deed had had the intended outcome. Confusion sifted through her terror, but she couldn't afford to worry about it now. She had to get to safety. But how? Reaching the cliff was not an option. The wall above her was too smooth. And below, waves crashed against rocks, spitting seawater high and wide. Screaming would be a waste of vocal chords and might attract the wrong individual.

Stretching her right foot in an outward span, she tried to find a foothold or handhold, something that would support her weight, buy her time. Pebbles skittered loose and clamored down the cliff, their clatter lost in the noisy surf. As the daylight ebbed, the cold intensified. Her hands grew numb, her prospects dying as certainly as she soon would.

The tree trembled. April gasped. Renewed terror shot through her. She grabbed tighter still to the thick limb. It felt as though the fir's roots were slipping from the soil. Panicked, she executed another foothold search, this one concentrated to her left side.

More pebbles avalanched. She listened disheartenedly as they chattered down the wall. However, instead of disappearing in the surf, she could have sworn she heard them clunk against solid rock.

With her throat constricting, April cautiously shifted her body, craned over her left shoulder and scanned the scene below. The waning light cast shadows across the whole area, but she could see enough to set her pulse skipping with hope. Less than fifteen feet down, slightly left, there was a wide flat ledge, the very step she'd been looking at when she'd been shoved from the cliff. If she could swing —

A loud crack interrupted the thought as the section of tree April was clinging to broke.

Seventeen

Panic seized Spencer. He spun on his heel and raced for the foyer wishing his mind would stop conjuring horrific images of April. Injured. Helpless. Perhaps dying. His blood flowed as cold as a mountain river.

Thane caught up with him at the front door and grabbed him by the shoulder. "Where the hell do you think you're going?"

Spencer jerked free of his twin's grasp, frowning at him as though he were an idiot to ask such a stupid question. "To find April."

"Without a jacket or a flashlight? Use your head! Turtle Rock is a mile from the house. It's freezing outside and what moonlight there is won't allow you to see beyond your big toe. How much good do you think you'll do April if you go off half cocked?"

The last thing Spencer wanted to deal with at this moment was logic. But Thane made sense. "My jacket's upstairs. Where's that big flashlight of yours?"

"I'll get it. But I'm coming with you."

Spencer charged up the stairs. Thane dogged his

heels, instructing, "Change shoes, too. And grab a blanket."

These last words sent icicles stabbing through his brain. April would be cold when they found her, from shock, from hypothermia, from . . . No! *April, please be all right,* he prayed, running down the hall to his room.

He was headed back to the foyer in less than three minutes, precious minutes he realized, that could make the difference between April's life or her death. The excited rumble of rapid activity throughout the upper floor barely penetrated his worried mind. Hastening down the steps, Spencer crammed a fleecy blanket inside his suede jacket, and worked the snaps closed.

"Here's the flashlight," Thane said from behind him. Spencer stopped long enough to grasp the object by its neck. .

In the foyer, August sat on the bench seat of the halltree, lacing his work boots. He glanced at the twins as they approached. "I've instructed the household, guests included, to change clothes and assemble in the kitchen." He finished tying the last knot and stood. "Karl's gone to the workshop for . . . Oh, here he is."

Karl came through the front door carrying an armload of various shaped and sized flashlights. "I didn't take time to check them." He sounded slightly breathless.

"I'll do that." August selected two of the newer-looking flashlights, determined they were working properly and handed one to Thane. The other he stuffed into Karl's coat pocket, then relieved him of the remaining bunch. "I'll organize the others, but we won't be as fast as you three. Go straight to Turtle Rock," he advised, hustling to the kitchen.

As Karl opened the front door, something struck Spencer in the back of the thighs and wrapped itself around him like a lasso. He lurched to a stop. "July?"

Keeping her arms locked about his legs, she gazed up at him with tear-blurred eyes. Her face was as pale as milk, and she wore her coat and boots. "I know the way to Turtle Rock. I want to go, too."

Disengaging her arms, Spencer knelt to embrace her. "Not this time, twerp."

"I don't want April to be hurt." Her voice wavered with tears.

Spencer felt his heart contract with renewed fear. "She's not hurt, sweetheart. She's probably just gotten lost in the dark." God, let that be the truth. Kissing the top of her head, he rose and turned toward the open doorway. He could see Thane waiting on the stoop.

As he reached the door July grabbed his pant leg. "I still want to go." Her little jaw lifted at a stubborn angle that heartbreakingly reminded him of April.

"July, you're not goin' anywhere. Now let loose of your brother this instant." Cynthia descended the staircase to her daughter and clamped her hands on the child's shoulders. "Sugah, you have to stay inside with Aunt March and Vanessa's grandmother."

"I'll let you know the minute we find her, twerp, I promise." Spencer tossed his mother an appreciative look and left. Pulling the door closed behind him, he effectively shut out the sound of his sister's sobs, but not the anguish they caused him.

"She'll be all right as soon as we find April," Thane said.

Spencer knew his twin was trying to ease his pain and he was grateful for any crumb of hope. You're right! Let's go find her." He fell into step with Thane, playing his flashlight beam across the ground. "Where's Karl?"

"He took the trail through the woods. I said we'd follow the cliff path."

"Good thinking. It's quicker."

"Not necessarily. In this weather it'll be as slick as slime, but we have two flashlights compared to his one."

Spencer didn't give a rip who had what advantage, or what kind of precautions Thane thought should be taken. He proceeded at a careless clip, shouting April's name every few feet. His ears were sensitized to every sound, every wave hitting the shore, every night animal startled by their approach, every crunch of gravelly soil beneath their feet. But nothing even remotely resembling April's beloved voice answered his frantic calls.

"I don't understand this, bro." Thane sounded as confused as Spencer felt. "There are no dangerous wild animals on this island, no poisonous snakes or insects—what the hell could have happened to her?"

"I don't know." He swallowed past the tennis ball-sized lump clogging his throat.

"Is she getting sick again?"

The question had been asked softly, but it sounded like a gunshot to Spencer. Denial sprang to his mind, his heart, his lips. "No!"

He shouted April's name again, and picked up speed, but he couldn't outrun Thane's question or the feeling that his brother had hit the nail on the head. Fear settled in his belly like a frozen brick as the night air closed in on him, damp and gelid and eerily motionless except for a few misty patches, swaying through the woods like eight foot spectrals.

They were halfway to Turtle Rock before Spencer realized what the dense mists represented. "Oh, God, it's getting foggy."

"Yeah." Thane answered brusquely. There was no need to dwell on the significance of this. They both knew what it meant. They had to find April soon, or be forced to give up the search until morning. Spencer swore, shouted her name, and whipped his beam across the landscape with the composure of a madman. Recklessly, he raced on, feeling the thickening mists swirl around his head and neck like a slowly tightened noose.

At long last, he spotted another light bouncing through the darkness ahead. Karl. "Have you found her?" he shouted, praying the answer would be yes.

"No!" Came the reply.

Running, Spencer reached Turtle Rock, skidded to a stop, and planted a hand on the humped top of the huge boulder to keep his balance on the slick ground. His hope was turning as bleak as the night.

"Watch where you're stepping, man!" Karl crabbed. "There's prints in the sand here—at least there were until you skated across them—that looked about the size of April's feet."

"Damn!" Spencer wanted to look, but feared if he stepped back he might further destroy what little evidence existed. He forced himself to stand firm. "Thane, check out the prints," he pleaded with a ragged voice. Leaning into his palms which were flattened against the rock, he braced his weight on his locked arms and strove to catch his breath.

Directing his beam around Spencer's shoes, Thane knelt and examined what was left of the prints. "All these prove are that she was here. The ground was so damned dry this afternoon there's no way to tell which way she went when she left."

"Shouldn't we assume she'd go back to the house?" Spencer had finally caught his breath and was trying to think with what logic he could muster. "After all, she knew Vanessa's family was coming for dinner."

Karl frowned, and picked up the thought. "Yeah, she couldn't've left the island. Her rental car's still parked in the garage, and she wasn't on board the ferry when I went to Friday Harbor for the O'Briens."

"Maybe she took the ferry after you came back." Thane looked as though he hated to even suggest such a possibility. "Have you checked?"

"Forget it, man. That's why I was late to the cocktail party. I was securing the ferry for the night. The keys are locked in the shed, and the spare set and the key to the shed are in my pocket."

"Hell!" Spencer growled, but the curse did nothing to release his tension. "Standing here speculating is futile. We're losing visibility by the second."

He shoved away from the rock and started to make for the woods.

Thane hooked his hand around Spencer's elbow, and yanked him to a halt. "Oh, no you don't. You aren't going off by yourself in this fog."

"The hell I'm not." He jerked his arm, hard, but Thane held on tight. Spencer glared at his twin. "Let go of me."

"No." Thane spoke with a quiet finality. "Dammit, you aren't the only one worried about April. Dashing haphazardly through this pea souper isn't

239

going to find her."

Spencer looked from his brother's face to Karl's and knew he wasn't being fair. Not to them, not to April. Every pore in his body craved haste, but if he didn't curb the impulses he would be more of a hindrance than a help in finding her.

Raking his hands through his damp hair, he sighed. "What do you have in mind?"

"There was no sign of her along the cliff. Retracing that would only waste time. We need to cover the wooded section between here and the house. Searching in a line, keeping within a flashlight's beam of one another is the best chance we've got of coming across her now."

Agreeing, the three men struck a synchronized pace, and began trekking between fir and madrona, alternately calling her name.

Branches slapped Spencer's cheeks and crunched beneath his shoes, he stepped in chuck holes and stumbled over logs, but he barely noticed as his gaze scoured the forest floor for a trace of April. Her face swam before his mind's eye, and with every step a painful band threaded tauter across his chest.

By degrees the fog grew thicker. At several points the three men were forced to lessen the distance separating them, each time narrowing their individual fields of search until eventually they were only a few feet apart.

Spencer guessed they'd gone about half a mile when he heard a voice calling. His head shot up. He eyed the swirling mist in front of him, finally detecting a dim light, then several more, all moving toward them.

"It's August and the others." Karl informed them unnecessarily.

Spencer hollered, "August, have you found April?"

"No." The fog seemed to muffle the word, but not its import. Suddenly Spencer couldn't breathe. The panic he'd struggled so fiercely to control ripped from its restraints and charged his bloodstream. He tore through the underbrush, screaming, "April! Where are you? Answer me!"

Right away, Thane was there, grappling with him. Spencer bellowed with rage and threw him off. He managed to run three more feet before Karl tackled him. He pitched through empty air, and landed with a painful thud on rough, wet ground. The wind poofed from his lungs, but the blanket inside his jacket buffered the impact to his rib cage. Spencer closed his eyes and tried to catch his breath, tried to shut out the annoying ringing in his ears. Slowly, as he lay sprawled like a ferret in a game trap, his senses returned.

When he opened his eyes he found Thane squatting beside him. The concern on his brother's face cut a swath of remorse through him. He offered a feeble, "Sorry."

"Are you all right?"

"I will be as soon as Karl lets me up," he grunted.

Karl straddled his body, holding him pressed to the moist, grungy earth with his superior weight. "Not until I'm certain you ain't gonna pull another stunt like that one."

"I won't," he said gruffly, then softer, "I won't."

With his flashlight beam trained blindingly on Spencer's face, Karl eased off of him, stood and backed away. "What the hell possessed you, man?"

In answer Spencer sent him a scathing scowl. "Get that blasted light out of my eyes."

Karl shook his head and retreated further still, obviously of the opinion that Spencer had lost his mind completely. And for a moment, Spencer realized, he had.

"What's all the commotion?" August was breathless and pale. Fear emanated from him. "Is it April?"

The other searchers converged around them, stepping through the eerie fog like wraiths on a nightly foray. The same dread was on all their faces.

"No." Thane informed them. "She was at Turtle Rock, but the trail grows cold from there."

Everyone seemed to speak at once, but August's voice rose above the others. "I don't understand." His shoulders sagged as he looked from one face to the other. "Where could she be?"

No one could tell him. They didn't try. But the possibilities were narrowing and they all knew it.

Cynthia moved to her husband's side and slid her arm through his. "Darlin', I know you want to keep looking, but the fog's gettin' too dense.

August shook his head. "We can't quit now."

"We must. We're all cold and wet. We need to get back to the house before we all get lost, or catch pneumonia."

No one wanted to accept this, least of all Spencer. But there was no choice. His mother was right. To continue searching in this weather would only put others at jeopardy. They'd have to wait until the fog lifted. Only God knew when that would be.

Spencer's heart hung in his chest like a worthless piece of tin as he stumbled after the others, heedless to time and place, knowing that with every passing hour the chances of finding April alive were dwindling. He was as powerless to help her now as he had been twelve years ago, but this time he couldn't block out the feelings.

He let himself be led into the house and seated at the kitchen table, let July sob inconsolably against his chest, let her go, reluctantly, when their mother insisted the child be put to bed. It seemed incredible that only two hours had passed. March pressed a mug of hot coffee into his hand. But he didn't drink. He stared at the dark liquid and saw April's face, watched the steam rise and felt her warm breath mingle with his.

August's shaky voice interrupted his tortured thoughts and the murmur of conversation going on throughout the room. "I've contacted the Coast Guard. They'll do a complete sweep of the island tomorrow. But they can't do anything before dawn."

The grim quaver of acceptance in his stepfather's tone sent shivers across Spencer's flesh. A sweep of the island meant August had concluded what he had concluded. April had fallen from the cliffs. The image this created in his mind refueled his panic. He scrambled to his feet and bracketed his palms against the tabletop, sloshing coffee and startling the people seated beside him. "I know you had to call the Coast Guard, but she's not there, August. She's not."

"I know how you feel, son. But we may have to accept the possibility."

"I can't." Spencer flipped his jacket from the back of his chair and began struggling into it.

August's hand landed heavily on his shoulder. "What do you think you're doing?"

"I'm going back out and find April."

"No." The word was softly spoken, but carried the weight of Turtle Rock. "I'm not going to lose

243

you, too."

For ten seconds they stared at one another, sharing a mutual anguish and love. Then Spencer nodded. Swallowing hard, he flopped his jacket back onto the chair and sat.

"Under the circumstances—" Dee Dee O'Brien scraped back her chair and stood, "I think we should call off the engagement party."

Although it was the sensible thing to do, the suggestion presumed the inevitable outcome of this ordeal. The group fell silent.

Dee Dee's little-girl-voice broke the quiet. "Vanessa?"

"You're right, Mother." Vanessa's face was as gray as Spencer's mood. However, she sounded relieved to have something to do. "I'll get our guest list and we can start making the calls."

"You can use the phone in August's den." There was an odd lack of inflection in Cynthia's tone. "I'll make my calls when you're finished."

Spencer's nerves were too raw, his temper too short, to sit here and deal with this. Lurching from his chair, he left it rattling on its metal legs and strode across the kitchen to the laundry room. Fog hugged the windows like puffy drapes.

He stared at the blanketed glass. *April, where are you? What in the world could have happened?* As worried as he was about her mental stability, he refused to believe she would have done herself harm. What then? His gaze shifted to the stairway, and he replayed with vivid memory the rejection he had handed her in the wine cellar. Could that account for this? God, he didn't know. Her doctor. He should return her call. Find out what she wanted. Tell her April was missing. Maybe Dr. Merritt would have some much needed insight.

"Are you sure April's not in the house?" Thane had approached so quietly Spencer flinched at the sound of his voice.

"Well, I haven't looked in every nook and cranny, but I did check the attic and the basement and her bedroom."

Nodding, Thane emitted a wistful sigh, and angled his hip against the washing machine. "I was just thinking. About the tunnels. Is there any possibility she might have gone exploring?"

Thinking back to their conversation in the wine cellar that morning, Spencer recalled April's abhorrence at the thought of the darkness and the rats. He shook his head. "I doubt it."

"Why? Vanessa would give her eye teeth to explore the damned things. Why should April be any different?"

Putting aside the fact that he could expound for hours on the differences between the two women, Spencer raked his fingers impatiently through his hair. "Even if it were remotely possible, how would she have gained access to any of the tunnels?"

The gleam in Thane's eyes seemed to imply Spencer was being extremely dull-witted. He shrugged. "Through the house, of course."

Spencer shook his head again. "Karl and I were just in the wine cellar. The access is boarded up tight."

Thane arched one eyebrow. "That's not the only entrance down there. Have you forgotten the one right behind where the staircase used to be?"

He had. Tilting his head, he asked, "Aren't there a couple more on the back wall as well?"

Smiling, Thane angled his face close to Spencer's.

245

"Isn't it worth checking out?"

"Bro', anything would be better than standing around twiddling my thumbs, waiting for this godawful fog to lift. Let's go."

"I thought you might say that." Thane reached to his back pockets, withdrew two flashlights, and handed one to his twin.

Spencer followed him down the stairs through the larder into the basement. The inadequate light bulb cast a yellow haze across the massive room. Both men switched on their flashlights. It was no wonder he hadn't recalled the other openings to the smuggling tunnels, Spencer thought, scanning the hulls of discarded inventions. The walls were all but hidden from view by the shrouded frameworks which stood like malformed dragons guarding the entrance to the secret passageways.

Thane seemed to agree. "These spooky-looking monsters would give a ghost nightmares." He chuckled and urged his brother to follow him.

As they strode across the floor, Spencer's pace slowed. He couldn't come into this room without being assailed by the memory of finding April alone in the dark, sobbing, nor could he pass this closed wine cellar door without seeing her sprawled beneath the racks.

On impulse he flung open the door and flipped on the light. The room was as he and Karl had left it. April was not there. Numb, he flipped off the switch, shut the door, and hastened after Thane.

Thane had reached the end wall. He skirted a cloth-covered structure and disappeared. A moment later, he shouted, "I've found one."

Hope quickened Spencer's step, but when he

caught up with his twin all he saw was a wall plastered with boards. He grabbed one of the planks and tugged. "Nobody's entered the tunnels this way in years."

"This isn't the only access."

A sudden curiosity grabbed Spencer, and he scanned the darkness beyond them. "Is there a walkway all around this skeletal graveyard of August's?"

"Yes. Sometimes he comes down here and steals parts off one or the other of these rejects to use on some new project. Come on." Thane veered to the right, fanning his light to the cement beneath his feet. "You know it's kind of strange how clean this floor is. Am I leaving any footprints?"

Spencer directed his beam along the concrete from his toes until it outlined Thane's heels. "No. In fact, it doesn't even smell particularly dusty back here. Shouldn't it?"

"You'd think so. 'Course, considering the cleaning frenzy Helga's been on, maybe we shouldn't be too surprised."

It was the first mention Thane had made of his canceled engagement party, and he was trying to make Spencer feel better. It made him feel worse. How could he have suspected his own twin of wishing April harm? He'd almost let the vile suspicions drive a wedge between them. Thank God that hadn't happened. If the news of April wasn't going to be good, he would need his brother more than anyone else.

"Ah ha. Another one. Crap! It's boarded up, too." Thane absently grasped the end of a plank. The board pulled away from the others. "Yikes!"

He jumped back a step. The board dropped to the floor and landed on his toes. "Ouch."

"What are you doing?" Spencer waved his beam over his twin.

Thane pointed to the boarded section, which was now missing a strip of wood. "I touched a plank and it came loose in my hand."

They concentrated both beams across the other planks.

Thane leaned closer, examining them. "Somebody's loosened all the nails."

Spencer's heart raced with hope. "Recently?"

"No. I'd say it was done years ago."

"Why?"

"You got me."

Spencer wasn't ready to give up yet. "How about that access you mentioned near the former staircase?"

"It should be over there." Thane stepped over the fallen plank and flicked his light along the wall ahead. "What's that?"

Spencer aimed his beam to the area in question, then frowned, doubting what his eyes told him. The texture of the wall altered drastically from rugged concrete to an unnatural smoothness.

"It's a blanket," Thane exclaimed, reaching it first. "Someone's hung an old blanket here."

"A blanket?"

"Yeah. It's the color of the cement."

Spencer hurried to his brother's side, clutched an edge of the blanket, and lifted. Even before he shined his light into the dark hole, Spencer felt the cool stale air, caught the odor of dank earth. His heart gave an unsteady leap.

"Well, I'll be . . ." Thane sounded more excited than he. Which just wasn't possible. For five whole seconds they stared at one another, contemplating what they'd discovered.

Finally, Spencer said, "Obviously someone doesn't want this access to be readily detected."

"But why isn't it boarded up like the others?"

"There's only one way to find out."

They stepped into the mouth of the cavern. The blanket flopped into place behind them, furled against their backs, then stilled. The crudely carved tunnel had been cut through the earth over a hundred years ago, and Spencer eyed the rafters dubiously. On closer inspection they seemed solid enough. The width and the height of the place was impressive.

Thane said, "Remember August saying that old Octavius used to run a pony and cart through one of the passageways to the cliffside to pick up whatever was being shipped in?"

"This has to be the one." Spencer glanced over his shoulder at the blanket. "How did the cart and horse get in and out of the basement?"

"Seems like August said the larder. I believe from the outside it once looked like any root cellar, but inside there used to be a narrow rampway."

At any other time, Spencer would have enjoyed the history lesson, but not now. "April!"

They had gone about ten feet, walking in silence, prodding the dark with their beams when an acrid stench assailed Spencer's nostrils. "What's that awful odor?"

"I don't know."

A flapping sound arose.

Suddenly something swooped off one of the rafters and dived for Spencer's hair. He swore. Ducking, he wrapped his hands protectively about his head. "What the hell was that? Birds?"

"Bats."

"That explains the smell, but how did they get in here?"

"They're all over the island. These tunnels are probably teeming with them."

"Shouldn't they be hibernating this time of year?"

"Yeah. But I read somewhere that they can be awakened when disturbed."

Eighteen

"April!" Heedless of sleeping bats, Spencer called her name every few seconds. The word resounded off the tunnel walls and throbbed emptily inside his ears without answer.

"Look." Thane had pulled to a stop.

Coming up behind him, Spencer splayed his light into the darkness ahead. The tunnel was cluttered by a wall of cobwebs that dangled from the rafters like shredded white hosiery. A scattered pile of rat or bat droppings littered the earthen floor, but he saw nothing to account for the wonderment in his brother's voice. Disappointed and growing impatient again, he griped, "What?"

"Not there." Thane grasped Spencer's flashlight and yanked it toward their right. "There."

Outlined in the limited beam he saw a man-sized slit in the dirt wall. Surprise and puzzlement curled through him. He moved closer, panned the light into the opening, then stepped back and played it across the entire section of wall. An almost imperceptible line circled what appeared to be a massive boulder.

Spencer touched the stone. The composition was as hard as any rock, but it felt different. He tapped the end of his flashlight against it. The clink of metal hitting metal rewarded the effort.

"What the hell is it?" Thane demanded, moving closer.

"It seems to be some kind of door. Hold this." He handed Thane his flashlight and applied his palms to the rock, shoving hard. It moved inward with such unexpected ease that Spencer lost his balance. He pitched to the ground. His knees banged painfully against the first of three crudely chiseled stone steps just inside the opening.

"Well, I'll be . . ." Thane said, stepping over him and fanning both beams into the dark cavity. The passage was barely wide enough and tall enough to suit the average man, and, not five feet in, it veered to the right, taking what appeared to be a 180-degree turn. "Isn't this interesting?"

Rising, Spencer brushed at his slacks. "I don't recall any mention of secret passageways opening into other parts of the house. Do you?"

"Not a one, but that pseudo-granite door has been there a long time. Probably installed by Octavius himself."

Spencer nodded. "Considering the smuggling that went on it makes sense the old guy would've built himself a few escape routes."

Thane handed back the extra flashlight and strode forward, hunching over to accommodate his tall frame in the low ceiling passageway. "Where do you suppose this leads?"

"I don't know, but judging the effortless way that door swung open it's been used and used recently."

"Do you think April could have found this and come in here to investigate?"

Knowing her terror of the dark, Spencer couldn't

imagine anything less likely than April traversing dark corridors of her own free will. And yet, what other hope did he have? "At this point I'm willing to consider just about anything."

The crouched position grew uncomfortable sooner than Spencer would have thought possible, but uncertain what lay ahead he knew they dare not move faster. "Unless my sense of direction has failed me, I'd say we're backtracking, skirting the house on the outside of the basement."

"Your sense of direction is right on, but the air quality in here could use improvement."

Just as he was getting used to the crick in his neck and between his shoulders, Spencer saw Thane straighten. His head disappeared from view. A second later he was stretching his own spine. They were standing in a ten-by-ten room.

"What do you make of this?" Thane asked.

Drawing a lungful of somewhat better air, Spencer wheeled his light across the coarse dirt walls and floor. Except for a rusted Coleman lantern sitting next to a rat-eaten mattress in one corner and a wooden ladder in the other, the chamber was empty. "Storage room, apparently."

"For opium, diamonds, wool, whiskey, or Chinese slaves . . . ?"

"Probably all of them, at one time or another."

"Lord, if only these walls could talk. Why is there a mattress down here?"

Spencer shrugged, and kicked at it with his shoe. Dust furled upward. "It's too new to have been for the slaves. At any rate, no one's lain down on it for a lot of years, I'll tell you that." Normally this discovery would have intrigued him, but it brought him no closer to finding April, and right now nothing else

253

mattered. He stepped to the ladder and shined his light against the ceiling. "Hey. Come here."

He was scrambling up the ladder, lifting the wooden hatch before Thane responded. It flopped back on its hinges, but any expected banging this should have caused was muffled. He clambered over the lip of the opening. One look at the tools hung on hooks and scattered about and he knew where they were. "So much for both our senses of direction," he told Thane. "We're inside the storage shed." The storage shed sat on the rise above the dock.

"No wonder it seemed like such a long walk." Thane joined him. "Did you know this trapdoor existed?"

"No." He glared at the gunny sacks that had reposed on its top. "It's obviously kept covered on purpose."

"The question is why?"

"Who knows." The very furtiveness of the camouflage made Spencer uneasy, for he felt certain this secret was not connected with smugglers or pirates. Inexplicably, he sensed it had something to do with April, and yet, he couldn't say how or why he felt this. Did she know about this tunnel, this escape hatch? Had she used them for some unguessable reason? He wanted to hope. Anything was better than the images he couldn't quite dispel of her broken body lying on the rocky shore of Haro Strait. He strode to the other side of the building and rattled the doorknob. The resistance scrapped his hope. "Karl was right. It's locked up tight."

"It's cold in here, too." Thane clasped his hand on Spencer's shoulder. "Sorry about the wild goose chase. Let's get back to the house. There may have been some word about April."

There wasn't.

Spencer's mother placed a fresh cup of coffee and a sandwich on a plate in front of him. Evidently Helga had sliced up the sirloin tip. The O'Briens ate hungrily. Spencer didn't begrudge them, but he couldn't sit here and watch them eat.

Carrying his coffee he retreated to August's den, and was grateful to find he had the room to himself. Apparently the party-goers had all been informed of the cancellation. He jerked open the drapes. The fog stared back, pressing against the French doors like a bloated-faced monster, ugly and drippy, wetting the glass as effectively as rain, thwarting his efforts to hunt for April. The second it started to dissipate he would be ready.

Behind him the telephone rang. He jumped and spun toward it. "Hello?" he answered tentatively, hoping the caller would be April, yet fearing it would be someone with bad news about her. "Calendar House."

"Finally. I apologize for the lateness of the hour, but I've been trying to get through for ages. I got so many busy signals, I was about to call the operator to see if something was wrong with the line."

"No. Nothing's wrong with the line. It's been in use." Probably another guest, he thought, not recognizing the woman's voice, nor wanting to deal with her petty complaints. "Who is this?"

"Nancy Merritt. May I speak to April Farraday?"

The doctor. He'd forgotten he was going to call her. Only now that she was actually on the phone he didn't know what to say to her. How did he tell April's psychiatrist they had lost her on an island the size of Farraday? Weary beyond his years, Spencer sank to the edge of August's desk and deposited his untasted cup of coffee next to the phone.

"Doctor, this is Spencer Garrick. I was the one you spoke to earlier this evening. I'm afraid there's a . . . a problem. April can't come to the phone."

"A problem?" He could have sworn her voice had raised a notch. "Has April suffered an . . . ah . . . relapse?"

Had she? Could the mixed signals he'd been heaping on April since the first day of her arrival here have sent her into a mental tailspin? Over the past few hours he'd considered and rejected this possibility so many times he no longer knew what to think. "Not that I know of."

"Not that you know of? What kind of problem are we talking about Mr. Garrick?"

The moisture drained from his mouth. Spence reached for his abandoned mug and swallowed a gulp of lukewarm coffee. Just as he started to speak, the doctor cut him off.

"April left a message on my answering machine sometime in the wee hours of last night." Dr. Merritt's obvious impatience punctuated every word. "She mentioned a mishap with a wine rack, but she said her wounds were minor."

"They were." So April had called the doctor. Was there something to be learned from an exchange of information? "This has nothing to do with the wine rack."

"Mr. Garrick, you're frightening me. What has happened to April?"

As succinctly as possible he explained everything he knew, including the family's assumption that April had fallen or jumped from the cliff. "We've called the Coast Guard, but the fog is so dense at this moment we've had to discontinue our own search."

"Oh, God." Nancy Merritt whispered, sounding stunned, but surprisingly resigned. "April's message was . . . I . . . I was afraid something would happen."

Spencer was suddenly furious. "Then why did you wait so long to call?"

"I'm in Seattle at a convention," she answered defensively. "I had only collected my phone messages shortly before I called the first time. And when you said everyone was about to sit down to dinner, I assumed you had seen and spoken with April and that she must be fine. But when she didn't return my call . . ."

"I see." The words fell from his mouth as flat as his hopes of finding April alive and well.

"Mr. Garrick, I can't say April couldn't have fallen from a cliff, but I have no reason to believe she was suicidal."

He rammed his fingers through his hair. "May I ask you what message she left on your answering machine?"

"You may ask. However, I assume you know that disclosing the confidences of my patients would breach my professional ethics."

"Doctor," he ground between clenched teeth. "I appreciate your reluctance to discuss this with me, but if April can still be helped, can't you see that every minute counts?"

Nancy hesitated, obviously debating the virtue of doctor/patient confidentially against patient welfare. Couldn't she see there was no contest? April had to come first. "Doctor?"

"All right. You understand I'm only doing this for

April's sake." He also understood from her tone that the damned woman wasn't going to tell him anything more than she thought he needed to know.

"The reason I asked if April had suffered a relapse was because of the way she described the incident with the wine rack. She said at first she thought someone had pushed it over on her, later she'd decided it must have been an accident, but by the time she called she'd come to the conclusion she was losing her grip on sanity altogether."

His scalp felt too small for his skull. "Is . . . is that what you suspect?" The line went blank and for a split second he thought the doctor had hung up. Then he heard her breathing. Considering. Spencer crammed his fist into his thigh. God, couldn't the woman think faster than this?

Finally, she replied, "I'd have to see and speak to April before making that kind of judgment. Tell me, during these past two weeks, has she shown any signs of regression?"

Now pounding his fist against his thigh, he recounted the episode on the attic stairs when April had acted disoriented, and the time he'd found her in the dark basement sobbing uncontrollably.

"Actually, those are both side effects of her illness, ones we discussed, and prepared for. They could mean she'd started remembering."

Spencer quit hitting his leg and scrubbed his face with his hand. "That's good then, right?"

"Yesterday I would have said yes. Tonight, I'm not so certain."

Fear heaved through his stomach.

"Mr. Garrick, would—would you know who might have sent an anonymous note April received prior to her departure for Calendar House?"

"An anonymous . . . ?" Like a man moving in slow motion, Spencer stood. He frowned at the phone as though he could actually see the doctor at the other end in her Seattle hotel room. "You mean a threat of some kind?"

"Yes."

"Do you think someone's been trying to frighten her?" He was shouting now. "For God sakes, harm her?"

"I don't know."

But she sounded as though that was exactly what she thought. Heat dropped from his face so fast he felt dizzy.

Nancy said, "I've rented a car. I'm driving to Anacortes to catch the first ferry. I'll be in Friday Harbor as soon as possible, but I'm at least five hours away. I'll call when I arrive. In the meantime, you might want to conduct another search of the house—every closet, every cupboard, anything big enough for April to fit into."

He gripped the phone so hard his hand hurt. "Am I looking for a place April might have crawled into on her own, or one where someone might have put her?"

"Yes."

Spencer's skin cooled to a temperature near the one outdoors. He dumped the receiver into its cradle, then stood staring at the phone, shaking.

Had someone hurt April, had she hurt herself? His mind spun. God, the incident in the garage, the family's assumption it had been a suicide attempt, Dr. Merritt's insistence April was not suicidal.

The electrician's words assailed him, "Someone shut off the main switch on purpose."

His heart squeezed with pain as he mentally compiled a list: the clean path around August's discarded hulls, the access to the tunnel through which someone could come and go whenever they pleased; April not just terrified in the dark basement, but hysterical; the missing poems; Lily's disemboweled trunk; the collapsed wine racks; and April dramatically plunking the Barbie doll on the breakfast table as if trying to catch someone off guard. Add to that an anonymous note. Considered separately these things appeared innocent enough, weighed together they suggested sinister goings-on.

He lifted the receiver and dialed the San Juan County Sheriff.

Spencer informed August that Dr. Merritt had called, but other than the fact she was driving up, he kept the theme of their conversation to himself. He spent the next two hours inspecting every inch of Calendar House. Alone. He confided in no one, trusted no one. How could he? April's life, or her sanity, depended on his discretion.

The others—the O'Briens in particular—probably thought he was rude, or crazy, insisting on rummaging through their rooms. So much for manners. Normally, he would have gone to great lengths not to offend Thane's future in-laws; tonight he didn't give a damn. The worst of it was, he hadn't found a trace of April.

Maybe she's in here, he thought, shoving through the doors of the west wing. Eerie darkness greeted his entrance up the three stairs and into the unused hallway. The thick carpet absorbed his footsteps, the dusty air his breath. He located the light-switch. The click was loud and ineffective.

He tugged the flashlight from his back pocket with a frustrated grunt, then played the beam into the dark corridor. He hadn't been in this wing of the house in years, eleven years to be exact. From the look of it, neither had anyone else. Still the doctor had said to check every nook and cranny.

Spencer proceeded to the old servants' quarters at the farthest end of the hall, quickly eliminated them, and moved on to the abandoned guest bedrooms. Every surface seemed coated with dust. Ignoring it, Spencer searched in, under, and around every item in each room, smudged his clothes and his face, and emitted several hearty sneezes.

Heavy-hearted, he headed back along the corridor, absently lighting his way with the flashlight beam, to the ballroom. It was the only place he hadn't looked. He approached the glass door with his hope in shreds, uncertain how much more of this he could take.

He stepped into the vast room. Cold and biting as the fog cleaving the enormous glass windows stole over him. Spencer shook off a shiver. Panning the light from corner to corner, he strode stealthily across the wooden floor. Nothing. Nothing, but empty spaces.

He pivoted, gradually circling. The beam fell on the furniture at the far end of the room. Lily's furniture. But why were the sheets tossed carelessly aside? Could April be hiding there?

He advanced on the huddled group of sofas, tables, and chairs, with a quickening pulse, the beam of his light now purposeful, now directed. "April? Are you here? It's me, Spence. I won't hurt you. You can come ou—" Inches from the sofas, Spencer stopped short. "What in the hell . . . ?"

He couldn't believe what he was seeing. The sofas were ripped open, every cushion cut, the tables tops lacerated with long and short gashes. What in the name of God was the reason for this? Slowly, reluctantly, he lifted his light to Lily's portrait. Shock held him rooted. Lily's delicate face had been scored like a piece of tough steak. The hatred behind the act was so evident it lingered in the gelid air around him as though the vandalizer were still here, standing just out of his line of vision. Uneasily, he fanned the light around the room one more time to assure himself he was actually alone.

His thoughts appalled him as much as the defilement. Had April come to the ballroom, remembered her hatred of her mother and done this? The notion turned his stomach.

He slid his finger into the pocket of his slacks, touching his mother's gold cross. Cynthia, too, had hated Lily. But why would she wait until April was home to destroy these things? Perhaps it was someone else, someone who hoped this carnage would be discovered and the finger pointed at April. It was a possibility he wanted to believe so badly his head throbbed. But if someone had meant April to look insane, why hadn't that someone found a way to expose this deed?

Because they'd found a way to dispose of April instead?

He left the west wing with the weight of the world on his shoulders. In all the elections he'd ever lost, Spence had never felt more defeated. He returned to the den. It was deserted. Had everyone else gone to bed? Most likely. Should he? Why bother? He was exhausted, yes, but sleepy, no.

He collapsed his long frame into one of the red

leather chairs. And waited. He'd thought the night he'd waited to search April's room for the poems had been the slowest in his life. He'd been wrong. He stared out the French doors at the unrelenting fog, then back at the sluggishly moving hands of his wristwatch. It was after 1 A.M. So early, so late.

Feeling as restless as a captive tiger, he abandoned the den and stalked through the lower level. He was surprised to come upon his mother, brother, step-father, stepaunt, and three of the five O'Briens in the living room. Their conversation was nothing more than a low murmur, accompanied by the nervous clack of March's knitting needles, audienced by the stealthy fog.

August sat slumped on one of the sofas, his face drawn with worry, his shoulders limp with resigna-tion, while Cynthia fluttered, the perfect hostess at this imperfect affair. Thane and Vanessa accepted her offered coffee. Walter and Dee Dee O'Brien hud-dled together on the opposite couch, uncomfortable participants in someone else's tragedy. Spencer joined them, but soon discovered he was unable to sit or carry on conversation for more than a few sec-onds. The strain of distrust kept him moving.

In the kitchen, he found Karl pacing, grumbling to Helga and Vanessa's aunt about the fog. The two men exchanged knowing looks, but Spencer wasn't ready to share his worry for April with the one man who undoubtedly knew exactly how he felt. He re-filled his coffee cup and left.

At length he found himself in July's bedroom. A bedside lamp had been left on, evidently to placate the terrified little girl. As he strode to the bed, he re-alized he no longer had his coffee cup nor any idea where he'd put it. Not that it mattered. He gazed down at the sleeping child. Poor kid. Overly tired, she had fought sleep until the last possible moment. She wasn't resting peacefully. Her tiny fingers were curled into tight fists, and, as he watched, she flinched and cried April's name.

With his heart wrenching, he sank to the bed beside her and smoothed a lock of hair from her forehead. July continued to sleep as he studied her dainty face. Until now, he hadn't noticed the uptilt of her nose was a duplicate to April's. A half smile tugged his tense mouth. Was this what he and April's children would have looked like had they ever been given the opportunity to have any? The thought tore at his ravaged spirits. He shoved his fingers through his hair, sprang to his feet and shuffled to the window.

Damn this fog. It hadn't given an inch. He wanted to ram his fist through the glass and tear the cursed mist apart with his bare hands. The foolish notion only served to heighten his frustration. Swearing beneath his breath, he spun around and paced the floor.

Although the four walls seemed to grow smaller with each passing minute he stayed in July's room, gleaning what little comfort he could being in the presence of the only person in the entire household he knew he could trust without reservation. But his limbs tingled from the enforced waiting, and again and again, he trekked to the window, treading the same path across braided rug and hardwood planks.

As the hour hand swept toward 4 A.M., Spencer thought he heard wind whispering against the house. The harder he tried to listen, the louder came the rush of blood in his ears, blocking the sound. A fast trip to the window told him nothing new. The fog was still intact. Wishful thinking, he decided. Probably just the house creaking and settling, as usual.

Disheartened, he pulled a chair to the bedside, turned it backward, straddled the seat, and laid his chin on the wooden backrest. As he stretched his legs, the toe of his shoe stubbed something solid beneath the fold of the bedspread.

Leaning over, he scooped a metal cylinder from the floor. It was an old flashlight. The plastic lens was cracked, a piece missing, and the beam of light cast by the tiny bulb hovered near death. He flicked it off and slid it to the bedside table, wondering what childish whim had driven his young sister to procure the worthless thing.

Behind him the door opened. He glanced over his shoulder and saw his mother standing in the doorway. She was dressed for bed. A white nylon nightie winked from the gap in her flowing black robe as she swished into the room on high heeled mules. With her long dark hair hanging loose about her face, she looked absurdly young, almost innocent.

Her brows furrowed with concern. "Is she still asleep?"

Turning to regard July, he nodded. Cynthia crossed the room so silently that when her hand touched his neck, he jumped. Instantly she removed it, but he sensed her hurt and hated himself for distrusting his family, his mother in particular.

"There's nothing we can do until this fog lifts. I've convinced August to lie down awhile," she said softly. "Don't you think you should try to get some sleep, too?"

"No." He spoke louder than he'd meant to.

July's body jerked and her eyes fluttered open. She squinted against the light. "Spence?"

He angled around the chair and gently caressed her cheek. "Go back to sleep, twerp. It's not time to get up yet."

"Mommy?"

"We're just checkin' on you, sugah." Cynthia adjusted the blankets at July's feet which the child had kicked free during her restless slumber.

"I was dreaming." As July struggled into a sitting position, her brows descended sharply. Fear and anguish telegraphed from her eyes. "April," her voice caught, "fell off the cliff."

"Oh, dear." Cynthia rushed to soothe July, reassuring her that she had had a nightmare, that April was probably only lost in the woods.

Spencer added his own assurances, but as much as he wanted to protect July, he pondered the wisdom of lying to her. He'd already experienced a dose of her perceptive powers. Had she sensed the tension among the adults and known they weren't telling her their true suspicions about April? Had that brought on the bad dream?

July let Cynthia plump her pillows and ease her back to a prone position, but her little fists were still curled tight. "I'm afraid."

Spencer's gaze met his mother's. He detested distrusting her, but had no help for it. Perhaps, he *could* help July. *Let me try,* he conveyed silently. Cynthia nodded.

Untangling himself from the chair, he set it aside and sank to the bed. His sister's eyes were the size of golf balls, full of fear and misgiving, without a trace of sleepiness.

Spencer smoothed his hand across the soft skin of her forehead and cheek. "I know your dream seemed real, twerp, but it was only a picture your mind made up because you're so worried about April."

She looked anything but convinced.

He tried again, repeating his mother's sentiment. "April is probably only lost in the woods." The second these words left his mouth he knew July would realize even he didn't believe this. Bearing that in mind, Spencer offered her the one truth he had. "As soon as the fog lifts we're all going to go out and find her."

"Can I come too?"

"We'll see."

Looking somewhat mollified, July laid her head onto the pillow. As her eyes drifted shut, he whispered to Cynthia, "I'll stay with her. Go see to August, and get some sleep."

She seemed about to offer him the same advice on sleep, but after a moment's hesitation, she only nodded and left.

Spencer directed his attention to July. She appeared to finally be relaxing. As he watched, her left hand uncoiled, slightly. A glint of color winked at him from the gap. Surprised, he leaned closer. He'd thought those fingers were curled from tension, now he realized she was clutching something in a life and death grip.

His curiosity aroused, he nudged the fingers farther open with his thumb. July snapped into a sitting position as though her head were attached to an invisible string on which he had just jerked. Her fist locked on the object. Alarmed, he frowned at her. "What is it, twerp?"

July threw him a guilty look and shook her head stubbornly. "Nothing."

"All right. You don't have to show it to me if you don't want to."

"I want to, but I can't." Cringing, July shrank into her pillow. A tear rolled down her freckled cheek. "I'll get in trouble."

"Not with me. It'd be our secret."

She looked uncertain. "Promise?"

"Promise."

Slowly, she unfisted her hand.

Rhinestones glinted at him in garish profusion from the turtle-shaped object in her tiny palm.

"April's turtle earring," he whispered. He smiled at July, his heart going out to the child who obviously wanted something of her big sister to hold on to. "It's all right, twerp. I know April wouldn't mind that you went into her room and took this."

July's face paled and, impossibly, her eyes grew wider. "I didn't get it from April's room."

A sudden premonition struck Spence. He felt his pulse wobble. "Was April wearing her turtle earrings when she went out for her walk?"

Pressing her lips into a flat line, July answered with a nod of her head.

His heart stopped, then restarted with a skip as he grabbed her by the shoulders. "Where did you find this?"

Tears puddled in her dark eyes. "You're m-mad."

"What?" He realized he was holding her too tight and loosened his grip. "I'm sorry. I'm not mad, sweetheart. I just need to know where you found the earring."

"I wasn't supposed to . . ." Sniffling, she trailed off and turned her eyes away from his.

With his heart threatening to escape his chest, Spencer hauled her out of the covers and onto his lap, hugging her gently this time. "No one's going to get mad at you, twerp. You've found the only clue so far that might lead us to April, but if you won't tell me *where* you found it, I can't help her."

He felt the tension in her body ease. Swiping the sleeve of her pajamas under her nose, she snuffled. "I found it on the cliff."

If Spencer hadn't already been sitting down, he would have collapsed. Somehow, for July's sake, he managed to keep his tone level. "Which cliff?"

"The one you can see from the living room."

His gaze fell to the flashlight on the bedside table, and he guessed what the child had done, why she feared punishment. She must have waited until the grownups were outside and Aunt March was occupied elsewhere, then helped herself to a leftover flashlight and, defying orders to stay indoors, conducted her own search for April.

Unwished for images of the horror they would find when the fog lifted, when dawn came, ravaged his mind. Clinging desperately to his young sister, Spencer tilted his head back on his neck and closed his eyes, fighting the bile burning up his throat. The blood in his veins flowed icy, yet his body felt sweaty. Shaking uncontrollably, he dropped his chin to his chest, grazing the top of July's head.

She crooked her neck and lifted her tear stained face to him. Her lower lip quivered. "April fell off the cliff, didn't she?"

Nineteen

The cracking branch resounded like a gunshot to April's terrified ears. As the limb broke free, she pitched away from the cliff wall.

Falling.

Her heart and stomach vied for position in her throat.

"Nooooo!" Grappling frantically, she struck out with her foot. It hit solid granite. She shoved hard. Her body lurched left. Was it enough to center her above the flat shelf?

Dear God, please!

April plunged.

Faster.

Crashing waves chanted her dirge.

Icy water sprayed her pant legs, plastering the wet wool cloth to her calves like manacles of death.

Hope slipped away.

Then her foot struck ground. The impact jarred her body, twisted her ankle. Slammed to a stop, April crumpled like a boneless corset, vaguely aware that she'd missed landing on the pointed tip of the torn tree branch by mere inches.

For several minutes, she lay there, afraid to move. Her breath refused to lengthen into more than gasps.

Her heart had skipped and skittered so often through this ordeal that she was amazed at the ferocity with which it now walloped her rib cage.

But the damp, pebble-thick ledge supporting her felt as blessed as a down-filled pillow. The idea made her laugh, a long, high-pitched giggle that had nothing to do with humor, and had all the suggestions of hysteria. April clamped her mouth shut. This was no time to fall apart. She'd survived the worst already.

As her mind started to function normally, she recalled Spencer's words about erosion and wondered how solid the ledge actually was. Slowly, April untangled her limbs, scooted her bottom into the mouth of the cave and pressed her back against the dirt and granite wall.

An oddly rancid scent wafted to her from inside the cavern. She peered uneasily into the inky depths. What could be in there that would create this odor? A dead animal? April shuddered. The only critters anyone ever mentioned in connection with the caverns were rats. The thought made her skin crawl. Maybe she should wait here on the ledge with the relative comfort of the moonlight and familiar twinkle of the stars through the swirling mists.

But wait for what—some passing boat to see her? And how long might that take? Days? Weeks? Long enough for her to starve or freeze to death? No—as the waves viciously crashing on the rocks below tauntingly reminded her—this black abyss was the only way to safety.

Besides, misty patches were rising across the water, growing thicker as the minutes passed. April knew the weather could get densely, bone-chillingly foggy with little or no warning. The thought of the warmth of Calendar House made her acutely aware of how cold she was. She started to stand. Pain seized her ankle and raced up her left leg. Oh God, had she broken something? The ramifications of this possibility penetrated her shock. It was one thing to fantasize about traversing the cavern through the dark, past pitfalls and rats, to reach one of the sealed accesses in the basement. But injured?

Wincing, she sank back to the ledge, gingerly lifted the pant leg as high up her thigh as it would go, bent at the waist and gently patted the length of her leg. Her fingers were numb with cold and prodded too roughly a couple of skinned areas. April hollered "Ouch!" each time this happened, finding the verbal release soothed her nerves. At the end of her search, she'd pinpointed the center of pain, but had encountered no places where bone protruded flesh. A pent-up breath rushed from her lungs.

Feeling fairly certain the worst she may have suffered was a fracture, she struggled to her feet and cautiously plied her weight to the aching limb. Pain zinged from the ankle in question, but if she was careful, she could stand on it, even hobble. It was probably only sprained. Still . . . could she negotiate the maze of passageways?

Quit thinking negatively, she warned herself. She'd made it this far. Why be defeated by dwelling on the difficulties ahead? April wasted forty seconds arguing with herself, then suddenly her trepidation dissolved in a blaze of rage. How dare anyone try to end her life? How could she even have considered letting them get away with it?

Scooping up the tree limb to use as a guide, or, if necessary, a weapon against small furry creatures, she limped into the dark hole.

Beneath her the ground dipped and rose in no particular pattern. She moved cautiously, deliberately, wielding the heavy stick like a blind person might a white cane, pausing when the pain in her ankle became too fierce. As the noise of the surf died away, the silence increased until the only company she had was the growling of her stomach.

She refused to let herself think of how hungry she was, or how terrified of the dark, or how frightened July, and maybe even Spence, would be when they found her missing. But she couldn't repress the haunting question of who had pushed her off the cliff.

Had the same person penned the anonymous note, left the headless Barbie on her pillow? She had been so convinced these were the deeds of a coward, as were the attempt in the garage, and the voice in the dark basement—for now she was certain there had been a real voice, not one dredged from her sick mind. But the wine racks and the shove from the cliff were acts of desperation.

A chill tore through April, and for a moment, she stood still and hugged herself. Who wanted her dead? And why? The blackness pressed in on her as menacingly as the adversary whose identity and motive she couldn't fathom. Was the faceless someone afraid of what she would remember when the past came back to her? Was that the reason behind the attacks?

She shook her head as though that would rattle loose another chunk of the blockage, but as usual, the harder she tried to remember, the greater the throbbing at her temples. Forget it, she instructed herself.

Clinging to her shredded courage, April limped on. Her arm was starting to ache from the weight of lifting the cumbersome branch to whisk away unseen cobwebs. She lowered it to the ground and tapped the unseeable passageway floor. Almost immediately gauzy fibers crisscrossed her face. April squealed and slapped at the webs. For several seconds she was subjected to shudders as she swung the limb through the area near her head.

Feeling only half convinced no spiders were crawling in her hair, she forced herself to start moving again. Her foot landed in a hole, jarring the tender ankle. A sharp pain shot up her leg. As much from frustration as agony, she swore as loudly as possible.

From somewhere ahead there came an answering rustle.

Eying the darkness apprehensively, April froze. The odd stench seemed even stronger here. She swallowed past the lump building in her throat and took a cautious step forward. Her pulse thudded in her ears. She took another step.

The sole of her shoe connected with something slick. Instantly, her right leg slid forward, the left backward, leaving her sprawled on the ground like a collapsed tepee. Something slimy and smelly smeared across her hand. Her nose wrinkled in disgust as she wiped it against her slacks. Cursing and moaning, she managed to stand. But the fall had exhausted her. For what seemed an hour, she leaned against the cavern wall, breathing too hard. As some strength returned, she pushed away from the wall and forced herself to move.

An agitated rustle split the silence around her.

April's heartbeat quickened. She had to get out of here back to the safety of the house. Feeling foolish, she started to whistle, much as Lily had whistled on that fateful day twelve years ago when she'd interrupted Spencer and April's first kiss.

A sudden flapping jerked her to a halt.

Her eyes widened, but saw no clearer. "Is someone there?"

A screech had April slamming her back to the wall. She heard the whoosh. Then flapping wings. Something grazed her hair. And another and another.

Bats!

She swung the branch, but the attacking swarm broke her grip. The limb fell. April covered her head with her hands and dropped to the cave floor, screaming.

The startled creatures screamed back.

Like a bolt from the blue, inside her mind April heard another's screams. Her mother's. Suddenly, behind her closed eyes, she started to remember, to see.

April realized she was reliving again the incident in the basement right after Lily had interrupted Spencer and her first kiss. Now, she was standing in the shadows of the basement stairs, listening to the clump of Spencer's shoes ascending the risers. When he reached the halfway mark, she heard Lily say, "Oh, darling, you startled me."

The footsteps continued upward to the landing.

"I need a little winy-poo for my empty glass." Lily's voice sounded slurred. "Lord, I didn't know how I was going to manage that spooky ole wine cellar alone, but as you can see, I'm desperate. Come along, darling."

"Don't you think you've had enough?"

"Had enough? Well, maybe you're right, darling." Lily had dropped her voice seductively. "What do you suggest instead?"

There was a whisper of fabric and then silence. April crept from her hiding place. The scene that met her eyes set her back on her heels. Spencer was kissing her mother.

But no.

His hands were on her upper arms, and he was trying to disengage her hold. Lily was the one doing the kissing. Jealousy and anger tangled inside April, but she held her tongue.

"Mrs. Farraday, don't," Spencer pleaded, his voice and good manners strained.

Lily ran the tip of one long nail across his lower lip. "Mrs. Farraday? No need to be so formal, dear. No one is going to hear us . . . or is that what you're afraid of? That we'll get caught here? You always were more shy than your brother. Well, I know a very private place. No one will disturb us there—because no one but me knows it exists."

"What?"

She tapped the empty wine glass against his chest. "Oh, I know what you're thinking. Lily won't leave the house. Well, to get to my secret place it isn't necessary to go outside. You don't believe me, do you?" She laughed and looped her arm through his. "Come on, I'll show you."

"You don't understand. I don't want to go anywhere with you, Lily."

"I beg your pardon?"

"I don't care about you in *that* way."

Releasing Spencer, she stepped back and raked her eyes over him, then arched one brow and peered at him tauntingly. "Are you trying to tell me you prefer—ahem—your own gender?"

"No!" Spencer roared. "I prefer April."

For five whole seconds, her mother stared at him,

clearly taken aback. Then she burst into laughter. "April! She's just a baby. A man like you needs a woman."

"April is worth the wait."

"You're making a big mistake, darling." Her words sounded more slurred than before, but the threat in them was distinct enough. "Reconsider—or I might have to tell August I caught you playing nasty with little April."

As though her feet were part of the concrete floor, April stood frozen in place, unable to look away, unable to block out the horrid words.

Spencer glared at Lily. "August wouldn't believe you."

"Don't underestimate my influence with him. If the notion struck me, I could convince him to send you, your brother, and your phony Southern belle of a mother back to whatever Texas rock you all climbed out from under." She moved against his chest again. "But I could be talked out of forgetting the subject ever came up . . ."

"No." Spencer set Lily away from him.

Lily bristled, swinging the wine goblet through the air. It hit against the banister. The lip of the glass broke. The sound reached April before a jagged chunk of crystal landed near her feet, but her attention remained riveted on the scene being played out on the landing above her.

"You'll be sorry. . . ." A vicious smile curved Lily's famous mouth. She glanced at the now dangerously notched rim of the wine goblet. She tossed her head haughtily and narrowed her eyes as though she were acting out a role and the weapon in her hand were a prop, not something that could inflict real pain, real death. For a heartbeat, she waved it menacingly at Spencer. Then, shrieking like a wounded cat, she lunged at him.

Spencer threw his arms up to protect himself and pushed her away.

Surprise wiped the smile from Lily's face. She reeled backward and struck the railing but failed to grasp it. She pitched out over the stairs. Spencer grabbed for her and missed. Lily screamed. And screamed.

As April watched in horrified shock, her mother started to tumble toward her. The wine glass fell. Crashed. Lily's body banged against the wood railing, thumped against the risers, as April ran forward and Spencer ran down. But neither reached her in time to stop her rough landing on the concrete floor.

April fell to her knees beside her mother. Lily was still alive, but even at fourteen April could tell she was hurt badly. Her eyes were glazed, and she seemed to be holding her neck at an odd angle.

Terrified, April clutched her mother's hand and glanced up at Spencer. He was staring dumbfounded at Lily. His face was dead white. "I didn't mean to . . ."

She nodded. "Go get Daddy. Hurry."

Spencer had raced up the stairs as if the devil himself were after him.

April blinked. The inkiness of the cavern surrounded her, pulling her from the past with a jolt. For a long while she stayed huddled against the ground, eyes closed, listening. At length, she realized the frightened bats had roosted elsewhere, as evidenced by the heavy silence.

Slowly she lowered her hands and opened her eyes. Several seconds passed, and the squeeze of fear that always came when she faced total darkness failed to take hold. Soon she realized she was not afraid and knew the answer was simple. There were no more secrets hiding in the shadowy depths.

She shifted to a more comfortable position, leaned against the wall and closed her weary eyes. Discovering she hadn't killed Lily had left her feeling oddly empty and strangely satisfied. Yet, oddly, a scrap of guilt still burrowed in her conscience. Why? Because she was the catalyst for the fight between Spencer and her mother which had led to the fall? Probably. She could live with that, but if she couldn't have Spencer, what good was knowing the truth?

Hot tears fell across April's chilled cheeks, and fear, worse than any created by the darkness, attached itself to her heart. For April was certain she finally understood Spencer's repeated rejections, the fleeting twinge of guilt in his haunted gray eyes. Undoubtedly he was reminded of his part in Lily's accident every time he looked at April. And he always would be.

She hugged her knees, lamenting into the black silence, "Oh, Spence, even with my memory back—Lily is going to keep us apart forever."

Twenty

The person who had pushed April from the cliff considered those gathered in August Farraday's den. Men, women, and child, all were present, dressed for outdoors. But until the fog and the darkness subsided, no one was going anywhere. A sense of agitated gloom hovered over the group like a thunder cloud. It was apparent they thought they already knew the dismal outcome of the search that lay ahead and dreaded its inevitability. Yet each appeared anxious to get on with it.

Fools. So, they'd found an earring. Well, soon they'd find her body. But the truth . . . they would never find that. It was as dead as April.

The person smiled inwardly, welcoming the impending search, no longer afraid of discovery. At some point during the sleepless night, the serenity had finally come. Probably with the acceptance that eliminating April had not only been necessary, but had brought the events of twelve years ago full circle.

And finding her and burying her would deliver the final release.

Twenty-one

In the background a radio station played static-laced elevator music as those gathered in the den awaited a weather report. Helga served coffee and sweet rolls. Spencer accepted a cup of the strong black liquid, but refused the pastry, knowing he'd never choke food past the lump in his throat. It didn't even smell good.

Gulping down coffee, he stalked to the window and stared at the smothering fog. July nudged his side. He draped his arm around her shoulder and pulled her against him in an awkward, comforting hug. Neither spoke. There was nothing to say. With half an ear, he listened to August's phone conversation with the Coast Guard, feeling like a motorless sailboat stalled in dead seas, waiting for a wind that wasn't going to come.

Hearing him say good-bye, Spencer turned around in time to see August shakily set the receiver in its cradle. A solemn resignation defined the elderly man's slumped form. After a long moment, he lifted his head. Tears stood in his dark blue eyes. "I told them to concentrate on the south shoreline."

No one said anything. Spencer's eyes met August's and he knew their thoughts were on a similar plane. It was twelve years, almost to the day, and now they would find April as they had found Lily.

Spencer's stomach hurt. The hot coffee exacerbated the pain. He released July, strode to the fireplace, and deposited the cup on the mantel. Grabbing up the poker, he prodded the dying flame. It hissed, then revived with a crackle and a spark. He added another log.

With his back to the growing heat he sank to the raised hearth and surreptitiously studied the faces of those so familiar to him. Which one—Thane, Karl, August, Helga, March, or Cynthia—was the consummate actor? Which one, professing fear and worry for April, might actually have been capable of shoving her from the cliff? For he was now convinced that was what must have happened. The only other alternative was that April had jumped, and her doctor insisted she wasn't suicidal. He'd been convinced enough to call in the sheriff, but he was practical enough to realize he might never be able to prove foul play.

Maybe if he understood the motive behind this hideous crime, he'd know which one to blame. Somehow, he felt it had to do with Lily. Was it because April looked so much like her mother?

He glanced at his own mother through hooded eyes, hating that he suspected her. But, for all her claimed concern, he kept recalling her resentment and jealousy of Lily. Did she look upon April as a constant reminder of the actress August had once loved? Even so, could she hate enough to kill? The very idea made his skin crawl. Yet . . . Before Lily, he hadn't thought himself capable of such thoughts either.

The old guilt soured his weak stomach. It was generous of Thane to insist Lily's fall had been an accident, but had it been? Although he'd never said it aloud, no matter how hard he tried, Spencer couldn't deny he'd despised Lily for the things she'd been saying and trying to do, couldn't deny he'd shoved her, and couldn't erase the vision of her sprawled on the cement floor with her neck broken, her eyes glassy.

August's tremorous voice sliced through this black introspection. "The man said there's a storm due in and the headwinds have already reached Friday Harbor. The fog should start lifting by noon."

"Noon!" Spencer leaped to his feet, dropping the poker with a clatter. "Hell, it's six-thirty. I'm not gonna cool my heels for another five and a half hours."

"You're not going to have to, man," Karl pronounced from his position at the French doors. "Listen."

Except for the fire, the room fell silent. Then Cynthia whispered, "Wind."

Spencer strained to hear it. A weak breeze. It wheezed against the ancient structure, erratically at first, panting into the blinding mists with the strength of a breathless jogger. But it gained force rapidly. Even before holes of visibility appeared in the dense fog, everyone had donned their respective coats.

Like a small army marching to certain defeat, they left the house. Spencer hadn't bothered to suggest that anybody stay behind, it was evident no one wanted to wait in the house.

Random patches of fog lingered, wavered in the wind, swirled and dissipated, chilling the air with frigid dampness. Overhead, the sky was as sullen and gray as the group moving to the cliff.

The binoculars around Spencer's neck banged against his chest with every step he took. Soon, the cold penetrated his clothing and stung his unshaven face. Ignoring it, he clung tighter to July's hand. He still couldn't believe she had come out here alone, in the dark, against strict orders to stay indoors.

Children had the oddest sense of indestructibility. She had no real idea how dangerously high these cliffs were, no concept of erosion. If something looked solid, it was. God, they might have lost her, too, he reflected, shivering at the thought. "Are you cold, twerp?"

"Nope." She strode ahead with all the aplomb of her seven years. The group followed at a solemn clip.

Nearing their destination, Spencer was struck by an unwelcome memory. This weather, like a bad omen, was unerringly similar to the dark stormy day that had been Lily's last. Sweat dampened his chilled flesh. Of all the details he couldn't bury about that dreadful day, why had one he'd completely forgotten come to haunt him now? He had no answer, only gut-wrenching dread.

Five feet from the precipice, he signaled for everyone to halt. Squatting, he asked July, "Where was the earring?"

She scanned the cliff in both directions, seemed to visually measure the distance from the house, then shrugged at Spencer. "I think it was right there." Her finger was aimed at a disturbed section of ground directly in front of them, but her face was twisted in confusion. "I left Barbie to mark the spot. Where is she?"

The doll was missing as surely as April. Spencer wanted to rush to the ledge, but made himself deal with July first. He gave her a hug, then set her away from him. "You've been a big help. I want you to stay back with Mom now. Okay?"

Her lower lip trembled, but July nodded, and retreated into her mother's waiting arms. Tension hung in the air as thick as the fog that had kept them from this moment throughout the night. The women stood back. The men proceeded to the precipice.

"Spread out," August instructed. He knelt and inched close to the edge. The others duplicated his moves. "Watch your footing. It looks to be eroded along here."

As if to stress this, a clod of soil beneath Walter O'Brien's hand fell away, unbalancing him. He swore and scooted backward.

"Careful . . ." August warned.

Like a marine in a battle zone, Spencer dropped to his belly. The leather strap of the binoculars dug into his nape, the glasses themselves jabbed against his chest. He pulled them free and snaked forward on ground that felt something like spongy sandpaper. Pebbles rattled down the bluff.

Taking a deep breath, he stretched his neck over the lip of the cliff. His eyes slammed shut. He was terrified to look, more terrified not to. Wet earth and brine invaded his nostrils as the roar of the surf reached up and hammered against his ears. How often in his life had these smells and sounds lent him comfort? Not now. For the first time the natural phenomena failed to ease his distress.

Bracing himself, he lifted his eyelids and scanned the rocky shore below. He saw rocks and water and two wheeling gulls, but no human body. Breath exited his burning lungs with a sputter.

Karl was to his right, and Spencer now noticed that a bushy fir tree seemed to completely block his view of the shore. He started to assure Karl there was no sign of April when the man turned puzzled blue eyes to him and pointed to the fir. "Whaddaya make of this?"

He'd spoken so softly Spencer doubted anyone else had overheard. Belly-crawling closer to Karl, he trained the binoculars on the tree. Its branches had fresh breaks and a few of its roots were partially dislodged as though something—or someone—had tugged—or clung—hard enough to the tree to cause this damage. April. With his heart contracting, he glanced at Karl and could tell he had come to the same conclusion.

Fear battered Spencer's soul as he slowly played the field glasses across the roiling waters below.

From his position just beyond Karl, Thane shouted, "Hey, that looks like a ledge down there. And there's something white on it.

"Barbie!" July shouted.

The ground shook with running feet.

Spencer felt his heart leap.

Heard his mother yell, "July, no!"

He whirled around in time to see the child sprinting toward Thane.

As Spencer scrambled to his feet, Karl lunged for her and missed. She darted too close to the bluff. Rocks rumbled downward. Horrified gasps rent the windy air, and everyone seemed to move at once.

A split second later, a wild-eyed Cynthia grasped the child by the shoulders and hauled her away from the bluff. "July Margaret Farraday, don't you ever do that again!" She reprimanded with a quavery, breathless voice that parroted the terrified murmurs of all present.

Now everyone hastened to Thane. Spencer reached him first. His heartbeat was as quick as July had been a moment before. He dropped to the ground and again stretched out on his stomach. "Karl, Thane, grab my legs. I want a better look at that ledge."

He lifted the binoculars and peered through them, concentrating on the face of the cliff. What little light there was originated at his back and altered the true character of the rocky wall. Shadows adopted false depths, and the last vestiges of the blanketing fog darted like teasing fan dancers, blurring and obstructing the thing he most wanted to see. He shifted positions several times.

Gripping the metal tighter, he attempted to stifle the frustration needling him, but only managed to pain the tender flesh circling his eyes. He was about to give up when a break in the cloud cover released a shaft of light. At last. He craned his neck for a better look. There, in the center of the round magnified lens, he spotted the doll.

"It's Barbie, all right," he told the men. "And she's definitely on a shelf of some kind." After endless hours of desolation, Spencer felt a stirring

287

of hope. April was not there, but this ledge would have supported her.

August squatted beside his shoulder. "Do you think it's an entrance to one of the tunnels?"

He sat up and shakily handed the glasses to his stepfather. "You tell me."

August wasted no time joining him on the ground, employing the binoculars.

Spencer felt a panic like claustrophobia. The wind wasn't strong enough to steal his breath, and yet he found it difficult to fill his lungs. Perhaps, he rationalized, the odd sensation arose from the close proximity of the group; everyone seemed to be huddled around August and him like sheep waiting to be shorn.

"Yes, by God!" August's shout startled him. "It is one of the original entrances to the caverns. And look . . ." He grasped Spencer tightly around the neck, stuffed the binoculars into his palm, and pointed to the ledge. "Right next to the doll. Is that what I think it is?"

Spencer held the field glasses in a death grip and perused the area around the doll. Suddenly, a glint of light winked at him. He blinked. His hand stilled. He could barely believe his eyes—it looked like. . . . A shuddery laugh escaped as he lowered the glasses and turned a hope-filled gaze toward his stepfather.

"Is it . . . ?"

"I'd swear . . ."

"Do you think it means . . . ?"

For a moment all Spencer could do was nod. Then standing, he dragged his stepfather up with him. "Pray it does, August. Pray it does."

"For heaven's sake, will the two of you tell us what you've found?"

At the sound of his mother's voice, Spencer cocked his head toward her. She had stepped forward, away from July, away from the huddled group. Her face was as ashen as the sky.

For the first time since this ordeal had begun a grin parted Spencer's lips. "It looks like April's other earring."

Twenty-two

Everyone spoke at once. Voices collided in surprise, then speculation tempered with hope. For all but one, the discovery of April's second earring was good news. For that person the find caused shock, then apprehension spiked with panic.

No! No! April couldn't be alive, wandering around in the caverns leading to Calendar House, perhaps making her way at this very moment into the basement, perhaps remembering. *Have to get back. Have to stop her.*

But . . . running ahead of the others would be a mistake; an open admission of guilt.

Must calm down. Must think.

The person inhaled slowly and deeply, then exhaled with restraint, all the while watching the others. No one had moved toward the house yet. Indeed, most appeared to not fully comprehend the meaning of the earring on the ledge. Absorbing this fact brought a lessening of tension, a sharpening of reason.

Need a head start. The woods are less than twenty feet away. And . . . not a soul has counted heads. In all this confusion, I could surely make it to the cover of the trees and return to the house *undetected*. Without another thought, the person edged to the rear of the group, dashed into the woods, and headed for the house.

No one knows the passageways like me. They'll waste precious seconds in that black maze. By the time they discover the right tunnel, it'll all be over.

Twenty-three

"Daddy, is April in one of the smuggler's tunnels?" July's expression was a tangle of hope and excitement.

August squatted before his young daughter and pulled her onto his lap. "Maybe . . ."

Spencer ignored the note of caution in his stepfather's tone, ignored the warning voice inside his own head. The hell with not getting his hopes up. April *had* to be in the caverns. She *had* to be alive. "Let's go find her."

Within seconds, they were hastening en masse toward the house.

August strode beside Spencer, his face crinkled in thought. After a moment he said, "We'll need crowbars to pry the boards off the tunnel accesses."

"Not necessary," Spencer informed him. "Last night, Thane and I found a cave opening that isn't boarded up."

"What?" August jerked to a stop. His brows dipped incredulously. "Are you certain?"

His surprise struck Spencer as being completely genuine, and he realized he had never really considered August capable of doing April harm. Urging him to continue walking, Spencer quickly and quietly explained discovering the blanket-covered cave access.

The only thing that kept August from stopping again was Spencer tugging him along. He sputtered, "What's going on?"

Spence shrugged. He had his suspicions, but now was not the place nor the time to share them. The wrong person might overhear.

Plus, August was too worried about his elder daughter to have to reckon with the fact that someone in the household might have tried to kill her. Let them find April first, then they could deal with the rest.

As they neared Calendar House minutes later, Spencer realized he was not going to be able to put off telling August about his call to the sheriff. Sitting on the porch steps were a man and a woman. He didn't know either. The man, however, was easily identifiable in his San Juan County Sheriff's uniform. As she rose and brushed at the seat of her brown corduroy pants, Spencer guessed the female might be April's psychiatrist, Nancy Merritt.

"Dr. Merritt," August confirmed, stepping toward the couple. He glanced at the deputy with lifted brows. "Murphy, what are you doing here?"

Before Deputy Murphy could answer, the doctor asked, "Has April been found?"

"Not yet," Spencer answered, impatiently. He felt like a racehorse being held at the gate against his will.

Forcing a polite smile, he introduced himself to the doctor, a thin woman, plain by nature and by design. Her brown hair was cropped around her face as unattractively as a stocking cap, but, for all their lack of enhancement, hers were the warmest brown eyes Spencer had ever encountered. "We have reason to believe April's in one of several old tunnels that extend from beneath the house to the cliffs beyond. We're going there now."

"By all means," Dr. Merritt said. "Let's proceed."

But the deputy wasn't about to be shuffled aside. "Mr. Garrick." He cut in front of Spencer, glanced down at a note pad then up. "I take it this April is the same missing person you called in about."

Spencer felt his mouth go dry. The last thing he wanted to do right now was answer any of this man's questions. "Yes," he said, dodging to one side of the guy in hopes of getting past him.

The officer countered his move. "What's going on? You all act like she might be alive, but according to the report you filed you suspected foul play."

Several gasps punctuated the morning air. Spencer felt heat rush into his face and out again in rapid succession.

Judging by the scarlet tinge of August's complexion he hadn't taken this news any better. His blood pressure was likely skyrocketing. "Spence, what's Murphy talking about?"

"August, Officer, I'll explain later. Right now I want to find April."

For a moment, it appeared the scowling deputy was about to pull rank. Dr. Merritt gave him no chance. "Officer, my patient may or may not be alive, but if she's been exposed to the cold all night — it's imperative she be our main priority. Can't your questions wait?"

"All right, but not indefinitely."

Spencer rushed into the house.

April was so cold and weary she hardly noticed the pain in her ankle anymore. Like a plane on automatic pilot, she proceeded through the cavern. Her pace was clumsy, but she didn't notice. The new memories monopolized her tired mind.

Although the accident was something awful to remember, she could only assume she had blocked it all out because she'd so often — as angry children did — wished her mother would die. And yet a niggling doubt kept jabbing her powers of reason. When had Lily died? In her recollection, she remembered being terrified as she leaned over her injured mother, but when had she become hysterical to the point of amnesia? If the blockage had been surmounted, why couldn't she recall this part? She needed to talk to Dr. Merritt. Nancy could help her straighten out this confusion.

April yawned. The air tasted unpleasant yet breathable, but every pore in her body seemed to ache. She needed rest. Exhausted, she lowered herself to the earthen floor and curled into a ball attempting to stave off the bitter cold. She wouldn't stay here long, she told herself. Her eyelids drooped shut.

Feeling sleep drift over her, she was struck by a thought more chilling and foul than the air. If she'd remembered everything, why had someone tried to kill her? April sat up straight, instantly wide awake. As far as she could see, nothing about Lily's death pointed to a reason. And yet someone *had* tried to kill her.

She rubbed her fingertips against her temples. It was ridiculous to think Spencer could imagine her any kind of threat. Surely he realized he'd shoved Lily away in self-defense. Had something else happened when she and Lily were left alone? Had she done something to end Lily's life?

Had someone else?

Terror gave April renewed strength. She shoved to her knees and began to stand. A light bobbed toward her. Hope squeezed her chest, but she choked back the urge to cry out. Was the person coming at her friend or foe?

Pressing against the wall, April tried to make herself small, invisible. The light hit her full in the face. A voice echoed through the darkness, speaking her name.

And suddenly April was fourteen years old again, in the basement, kneeling beside an injured Lily, hearing this same person speak her name, seeing this familiar figure emerge—not from the shadows of the cavern—but from the larder.

Twenty-four

Tightly clutching her mother's hand, April stared at the person emerging from the larder doorway. As light fell on the familiar form, she choked on a sob. "Helga! Lily fell down the stairs. She's hurt. Help her. Please, help her."

Concentrating once again on her mother, April saw Lily's beautiful face was a twisted mask of pain. Tears were seeping from her large aqua eyes, rolling across her temples into her long hair which lay swirled about her head like a golden fan.

The housekeeper rushed forward and dropped to her knees. "She's shivering. Probably shock. Quick, child. Run and get a blanket."

Panic bunched inside April and, for precious seconds, the instructions failed to penetrate her stunned mind. Then she tried to move, but Lily moaned, clinging to her hand with a strength that was surprising under the circumstances.

Helga gaped at her in disbelief. "I said hurry, child."

April managed to free herself and stumble to her feet. She backed away from her mother, recoiling from the awful spectacle of her agony, her whimpering cries. She lurched for the staircase. *Hurry!*

But her heart was pounding so fast she could barely breathe and her legs were as stiff and heavy as lead pipes. The landing seemed a mile away.

Lily moaned.

Petrified, April froze. Could the doctor get here in time? The question seemed to lift her lethargy. She sped up the last of the stairs and crossed the landing, all the while listening to her mother's muted weeping and Helga's droning responses.

April assumed the housekeeper was trying to calm Lily, but as she opened the door leading into the kitchen, she detected fury in Helga's voice. Surprise brought her spinning around. She forgot about the blanket, forgot about the probable shock, and let go of the door. As it bumped shut behind her, April peered over the railing, listening.

Helga wasn't trying to calm Lily. She was angry, accusing. Something about Lily and Jesse. Something about a secret room beneath the toolshed. Alarm bells rang inside her head. April scooted to the staircase.

"I used to have such respect for you—Miss Lily Cordell—Miss World Famous Movie Star. To think, I was your biggest fan." Helga spat the words at Lily. "Except for my Karl, working for you has been the greatest joy of my life. Believe it or not, I could even understand and forgive Jesse for falling under the spell of your beauty and charm."

April moved onto the stairs and started a quiet descent. Helga gripped Lily by both upper arms.

Lily groaned.

Helga seemed oblivious to the actress's evident pain. Her eyes narrowed. "Now you've showed your true colors. You didn't care a whit for my Jesse.

He hasn't been dead two months and here you are seducing young Spencer. For the love of God," Helga raged, shaking Lily by the shoulders. "He's only eighteen years old. Next thing, you'll be after my Karl."

An agonized gasp issued from Lily.

Horrified, April lunged down the risers. "Noooo! Helga, don't move her!"

Her warning came too late.

The whisper snap of Lily's neck seemed the loudest sound April had ever heard. "No!" She raced to her mother's sprawled body.

Helga staggered backward, obviously appalled at what she had done.

April collapsed beside Lily, and clutched one limp hand to her heart. "Mommy?"

Lily didn't answer. She couldn't. As this realization sank in, all the remembered resentments, hatreds, attacked April's conscience, indicting her for her mother's death. *Be careful what you wish for. It might come true.* April shook her head. She hadn't really meant for her mother to die. Had she?

Helplessness and guilt welled inside her, knitting together in a snarl of horror so great her mind could neither comprehend nor deal with it. "I'm sorry, Lily. I'm sorry. I'm sorry . . ."

That was how they'd found her. Kneeling over Lily, murmuring those words.

Helga must have retreated into the larder until the others had arrived.

April took a deep shuddering breath and laid her head against the dank cavern wall. She felt as though a weight the size of Calendar House had been lifted from her. The niggling guilt was gone. Lily Cordell had been a tragic woman, who had died a tragic death, but it was not her daughter's fault. At long last, April could truly forgive her mother all the injustices that had been inflicted on her and let go of her anger.

"You've remembered, haven't you, missy?" Helga's voice was menacing.

It cut through April's thoughts with chilling precision. She lifted her hand to block the beam of light poking her eyes, and, keeping her movements slow and careful, she stood. "You sent the anonymous note, didn't you?"

"You shouldn't have come." The housekeeper's tone was accusing, implying that April, instead of she, was to blame for her murderous actions. An icy squiggle of fear crawled through April's belly. Helga stood less than three feet away, blocking the tunnel which led to the house.

There was something long and shiny in her other hand. A butcher knife, April realized with stunned horror. Likely the one she'd used to trash Lily's furniture and portrait, likely the one Karl had been sharpening the other day. A scream tore from her.

Helga laughed. "Go ahead. Yell 'til you're hoarse. No one's gonna hear. They're still out on the cliff trying to figure out what to do."

Moisture evaporated from April's mouth and sprang up on her hands. Terrified, she staggered backward, twisting the tender ankle.

The knife's blade flashed in the light as Helga slashed it through the air separating them. "Everything was fine as long as you didn't remember."

This reasoning made no sense to April. "You're

wrong, Helga. It's good that I've remembered. Now I can tell the others it was a mistake. You didn't mean to kill Lily."

"Can't you see that won't matter? Your ma was a movie star. Somebody like me can't just take the life of a Lily Cordell and not pay for it."

"But it was an accident. Why didn't you tell them?"

"Who was gonna believe me? If I'd told the cops why I was so angry, I would've had to explain about Lily and Jesse. That'd be handing 'em my motive on a fancy platter. And you couldn't even speak your own name, let alone testify for me."

"We'll go to the sheriff now and set the record straight."

"No! I won't have Jesse's name dragged through the tabloids. Those reporters don't care whose name they dirty, or who gets hurt by their nasty words." She slashed the knife at April's middle. It snagged her parka. Fabric tore.

Shrieking, April hobbled away, managing to put a good yard between them. Helga advanced on her. "That's right. Turn around. You're going back the way you came."

Too frightened to argue, April favored her sore ankle, racking her brain for some way to save herself. Too bad she'd lost the tree limb. Buy time, keep Helga talking. . . . "You don't need to kill me."

"Oh, I didn't want to. If you'd just stayed in Arizona, if you'd just left the secrets of the past buried. But you couldn't do that, could you?"

"I had to rememb—"

"Why? Everyone was perfectly happy with things

301

the way they were."

April jumped at the swish of the knife slicing the air behind her. She struggled to keep her tone level. "I had to remember in order to get well—in order to bring this nightmare to an end. For both of us."

"No. Your remembering ain't ended a thing for me. It ain't bad enough you gotta look like her. How come you gotta act like her? I'll only have peace when you're silenced for good."

The woman had lost all rationality. As scared as she was, April realized there was no reasoning with Helga. Still she couldn't help but try. "Just because two people look alike doesn't mean they're alike on the inside."

"There's more similarities 'tween you and your ma than mere looks. I've seen you with Spencer. One man ain't enough for you either, is he? You had to go after Karl, too—leading him on, trying to steal him from me same as your ma stole my Jesse."

So, Helga *had* been eavesdropping as April cried on Karl's shoulder. Eavesdropping—and misinterpreting the situation. April glanced over her shoulder.

Was that a light in the deep distance behind Helga? Or was desperation making her imagine flashlight beams where there were none? She couldn't tell. Nor could she rely on someone coming to her rescue. She was going to have to save herself. "You're wrong, Helga. I'm not leading Karl on—"

Helga cut her off again. "Hah! Like your ma didn't lead Jesse on? He spent hours working on that fancy sports car of hers, keeping it in tiptop shape because she'd convinced him she was going to leave Farraday Island in it with him. Instead, the car slipped off a jack and crushed the life out of the besotted fool.

"He should've knowed she wouldn't go anywhere outside. Especially since he'd had to have liaisons with her in the storage cave beneath the toolshed. Your ma not only led him on, she as good as killed him."

"Helga, no one cares about those things any more."

"Karl will care."

Now April understood. "Maybe at first. But he'll see you didn't mean to kill Lily. Karl will forgive you. And he'll get over it."

The housekeeper fell silent and April prayed she was still rational enough to see the wisdom of this. She chanced a glimpse at the woman.

In the spill of light from the flash, she saw Helga wag her head. "It's too late. I've tried to kill you. They'll lock me up for sure. There's only one way to end this now." She threatened with the knife. "No more talking. Get moving."

The finality of these words numbed April's brain. Feeling as helpless as she had watching her mother die, she shambled on, reflexively keeping ahead of the knife blade.

Shortly, the muted roar of the surf reached through the tunnel and whispered against April's ears, penetrating her stupor. She stiffened. If Helga succeeded, she wouldn't be alive to hear this wondrous, vital sound tomorrow. Was she just going to let this happen?

Sudden white hot rage licked through her. Cow-

303

ardice had robbed her of twelve years. She might not be in charge of this situation, but she wasn't dead yet. And by George, if she were meant to die at this woman's hand, it wouldn't be submissively.

With the anger came action. She unzipped her parka and shrugged it off in one smooth motion, clamping onto the right wristband.

"What are you do—" Before Helga could finish the question, April rounded on her.

She slapped the jacket at the housekeeper's hand. The woman hollered and let loose of the object she was gripping. The clunk of metal hitting solid dirt echoed around them. April's heart nearly stopped. The flashlight was lying on the ground, not the knife.

A guttural yowl tore from Helga's throat. She lunged at April.

April reared back and tripped. She hit the ground hard. Before she could move, Helga had straddled her, the knife poised high over her head.

Gasping, April lifted the parka like a shield, trying to wriggle away. Vaguely, she heard the thud of running feet. Help. They would arrive too late.

As Helga brought the knife in a downward stroke, bright light fell across the two women and glinted off the knife's razor-sharp blade.

"Ma! Don't!" Karl's voice altered Helga's expression from fury to shock and confusion. Her arm froze in midswing.

But April knew how far beyond the line of sanity the woman had gone, knew she could not be trusted to comply with her son's request. Using all the strength she could muster from her awkward position, April slapped her jacket at the deadly

304

butcher knife. Her aim was accurate. The knife flew free and spiraled through the air, landing with a clatter out of the housekeeper's reach.

The loss of her weapon seemed to drain the fight from Helga. As several bobbing lights neared, April watched her take on the appearance of a giant rag doll and feared she might collapse.

However, April hadn't the strength to stand, let alone go to Helga's aid. The combined lights pained her eyes. She dropped her head into her hands, heard Karl arrive at his mother's side, heard Spencer, her father, and Nancy Merritt's worried voices — all calling her name. Their chants resounded in her ears like a song that she was too tired to join in.

The last thing April felt were her own hot tears seeping against her palms before she succumbed to the welcome blackness of exhaustion.

Twenty-five

Spencer sat in the den with August, Cynthia, Thane, and March, who all, he concluded, looked as near exhaustion as he felt.

The sheriff and his deputy had asked their questions, taken Helga into custody, and left. July was napping. Vanessa, her parents, and grandmother had insisted on seeing to dinner, graciously giving the Farradays and Garricks a chance to sort through the aftermath of discoveries and events. For the past few hours that was what the five had been doing.

"Son, I've never blamed you for Lily's fall." August, seated on the sofa beside Cynthia, puffed at his pipe. The rich aroma lent a singular touch of normalcy to this abnormal day. "I would have said something a long time ago, but it just never occurred to me that you might be blaming yourself."

Spencer favored him with a grateful smile. Incredibly, April had been right about her father. August was aware of all of Lily's dalliances, and he held no animosity toward either of his stepsons.

"What will become of Helga, now?" Thane queried. This was the first time he'd spoken since August admitted knowing of his brief affair with Lily, and Spencer suspected his twin had been mentally laying old ghosts to rest.

"That's up to the county psychiatrist," August replied.

"I still don't understand why she stole Thane's poems from April's room, then gutted the trunk in the attic." Spencer shook his head, not really expecting anyone to answer.

The clack of March's knitting needles ceased. "Lordy, that's as plain as the nose on your face. She was afraid Jesse had written love letters to Lily, too."

"Poor woman." Cynthia sighed. "Livin' twelve years with the guilt of Lily's murder. It's no wonder her mind snapped."

"Indeed." August plonked his pipe against the ashtray. "She must also have felt directly responsible for April's illness, and, I suppose, somewhere along the way she probably started to question how 'accidental' her actions were."

"Pity—"

"Humph!" March cut Cynthia off. "Don't be wasting pity on that one." She waved one long knitting needle through the air for emphasis. "Or, go thinking she didn't resent our demands on her—our criticisms of Karl. Noooo. Helga didn't stay here because she loved us. Mark my words, she did it out of fear—fear of losing her livelihood, her home, her son."

Spencer agreed with March. Protecting Karl had obviously been Helga's motive. But the lengths she'd gone to . . . Damn the woman! He bit back the rage that wouldn't dissipate, and stole a glance at his mother. Heat crawled across his face. Helga wasn't the only one with sins to account for. It would be a long while before he forgave himself for suspecting his mother could in any way have been responsible for the atrocities the housekeeper had committed. He reached into his pocket and dug out her gold cross. He could only speculate why Helga had put it in the wine cellar.

"Here mother. I came across this in the bathroom last night while I was searching the house for April," he lied, seeing no reason to put his mother through any further anguish.

Cynthia's face lighted up as she caught hold of the necklace. "Oh, I'm so glad you found it. August gave me this when July was born." She patted her husband's knee. "I feel like the luckiest woman alive. Gracious, when I think how close we came to losin' April . . ."

A chill swept Spencer. Although no one had broached the subject of April's mental stability, he sensed the worry floating just below the surface of their conversation. "You're sure she's all right?"

Leaning toward him, his mother gave his hand an indulgent pat. "I've already told you—except for some major exhaustion, some minor bumps and scrapes, one rather colorful eye, and a sprained ankle, the little darlin' seems to have survived the ordeal intact."

"But . . . ?" He didn't need to express the root of his fear.

"Sweetie, only Dr. Merritt can tell us that. And until April is rested, and they can talk . . . Well, we'll just have to hold a good thought."

But good thoughts dissolved in the acid solution of worry and impatience that had claimed his brain. Spencer jerked to his feet. Carrying his coffee cup, he went to the French windows, undid the latch, and cracked the door open.

The storm had arrived as the searchers were entering the house, and from the mess on the grounds, it appeared to have swept across the island with an unleashed fury not unlike the maelstrom which had transpired at the same time inside the cavern. Clouds still lingered, but the air had a clean scent as though purged of all malignant factors. He felt the same sense inside the house.

Yet he couldn't relax. Spencer gulped at his coffee. Cold. He grimaced. Even his relief at discovering he hadn't killed Lily was dampened by not knowing how April felt about it. Would she realize he'd merely repulsed her mother's drunken advances, not meant to push her down the stairs? Or had Helga's attack permanently damaged her whole outlook?

Dusk began to creep across the landscape. He shut the doors against the encroaching cold and stalked to the fireplace. Surely, it was taking Dr. Merritt too long to evaluate April. It was a bad sign. He knew it.

At the sound of footsteps approaching, he jerked his attention toward the doorway. Directly, as though materializing at his silent behest, Nancy Merritt appeared.

He lurched at her, sloshing cold coffee on his clean slacks. "How's April?"

"Better than you, I'd say." The doctor smirked at him, accentuating the deep creases at the sides of both her warm brown eyes. She looked as tired as the rest of them, but not as troubled. "April has penetrated the memory block. We may need to talk again, but I don't anticipate any problems she won't be able to overcome now."

Exuberance and relief burst through Spencer. He shouted, "Yes!"

His happiness was echoed by the others with words of rejoicing, smiles, and tears of joy.

"It just goes to prove what I've always thought." March's crusty voice rose above the others. "There's nothing crazy about that girl. Why, she's a true Farraday."

Cynthia chuckled and dabbed at her wet eyes. August hid a grin by relighting his pipe.

Undaunted, March heaved to her feet. "I don't know about the rest of you, but I could use something a lot stronger than this cold coffee. Thane, let's go see how those in-laws of yours are doing.

Thane gave Spencer a thumbs-up, then offered the elderly woman his arm. "Ma'am . . ."

As the two made their way from the room, Dr. Merritt turned to Spencer. "By the way, April is awake and asking to see you."

Instead of delighting him more, the news dulled his elation. Ever since they'd found April with Helga, ever since he'd carried her unconscious to her room, he had been, in turns, anticipating and dreading this moment. The doctor's expression offered no clue as to what April wanted to see him about. His part in Lily's fall? The possibility no longer seemed likely. With the return of her full mental faculties, April would doubtless realize the truth on that score.

Spencer's pulse skittered. He knew what was really frightening him. Although mere hours had passed, April may have grown up completely, and come to see her feelings for him were nothing more than old memories. Perhaps the reason she wanted to see him was to let him down gently. Did Dr. Merritt know? He couldn't bring himself to ask.

"I want to see April, too." Grinning, August laid down the pipe and stood. "And finally give her her mother's jewelry."

"August," the doctor interceded. "Your daughter isn't heading back to Phoenix for at least a week. Couldn't that particular surprise wait another day or so?"

Rising, Cynthia crooked her arm through her husband's and gazed up at him with loving eyes. "Nancy's right, darlin'. I think we ought to give Spence and April some time alone."

"Why?" August sounded disappointed and, for a second, Spencer thought he was going to insist on coming along. But a dawning appeared in his wizened eyes. "Oh, I see." He winked at Spencer, offered his other arm to Nancy Merritt, and guided the two women to the door. "Ladies, an occasion like this calls for a bottle of my best champagne. Maybe two."

Trailing behind them, Spencer wiped his sweaty palms against his slacks.

"August," Cynthia sighed happily. "I've decided to redecorate the house this Spring. Get rid of all this dreary black . . . use some natural woods . . . some light, airy colors. What do you think?"

"It's about time, my dear."

In the foyer, August glanced over his shoulder. "We won't wait dinner on you, son."

Spencer hastened up the stairs, plagued by the

311

awful fear of pending rejection. As he reached the landing, another thought crept from the recesses of his mind to taunt him. What if Karl's claim about April's feelings for him were true? Dear God, had he pushed her away—into Karl's arms—once too often?

He headed into the endless hallway, unable to outpace his anxiety. It was one thing to harbor the hope he could win April's love again, but it would be a totally different matter if it was Karl she cared for. The possibility drove a nail through his heart, but he realized he'd have to accept whatever her choice was. His consolation would be her happiness.

Her door loomed in front of him. The time had come to lay his cards on the table, to gather in the winning chips, or to accept his loss graciously. He swallowed hard and lifted his hand. The sound of his knock rang as hollowly in his ears as the sorry images of what his life would be without her.

"Come in."

Spencer entered April's bedroom.

Propped against pillows with the covers tucked beneath her arms, April sat in the center of the bed, looking like a battered angel.

Spencer's throat tightened.

Her right eye was bruised and slightly swollen, and scrapes and scratches marred her normally smooth chin and forehead: ugly reminders of an ugly ordeal.

Saying a silent prayer of thanks that her life had been spared, he closed the door and moved toward her. Never had he felt more guarded. His future rested in this woman's hands, in the disposition of her heart. "Hi."

"Hi." April couldn't recall having ever been more aware of another person's mood than she was of Spencer's at this moment. Something was dreadfully wrong. Self-consciously, her hand went to her face. "Guess no one would mistake me for Lily Cordell right now."

She'd made it sound like a casual observation, but April was shaking inside. Before he'd arrived, she'd convinced herself her resemblance to her mother would no longer be a reminder to him of a murder neither of them had committed, nor could have prevented. But the discomfort she sensed from him suggested otherwise.

The bedsprings twanged as he sank to an area near her thigh. Distractedly, Spencer watched her golden hair spill across the ruffled collar of her yellow flannel nightgown. She was a ray of sunshine piercing his bleak outlook. Unbidden, his fingers reached to fondle the shiny tresses, but catching himself, he pulled back and dropped his hand to his leg.

The only thing he dared allow to touch her was his gentle gaze. "After all you've been through, I can't believe you're still hung up about looking like your mother. Take it from a twin. Sharing similar features with someone doesn't make you alike in any other way, and anyone who can't differentiate doesn't deserve your attention."

"As blunt as always, I see." The tautness in her chest eased enough to pull a smile from her. If her resemblance to Lily wasn't bothering him, then what was? "It's nice to know some things don't change."

"But others do."

His voice held such resignation, April's hope sagged beneath its weight. A lifetime had passed in the last few hours. It was naive of her not to realize he'd been affected as sharply as she had. High drama wrought changes in people, put priorities in order, and revealed unsuspected truths. Her heart thudded precariously. Had Spencer discovered he no longer loved her as he had at eighteen? That the intimacies they'd shared since she'd come to Calendar House had been nothing more than a halfhearted attempt to recapture their stolen youth?

He was searching her face. Searching for a way to tell her? The thought tore at April, but she'd learned she couldn't run away from reality and survive. "Spence, I—"

"It's Karl, isn't it?"

"Karl?" she asked, confused. "Has something happened to him?"

"No," he answered curtly. If she'd rammed a spear through the center of his chest, it couldn't have hurt Spencer more than the obvious concern for Karl he could see growing in her round aqua eyes. Well, at least now he knew where he stood with her. "Karl went to Friday Harbor with his mother."

April stiffened and dropped her gaze to her entwined fingers, wrestling to control the anger which arose at every mention of Helga. Although a part of her understood and pitied the woman, she imagined her body would heal before her mind supplied the insulating layers that would eventually distance her enough from the raw pain of the ordeal to put it into perspective. Right now, she couldn't bear to think of Helga, much less discuss her.

A new awkwardness hovered between them, and Spencer thought about leaving, but couldn't pull himself away. Despite her wounds, she was impossibly more beautiful than before the hell she'd been through. God, how he yearned to crush her to him and declare his feelings, but he knew now that it was not what she wanted. "Are you in much pain?"

"Nothing a few days and lots of Tylenol won't cure." And another hundred years to get over loving you, she added to herself, trying unsuccessfully to tear her gaze from his sensuous mouth. Longing swirled through her. "I suppose none of this can be kept from the press?"

"Not a chance. One zealous individual showed up today to find out why the engagement party was cancelled. The little weasel arrived as the sheriff and his deputy were leaving with Helga."

"Oh, no." Lily's death would be fodder for every trashy and legitimate news source around the world. Her last hope of claiming Spencer's love slipped away. It was so unfair. Now that her memory had returned, everything she had ever desired could be hers for the asking.

Everything, but this man.

He'd made it abundantly clear how he felt about this sort of publicity, and a man in public life could ill afford a wife who had a history of years spent in a sanitarium. There would always be another "little weasel" to ferret out the story to use against him in one election after another. "I'm sorry."

The misery in her voice went straight to his heart, and instinctively, he covered her hands with his. "It's not your fault, sweetheart."

April stared at the hands covering hers, intoxicated by the sudden tingles coursing up her arm. Sweetheart? A brotherly endearment? It didn't feel brotherly. *Don't read something into this,* she warned herself. "Aren't you concerned about next November's elections?"

"Not really." Recklessly, he slid his hands across the cuffs of her fleecy nightie, up the length of her arms to her shoulders. "I imagine the sensationalism of Lily Cordell being murdered will grab headlines for a few days, but then it should fade into obscurity . . . at long last."

"Until the trial." April tilted her head and closed her eyes, savoring the delicious feel of his warm hands. A small moan slipped between her parted lips. "Won't that hurt your chances of becoming mayor and Thane's of being elected state representative?"

"Don't worry about Thane." His voice rasped with desire, and, too late, Spencer realized his mistake in touching her. But he couldn't bring himself to stop caressing her arms, her hands, couldn't squelch the ache he felt to kiss her sweet mouth. "No one outside the family will ever learn of his affair with Lily. And knowing my brother's luck and charm, all the hoopla will work to his advantage."

April's breath quickened. "But will the citizens of Bellingham want a mayor with such a checkered background?"

"If they do, they'll have to look elsewhere. I've withdrawn my bid for mayor."

A soft gasp escaped her. "Why?"

"Because I'm sick and tired of smiling at people until my face hurts in order to get votes. I don't want to do that for the rest of my life." Spencer's pulse raced as he brashly lifted a hand to her temple and gently traced the curve of her cheek. "And thanks to you I'm not going to."

"I don't understand." Like a cat being stroked by its master, she stretched her face toward his petting hand. "What did I do?"

"These past few weeks you've made me realize I'd been stumbling through my life—not living it." Incautiously, he massaged the sides of her neck with his thumbs.

The effect on April was dizzying. "What career are you planning to pursue?"

"Something better suited to my 'blunt honesty,' as you call it. I'm going to dust off my law degree and look at my options. I'd like to be a prosecutor."

April couldn't believe what she was hearing. All the obstacles to their having a future together were gone and yet he hadn't said a word about wanting her in his life. "You'd make a great prosecutor."

"Do you really think so?"

"Yes." She brushed a strand of his coffee-brown hair from his forehead, knowing she would miss this man more than she could bear. Something in his intense gray eyes froze the thought. She'd been blind not to see it. Desire, a trace of fear, and . . . Yes! Her heart reeled. Spencer loved her. She nearly laughed with joy.

April caught his face gently in both hands and lifted her mouth to his. A startled moan escaped him, but he leaned into the kiss, obviously enjoying her tender assault. Passion stirred deep inside April.

Too soon, Spencer broke the heady spell, gripping her by both upper arms and holding her just far enough away to ask, "What about Karl?"

"Karl? What has Karl got to do with us?"

"I thought . . . he said . . ."

"If you can't judge a person better than this, how do you expect to be a good prosecutor?" Freeing one hand, she traced his mouth with her fingertip. "I love you, Spence."

A heartfelt sigh broke from his grinning lips and he gathered her into his arms, hugging her so possessively, April could barely breathe. She didn't care.

"April, do you have any idea how long I've waited to hear you say that?"

"As long as I've waited to say it."

"Oh, God, I love you." Starting at her chin, he began kissing every curve and valley of her face with slow, mind-boggling thoroughness. He had almost lost her twice already. Never again. "We are going to make this legal, aren't we?"

April felt as though her heart would explode with happiness. "Absolutely counselor," she answered, sliding her arms around his neck, and pulling his lips back to hers.

Once again Spencer pulled away. "Before Thane and Vanessa—as soon as possible?"

"Uh huh." Her voice was as thick as the desire coursing her veins.

Their open mouths welded in abandon, tongues touching, tasting, savoring. His hands drew sensu-

318

ous paths across her back, her waist, her breasts, stirring a honeyed torture inside that begged to be fulfilled. She tugged his shirttails free and began undoing the buttons.

Again Spencer pulled away. "This isn't right. . . . You aren't ready. . . . Someone might come in. . . ." His objections seemed ridiculous in light of the desire glazing his eyes. "We should wait—"

"Wait? Wait!" April caught him by the shirtfront and drew him so close his heated breath mingled with her own.

"First you had to wait for me to grow up."

Loosening the remaining buttons, she slipped the shirt from his shoulders and down his arms. "Then you had to wait for me to get well."

She rubbed her hands across his lightly haired chest and down his flat stomach. He groaned in obvious pleasure. "Well, I'm all well . . . and in case you hadn't noticed—"

She reached for the waist band of his trousers and tipped her mouth to his. "—All grown up."

"I noticed. . . ." His voice was ragged as he gave the blankets separating them an impatient tug.

"I've waited a lifetime for you." April scooted lower on the pillows and opened her arms to him. "And I'm not willing to wait another minute."

A wicked smile lifted the corner of Spencer's mouth. "In that case—I've better manners than to keep a lady waiting."